PENGUIN BOOKS

WALKING BACK THE CAT

Robert Littell was born, raised, and educated in New York. A former *Newsweek* editor specializing in Soviet affairs, he left journalism in 1970 to write fiction full time. Connoisseurs of the literary spy novel have elevated his books to the genre's highest ranks, and Tom Clancy wrote that "if Robert Littell didn't invent the spy novel, he should have." He is the author of fourteen novels including the critically acclaimed *The Company*, *The Once and Future Spy*, *An Agent in Place*, *The Defection of A.J. Lewinter*, *The Sisters*, *The Amateur*, and *Vicious Circle*. He currently lives in France.

WALKING BACK THE CAT

Robert Littell

PENGUIN BOOKS

PENGUIN BOOKS

Published by the Penguin Group
Penguin Group (USA) Inc., 375 Hudson Street, New York, New York 10014, U.S.A.
Penguin Group (Canada), 90 Eglinton Avenue East, Suite 700, Toronto,
Ontario, Canada M4P 2Y3 (a division of Pearson Penguin Canada Inc.)
Penguin Books Ltd, 80 Strand, London WC2R 0RL, England
Penguin Ireland, 25 St Stephen's Green, Dublin 2, Ireland (a division of Penguin Books Ltd)
Penguin Group (Australia), 250 Camberwell Road, Camberwell,
Victoria 3124, Australia (a division of Pearson Australia Group Pty Ltd)
Penguin Books India Pvt Ltd, 11 Community Centre, Panchsheel Park, New Delhi – 110 017, India
Penguin Group (NZ), 67 Apollo Drive, Rosedale, North Shore 0632,
New Zealand (a division of Pearson New Zealand Ltd)
Penguin Books (South Africa) (Pty) Ltd, 24 Sturdee Avenue,
Rosebank, Johannesburg 2196, South Africa

Penguin Books Ltd, Registered Offices:
80 Strand, London WC2R 0RL, England

First published in Great Britain by Faber and Faber Limited 1996
First published in the United States of America by The Overlook Press,
Peter Mayer Publishers, Inc. 1997
Reprinted by arrangement with The Overlook Press, Peter Mayer Publishers, Inc.
Published in Penguin Books 2008

1   3   5   7   9   10   8   6   4   2

PUBLISHER'S NOTE
This is a work of fiction. Names, characters, places, and incidents are either the product
of the author's imagination or are used fictitiously, and any resemblance to actual persons,
living or dead, business establishments, events, or locales is entirely coincidental.

THE LIBRARY OF CONGRESS HAS CATALOGED
THE HARDCOVER EDITION AS FOLLOWS:
Littell, Robert
Walking back the cat / Robert Littell.
ISBN 0-87951-764-6 (hc.)
ISBN 978-0-14-311357-7 (pbk.)
p.   cm.
I. Title
PS3562.17827W35   1997   813'.54—dc21   96-49507

Printed in the United States of America

For my brother, Alan

Us Apaches don't believe the world will last forever. We say that the rocks and the mountains will be around a long time, but even they will disappear. And when they have all gone—the rocks and the mountains and the Apaches and the white man—what will be left?

What will be left are our deeds.

—ESKELTSETLE

WALKING BACK THE CAT

PROLOGUE

The young man, pale as Lazarus returned from a grave, rose from the hole in the sand to thaw himself in the first light of the cool desert sun. He carried a pump-action shotgun diagonally across his back on a sling. He was about to launch a small helium-filled balloon to plot the morning's ground winds when he heard the snorting of the horse. Startled, he slipped the shotgun off his back and worked a shell into the chamber. Squinting, he made out the horse pawing at the sand between him and the washed-out sun edging over the dunes. The animal, saddled, bridled, off-white and pure Arabian, loped closer. Talking soothingly under his breath, holding out a palm as if it were filled with sugar cubes, the young man drifted toward the stallion. Snorting through its nostrils, the horse tossed its head but stood its ground. When the horse started sniffing his hand, the young man snatched the bridle, flung himself onto its back and jammed the heels of his Special Forces desert boots into its flank.

"Waaaaaaaa!" he cried.

The squad's CO, a black second lieutenant, emerged from another hole. "Watch out for—" he cried as the stallion, its ears pasted back, its hooves kicking up silent storms of sand, flew past and headed for the dunes.

Bent low over the stallion's back, clinging to its braided mane with one hand, brandishing the shotgun with the other, the young man—who had never been on a horse in his life—discovered he could ride the demon.

And then the stallion's hoof came down on a small round plastic canister buried in the sand and the mine exploded, ripping off the animal's right front foot, bursting open its stomach. The rider leaped clear as the horse slued sideways into a drift of sand. Lying on its back, foaming at the mouth, it flailed away with its three good legs and the stump of the fourth as if it were treading air.

A helicopter throbbed in low overhead and marked with a green flare the spot where the young man stood riveted to the floor of the desert. A quarter of an hour later the sweepers from Charlie Company, their long-handled detectors twitching like antennas on an insect, approached from the west and cleared a path to him through the mines.

The black second lieutenant came up behind the sweepers. Firing his M16 from the hip, he put the stallion out of its misery. The young man started to apologize for all the trouble he had caused, but his CO cut him off with a wave of the hand. "Everyone needs to have a philosophy," he called across the sand. "Mine is: I don't want to know what happened. But I want to make damn sure it doesn't happen again."

PART

The agent known by the code name Parsifal discovered the message, printed in a child's scrawl of large block letters, inside the wrapper of his local newsletter. It specified a time he was to be at a public phone in the town of Hatch, New Mexico, under a billboard that read: "Laundromat—American Owned." At the appointed hour the phone rang in the booth, which reeked of a cheap underarm deodorant that Parsifal found more revolting than underarm secretions. Pressing a handkerchief to his nose, he snatched the receiver off the hook. "Can't you come up with public phones in expensive restaurants?" he complained. "A person could be asphyxiated in these booths you pick."

Le Juif, an electronics wizard who provided Parsifal with the odd bit of gadgetry and served as the cutout between him and his handlers, didn't waste time on small talk. "Sweep your trail, meet me at ——." He named a day and used the code word for the reading room in the Albuquerque Public Library, which was invariably deserted ten minutes before closing time.

Parsifal had met Le Juif face to face only once before, a month after the American authorities in Trieste granted Parsifal political asylum and flew him to the United States. That had been fifteen years before. Settling into a seat across the table from Le Juif in the high-ceilinged reading room, Parsifal was startled by the appearance of his cutout. He had always been gaunt, with the bone structure of a sparrow, but now he was cadaverous; his skin, turned the color of sidewalk, seemed to hang in folds off his bones.

Sniffing the air, Parsifal thought he could smell the cancer eating away at Le Juif's intestines. "Are you ill?" he asked, but Le Juif, staring at him with watery, sunken eyes, ignored the question.

"Talk shop," he murmured. "Admit it—you thought they had forgotten we existed, misplaced the files, stranded us in this godforsaken country, but they haven't. We have got ourselves a new Resident." He spoke with unaccustomed intensity, stressing each word as if it were a pearl pried with enormous effort from a reluctant oyster. "His code name is Prince Igor." Le Juif bared his tobacco-stained teeth in a malevolent smile. "You see what I am driving at? Parsifal redux!"

"This new Resident—you have met him?"

"There is a cutout in place between me and the Resident. It is the woman with the code name of La Gioconda. She has met him. I can vouch for her—we have been assigned to the same network since coming to America."

"A cutout between you and the Resident is unusual."

"The situation is unusual. The world is unusual. The century is unusual."

"How can you be sure the new Resident is genuine?"

"La Gioconda conveyed his bona fides. She passed on an identifying cryptogram known only to me and our masters in Moscow Center. It is the signal we have been waiting for. The period of hibernation is over. The Training Villa has been taken over by the KGB Veterans Association. Wetwork is being run out of our old Moscow seminary." Le Juif's body, racked by a silent cough, stiffened. He dragged a very large handkerchief from a pocket of the jacket draped over his scarecrow shoulders, spit into it, inspected the phlegm, then, satisfied that his condition had not deteriorated, folded the handkerchief away. From between his books he produced a small package and slid it across the table. "New one-time pads. New cryptograms. A vial of ricin. A remote radio detonator for explosive charges; it has a range of up to two and a half miles. I should know. I fabricated and tested it myself. Also money for operational expenses."

A buzzer sounded over a loudspeaker. "Five minutes to closing," announced the brittle voice of a woman who worked with one eye glued to the clock she was punching.

Le Juif started to gather up his books. "This is a heroic day," he whispered. "Marx, Engels, Lenin, Bukharin ... our work in progress, our dream." He reached across the table and gripped Parsifal's wrist with his clawlike fingers. "Whatever happens to me, you must hang on to the dream. If you don't, it will float up like a helium-filled balloon, it will soar into the stratosphere, growing smaller and smaller until it is lost from sight." He looked up at the lights recessed in the ceiling, which were starting to dim. "La Gioconda describes Prince Igor as a visionary. He is preparing a great exploit, something that will make wetwork history, something that will shake the world. I cannot tell you more now." Scraping back his chair, Le Juif heaved himself to his feet. He plucked a sealed envelope from his breast pocket and dropped it on the table in front of Parsifal. "Inside you will find the details of your first assignment from Prince Igor—an address in Dallas, an apartment number, a cryptogram to get you past the door."

Fixing his moist gaze on Parsifal, Le Juif nodded as if he had access to the secrets of the universe. "You do see it, don't you? Capitalism, unrestrained by the existence of an alternative, is doomed. Greed will smother justice and generosity. We must strive on."

Turning abruptly, he scurried like a crab from the reading room.

G lancing at the faded letters on the doors, Parsifal made his way down the murky hallway. The moth-eaten carpet smelled of mildew, the walls reeked of disinfectant; from one apartment near the elevator came the irritating odor of cooked cabbage. His nostrils twitching in disgust, he passed an abandoned refrigerator crammed with empty beer bottles and, further along, sacks of garbage that spilled out of the incinerator room one door down from 14G.

Parsifal had an animal's nose for scents, which intrigued the medical researchers who discovered he was able to distinguish smells that laboratory instruments could barely detect. They eventually traced the phenomenon to a rare glut of olfactory cells in the mucous membrane of his nasal cavity and the extraordinary sensitivity of the olfactory lobes in his brain. (One of the doctors wrote a scientific paper on their findings, but the organization Parsifal worked for, citing "state security" guidelines, suppressed its publication.) For Parsifal, almost everything—books, rugs, weapons, clothing, wax melting on a lit candle, water dripping from a tap, a dog in heat, a woman nursing a baby—had a telltale odor.

There were moments when, inundated by odors, he felt he was going mad.

Stopping in front of 14G, he rapped the knuckles of his free hand on the door. It occurred to him that in America there were how-to books on every conceivable human activity—lovemaking, child rearing, vegetarian cooking, cholesterol-free dieting, homeowning, tree pruning. But there was no how-to book on wetwork. Like foreplay, it had to be invented as you went along.

He was inventing it now.

He heard a scraping sound inside the apartment, got a faint whiff of jasmine perfume as someone studied him through the peephole. He
scratched impatiently at his week-old beard; when time permitted, masking your face was routine wetwork tradecraft. He would feel human again
when he shaved off the mask; when he recognized the face that gazed
back at him from the mirror.

Parsifal knew he had knocked on the right door when it opened the
width of a black safety rod. Low-rent apartment buildings on the bitter
edge of a Dallas ghetto didn't protect their tenants with tungsten safety
rods. A haggard woman wearing a cream-colored blouse, a tight black
knee-length skirt and no stockings peered out at him. She took in the
handkerchief spilling from the breast pocket of his sports jacket, the razor-
sharp crease in his trousers, the soft loafers. "So: What is it you are selling?" she asked in a voice husky with fear.

The instructions in Le Juif's envelope had led Parsifal to expect someone in the mid-forties. He hadn't been told it would be a woman. Not that
it changed anything except the odors reaching his cranial nerve fibers,
which dispatched olfactory information to the brain; even without perfume women never smelled like men. He delivered his half of the recognition signal with some embarrassment; it was a shade too literary for his
tastes. "Voltaire, on his deathbed, was asked by a priest to denounce the
devil. I was led to believe you would know the story."

The woman completed the cryptogram. "Voltaire tells the priest to fuck
off. Voltaire says, 'This is not the time to make enemies.' "

The woman's watchful eyes stared out from deep shadowy sockets, giving
her the appearance of a hunted animal; she looked ready to slam the door
shut if her visitor made one false gesture. She kept one hand hidden behind
her back. Parsifal wondered if she had a firearm in it. "The hallway stinks of
garbage," he told her, tapping a forefinger against the side of a nostril to il-
lustrate the offense. "You ought to complain." He rambled on; small talk
often lulled people into letting down their guard. "The odor almost asphyxiated me. I could never live in a building like this. Garbage is the perfect
metaphor for the twentieth century; the stench of garbage could be said to
come from the rot of civilization. How do you put up with it?"

"The stench of garbage or the rot of civilization?"

Parsifal offered her what he hoped was a disarming grin. "Both."

The woman barricaded behind the tungsten safety rod didn't crack a
smile. "The garbage in the hall is sealed in plastic sacks. I do not smell a

thing. The odor of civilization rotting is something you grow so accustomed to you are no longer aware of it." She sized up the man who had rung her bell. "So: what has happened to the agent who calls himself Dewey?"

Parsifal, a stickler for detail, spotted two long gray hairs on either side of her eyebrows curling off in the general direction of her ears. He smelled her lipstick and noticed that it had been sloppily applied, deforming her mouth. He heard tinny big-band music coming from the apartment. "I was not instructed to tell you what happened to Dewey," he answered.

The woman glanced down at the leather attaché case in Parsifal's right hand, at the thin square carton tucked under his right arm, then up again at his eyes, which were all she could see of his face. "Tell me anyway," she ordered.

Whoever she was, she was clearly used to being obeyed.

"Dewey came down with German measles. Caught it from a neighbor's daughter. Didn't want to pass the germs on to you."

She nodded at the package under his arm. "What is that?"

"Wheat-germ pizza."

"Who is it for?"

"Me. You. Whoever."

"In the four months I have been here, I have up to now been contacted by your Mr. Dewey," she insisted nervously. She didn't add that Dewey had always turned up with a pizza under his arm; that they had shared it while he delivered the money and she filled in gaps in the ongoing debriefing.

Parsifal shrugged with his eyebrows. "Variety is supposed to be the spice," he remarked offhandedly. When she looked at him vacantly, he added with a smile, "Of life." He took pride in his ability to speak English like a native-born American; to season his English with idiomatic expressions.

A grimace flickered onto the woman's painted lips. "So: money is the spice of *my* life. You brought some?"

Parsifal caught a glimpse of a gold incisor shimmering in her mouth. For answer he hefted the attaché case.

She tested him. "How much?"

"Three months' worth. Nine thousand dollars. In crisp twenty-dollar bills. Each bill has been folded lengthwise down the spine as if someone started to turn it into a paper glider."

When the woman still hesitated, Parsifal backed away. "If you'd feel more comfortable waiting for Dewey . . ." He left the sentence hanging in the air between them. It was an inspired touch.

She came to a decision. The door closed. The safety rod slipped out of its runner. Then the door opened wide. His nostrils flaring in irritation, Parsifal plunged through a cloud of jasmine perfume into the apartment.

The woman followed him into the living room, which was furnished in Salvation Army modern and sliced with bars of shadow and light cast by half-drawn venetian blinds. Without a trace of embarrassment she brought the hand out from behind her back and set a red brick down on the coffee table. She snatched warm-up pants and a sweatshirt off the back of the couch (Parsifal had detected the faint odor of dry sweat) and tossed them through a half-open door. "I could heat up the pizza," she said awkwardly. Her fingers worked through her hair, which was uncombed and smelled of henna. "We could talk. I do not have many visitors. I do not see . . . many men."

Parsifal, a heavy man who moved easily, cranked up an expression that could pass for a smile as he took a turn around the room. "I don't mind," he said finally, winding up in front of her, handing her the carton. "Only fools refuse to mix pleasure with business."

"Do you have a name?"

"Everyone has a name. Mine is Howard."

She offered her hand. "It is a pleasure to make your acquaintance, Howard," she announced with formality.

He held on to her hand a moment longer than he had to. "Howard is my surname."

"American names mystify me. I still do not understand if Dewey is a first name or a surname."

"My friends call me O.O."

"O. O. Howard." She shook her head; she might as well have defected to the moon as America. "Are you crazy for Italian opera too?"

"Too?"

"Dewey is a crazy man for Italian opera. He always turns up with a tape and plays it on my machine while we eat."

"The radio is music enough for me."

"You can leave the money on the table," she called over her shoulder. She disappeared through a swinging door.

Parsifal watched the door jerk back and forth, then set the attaché case down on the back of the couch and dialed in the combination. The lid clicked open. He pulled on a pair of latex surgical gloves and removed the eleven-millimeter Chamelot & Delvigne 1874 French military revolver fitted with a short, stubby, jury-rigged silencer. On the radio a pilot broadcasting from a helicopter was in the middle of his midday traffic summary. "If'n you're heading out towards Dallas–Fort Worth airport on the interstate, let's hope you're not racing to catch a plane. A seven-car fender bender's backed cars up for miles . . ."

The woman pushed through the swinging door into the living room. "The pizza will be ready in—" She caught sight of the pistol, which was gripped in two hands and aimed at her heart. Hugging herself, she started to tremble. "Who are you?" she whispered hoarsely. "Which side wants me dead?"

"I was not instructed to have a conversation with you before I killed you."

Parsifal had to hand it to her, the woman put on a class act. With a shudder she regained control of her body, of her emotions. "So: tell me anyhow," she ordered, her painted lips pulled back in a mocking sneer. "I promise to take your secret to the grave with me."

From an almost forgotten past Parsifal dredged up an identity she could recognize. "I am what the Apostle John identified as the rider of the pale horse: death. As to who wants you dead, it is the Russians."

"I have put money aside for a day of rain . . . thirty-five hundred dollars." She managed a fragile smile, which Parsifal associated with broken china that had been glued back together. "Today could come under the heading of a day of rain."

The woman was clearly a professional, and very proud; she read in his face that there was no possibility of talking her executioner out of fulfilling his contract. Her hands fluttered over her skirt, ironing out wrinkles. Then, bunching the fingers of her right hand, trembling slightly, moving deliberately, she touched her forehead, her chest, her left shoulder, her right shoulder. Murmuring something in Russian, she filled her lungs with the last breath she would ever take and nodded imperceptibly, granting Parsifal permission to shoot.

He squeezed the trigger. The revolver erupted in his hands, spitting out its lethal seed. The woman, flung backwards into the swinging door, crumpled to the floor, jamming it open. An ink black stain spread across the front of her cream-colored blouse.

Squatting next to the twitching body, Parsifal got another whiff of her jasmine perfume. Was it his imagination or had the scent started to grow stale? With the ball of his thumb he worked back an eyelid. He squeezed her thumbnail between his thumb and forefinger until her nail bed turned white, then released it. The blood seeped back under her nail. The woman was clinically alive, but she wouldn't be for long. Reaching for her wrist, he reset the tiny watch strapped to it two hours ahead, then slammed her wrist against the floor, shattering the watch, stopping time.

Stepping over the body, he went into the kitchen. Now came the creative part of wetwork: the signing of the execution with someone else's signature, the messing of the sheets to make it look as if someone else had slept in the bed. He turned off the oven and tossed the pizza into a corner and half-burned the carton in the sink so the Dallas police would conclude that a delivery man had talked his way into the apartment and murdered the woman, and tried to cover his tracks. Then he systematically opened every container and jar to make it appear as if someone had ransacked the apartment for hidden money or jewelry. He swept the frozen food in the freezer onto the linoleum and ripped open each item; he emptied the contents of the small plastic garbage pail into the sink; he pulled out all the drawers and tossed the forks, knives, cooking utensils and the thick wad of supermarket discount coupons into the empty garbage pail.

Returning to the living room, Parsifal slit open the cushions on the couch with a kitchen knife, flung clothing that smelled of camphor out of a closet and a dresser and pulled up the frayed rug. He emptied the medicine chest in the tiny bathroom and shredded the mattress in the tiny bedroom. He pulled frames from the walls and cut pictures from their frames. Behind one picture he came across the $3,500 in crisp twenty-dollar bills—each bill folded lengthwise down the spine as if someone had started to turn it into a paper glider—wedged into a crack under a flap of wallpaper. He let several bills flutter carelessly to the floor as he pocketed the money. He found the woman's purse, took the handful of twenty-dollar bills in it and dropped the purse and some loose change near the body wedged in the swinging door.

Three-quarters of an hour after shooting her, Parsifal knelt next to the body. The scent of jasmine had been replaced by a distinctly acrid effluvium. Parsifal's nostrils flared in revulsion as he identified the odor;

the woman had been menstruating. Breathing through his mouth, he squeezed the woman's thumbnail between his thumb and forefinger once more.

This time the blood seeped back into her fingernail bed with excruciating slowness.

arsifal loathed telephone booths. He broke out in a cold sweat every time he fitted his heavy body into one. It wasn't so much the odors, though they were vile enough; the booths invariably reeked of cold sweat and stale tobacco and (he had convinced himself) awkward conversations. It was more a matter of obliging him to relive the day and the night he had spent wedged in a sewage pipe, waiting to cross the frontier at Goritzia, near Trieste, some fifteen years before. He thought of it as the most revolting experience of his life. Just before dawn, when the border guards who weren't in on the scheme were likely to be dulled by fatigue, he had crawled out of his hiding place and started to swim down the river that meandered through the town straddling the frontier separating Slovenia from Italy, separating the Communist world from the capitalist world. The barbed wire blocking the river had rusted away enough for someone to squirm through the coils stretched under the bridge at the frontier. The American soldiers who pulled him out of the water had taken one look at his clothing, shredded by razor-sharp barbs and stinking of sewage, and decided the defection was genuine. When the CIA station at Trieste verified that the young defector had spent three years in a Siberian gulag for distributing a samizdat criticizing the Soviet system, political asylum had been instantly granted.

Which was how Parsifal, a wetwork virtuoso for the Komitet Gosudarstvennoĭ Bezopasnosti, better known by the initials KGB, came to install himself in a mobile home on the bank of the Rio Grande in the town with the unlikely name of Truth or Consequences, New Mexico.

Now, crammed into one of the last coin-operated telephone booths in the Dallas–Fort Worth airport, breathing with difficulty, Parsifal heard the phone ring across the state in Houston. Half a dozen rings later someone picked up the receiver. Parsifal fed quarters into the slot. "Is this ——?" He read off the phone number of the booth.

"You have a wrong number," a man announced, and hung up.

Ten minutes later, the time it took for the cutout in Houston to get to a public booth, the phone under Parsifal's fingers rang. He snatched the receiver off the hook.

"Did the deal go through?" a voice asked. It was pitched high and had a metallic sound, which meant that a speech-altering device was being used. "Did you acquire the Starr single-action 1865 percussion revolver in question?"

"The person I negotiated with turned out to be a woman."

"Women have been known to sell rare guns too."

"You led me to believe the seller was American."

"I pass on what La Gioconda tells—" The voice from Houston was drowned out by the roar of jet engines revving on the runway.

"I lost you," Parsifal yelled into the phone.

"What La Gioconda tells me, I pass on. How do you know the seller was not American?"

"She spoke with an accent."

"America is a melting pot. Lots of people speak with accents. Me, for example."

"She had a gold tooth in her mouth. An incisor. Americans don't have gold incisors; they have porcelain incisors."

"So she was European."

"She was wearing a wristwatch. I recognized the mark. It was a Lake Baikal. Lake Baikals are manufactured in Russia."

"Nowadays Lake Baikals are exported."

"Just before we concluded the deal for the revolver, she crossed herself."

"A lot of people turn superstitious in the presence of lethal weapons."

"She crossed herself the way someone who is Russian Orthodox crosses herself, with three fingers of the right hand bunched to represent the Holy Trinity. Then she said something in Russian."

"She was praying you would pay top dollar for the Starr. Not many of them turn up on the market."

Parsifal was irritated. In the old days, when his instructions had come directly from Moscow Center, he had been trusted with the identity of his targets. Now that his instructions came from Prince Igor, he seemed to have been cut out of the loop, as the Americans put it. "She wasn't praying," he remarked in a tired voice. "She spoke Russian like a native. She said, '*Ya by otvergalo diavola no eto ne vremya iskat vragov.*'"

There was a snicker on the other end of the phone line. Le Juif was savoring a private joke. "'I would denounce the devil, but this isn't the time to make enemies.' Sounds as if she had a sense of humor. Get to the point, make a long story short. What do I tell La Gioconda? What does La Gioconda tell Prince Igor? Can he add an 1865 Starr Arms Company revolver with the inspector's 'D' stamped on the barrel to his collection?"

"She was about to sign a bill of sale when she developed a medical problem. Her fingernails turned pale as death."

"Why didn't you say so in the first place? La Gioconda will be sorry to hear it. Prince Igor will go into mourning." There was a pause. "Are you still in the market for rare guns?"

Parsifal bristled. "What kind of a question is that?"

"You cracked once . . ."

"That's ancient history. I'm open to propositions."

"Have you given any thought to the Jogger?"

"It could be done."

"When? Where?"

"The governor has asked him to come to New Mexico—there's a fundraising dinner, a police academy graduation, a groundbreaking ceremony. It's not the kind of invitation the Jogger would turn down."

"You're our wetwork specialist. Come up with a scenario."

The phone went dead in Parsifal's ear.

PART

11

4

From the Pacific Rim came a rending of garments, a tearing of skin that gradually transformed itself into an open wound, then quickly darkened as the orange of the blast furnace was blotted up by the silver of the sea.

Oblivious to the sun setting over his shoulder, Irish Stu, who'd been piloting hot-air balloons before Finn was born, sniffed anxiously at the wet wind. "The barometer's plunging," he shouted, struggling with the currents rippling through the yellow-and-black air bag stretched on the ground. "Low pressure's going to kick up some god-awful gusts." The big Irishman eyed the massive cauliflower-shaped thunderheads looming over Seattle to the north. "Give it up, lad. You cannot run from the demon in the pit of your stomach."

"What sheriff'd buy the story of an ex-con?" Finn yelled back. He was still wearing the rumpled, once-white three-piece suit that he'd gotten secondhand in a thrift shop the day Irish Stu hired him. His dirty blond hair was pulled back into a short ponytail. A small silver earring glinted in his left lobe.

"I bought the story of an ex-con," Irish Stu shot back furiously. He clearly held Finn's going against him.

"I didn't start the fight—"

"You sure as hell finished it," cackled the thin Chicano kid Jesús.

Finn had let Irish Stu down. He needed to justify himself. "I broke his wrist when he pulled the knife . . ."

"The cops didn't find a knife," Irish Stu said.

"Oh, it was beautiful," Jesús told the Irishman. "One second Finn here was closing on the Swede so fast he was all blur, the next he was leaning back and breathing hard and watching with this funny look in his eyes.

Everybody in the pool parlor heard the bone crack. The Swede fell back, his shirt was hanging off his shoulder, he was staring down at his right hand dangling from his right wrist. He couldn't fucking believe it!"

Finn was determined to go ahead with the flight. Of medium height, lean and hard, he wrestled the last of the four propane canisters into the old wicker gondola with *The Spirit of Saint Louis* painted on the thin copper plaque bolted to its side.

His face a mask of anguish, Irish Stu turned on Finn. "For the sake of the blessed Virgin, abort the bloody launch and take what you got coming."

"If they send me up I'll lose the *Spirit*."

Finn buckled the propane canister to the gondola's aluminum frame with army surplus belts, then wrapped the twelve-gauge pump-action shot-gun in newspaper and stashed it in the duffel bag lashed to the frame. He waved at the Chicano kid Jesús who dried the dishes Finn washed at Irish Stu's all-night diner. Jesús kicked the toggle, starting the giant fan that worked off the car battery. Then he held up the hooped crown the way Finn had taught him so that the fan was aimed into the hollow of the air bag.

Its nylon skin still rippling, the balloon stirred, then lifted lazily off the ground. Cursing the sins of saints under his whiskey breath, Irish Stu fought to free two fouled lines. A sudden gust stirred up dust in the field behind the diner, pushing the envelope to a forty-five-degree angle. Finn lit off the two propane burners, worked the nozzles until they were di-rected at the crown and turned on the blowtorchlike flames. A bubble of hot air seeped into the balloon. It reeled drunkenly, then billowed and swung upright as the sixty-thousand-cubic-foot envelope filled with air heated a hundred degrees hotter than the outside air.

The Spirit of Saint Louis strained against its mooring lines.

Laughing wildly, Jesús pitched Finn's banjo into the gondola. "Hey, man, you don't wanna go to heaven wit'oud your music maker."

To the north, the thick sullen sky closed over Seattle like a fire curtain. A soundless spark of lightning knifed through the towering thunderheads. "This is a bloody crazy way to travel," Irish Stu cried. "You'll be wanting the luck of the Irish only to clear the power lines."

"If I can get her off the ground fast," Finn said, following his own thoughts, "I ought to stay ahead of the thunderheads and joyride the jet stream."

Below them on the valley road a blue-and-white sheriff's cruiser came tearing up the long pitch toward Irish Stu's. The light on the cruiser's roof was throbbing like a pulse, which meant the cruiser's siren must be on, though its shrill wail was lost in the whine of the wind.

Jesús caught sight of the police car heading up the hill. "Go, go, go for it, man!" he whooped. Darting excitedly around the gondola, he slipped the mooring lines attached to stakes set in the ground.

"Watch out for the thunderhead breathing down your neck," Irish Stu screamed into the wind. "The bastard'll suck the *Spirit* up to thin air. If your blood don't freeze you'll suffocate for lack of oxygen."

Its siren shrieking, then suddenly coughing off, the police cruiser bounced across the dirt field and skidded to a stop yards from Irish Stu. Two burly deputy sheriffs vaulted from the car and leaped for the lines trailing from the wicker gondola. One of them managed to catch hold of a line, but it rope-burned through his fingers as the nylon air bag lifted off at a sharp angle, the gondola trailing after it like a pendulum jammed at one end of an oscillation. Drawing his pistol, the second deputy sighted on Finn, but Irish Stu lunged for his wrist and wrestled the weapon aside. Dancing furiously around them, the Chicano Jesús cursed in Spanish the deputy sheriffs and their mothers and the mothers of their mothers.

From the gondola, Finn flung fragments of phrases back at the earth. ". . . to rise above the demon . . . ," he yelled. ". . . to start fresh . . ." He shouted something else about needing to find a backwater where he could put the violence behind him, but his words were drowned out by the gas sizzling in the nozzles.

Out of the corner of an eye Finn spotted the neon "Irish Stu's" atop the diner roof careening toward him. He braced for the collision, but it never came. Whipped by the wind, the gondola snapped off a television antenna, then grazed the top branches of the poplar beyond it on its way up.

"Oh work the bloody nozzles!" Irish Stu screamed. Catching his breath, he crossed himself fiercely. As the gondola suspended from the yellow-and-black balloon skimmed over the high-tension lines, he let the air seep out of his lungs. "Holy Mother of God," he whispered hoarsely, "a man could wind up stone cold dead trying to rise above the demon."

Behind Irish Stu, the Chicano kid Jesús scratched angrily at his pock-marked cheek as he gazed after *The Spirit of Saint Louis*, now a bright speck clawing like a crab across the grim sky. He was bitterly sorry he hadn't coiled one of the mooring lines around his wrist and hung on for dear life; sorry he hadn't said fuck you to gravity too.

5

R iding a fast-moving barometric high in a great south-southeasterly curl, Finn managed to outrun the sea of thunderheads. At first light of the first full day into the flight of the *Spirit*, soaring on twenty-five-knot winds, he looked back at an inverted sky filled with towering cumulonimbus glaciers. Through a pasty ground haze he could make out the last of the Oregon mountains. Underfoot, ocher stretches of Nevada desert, etched with long tarmac ribbons, shimmered through a low cirrus gauze. Stamping his feet, flexing his fingers inside his woolen gloves, Finn checked the temperature of the air. The thermometer read minus five degrees. He could feel the bitter cold burning his nose and toes and ears and fingertips. It reminded him of the nights he'd spent on perimeter patrol in the Saudi desert: the endless expanse of sky studded with more stars than he dreamed existed, the endless expanse of dunes that shifted with each whisper of wind, the numbing cold, the sensation of thawing out when the swollen sun finally inched above the horizon where the enemy waited. Lieutenant Pilgrim's rule of thumb on frostbite, delivered with a raunchy laugh when the perimeter guards emerged like zombies from their mole holes in the sand, echoed in his ears: If you can still feel pain, it means you're operational.

Hugging himself to keep warm, Finn looked up into the hollow of the air bag, then at the patchwork of wispy white contrails high above it. He was wearing every garment he owned: a sleeveless sweater under his suit jacket, a khaki desert jacket with "Lance Cpl Finn" stenciled above the breast pocket, a khaki raincoat over the desert jacket, his woolen army gloves, the sailor's watch cap his mother had knitted on her deathbed. He turned to face the rising sun and strummed his banjo at it to work off the numbness, but his fingers moved awkwardly. The few notes he produced were whisked away by the wind. He thought of lighting off the one-burner camp cooker and brewing instant coffee but decided it was too risky; his fingers were too stiff, his gestures too clumsy, he might set fire to the gondola. Crouching, he nibbled a granola bar instead and studied the *National Geographic* map taped to one of the canisters.

His pocket compass showed the *Spirit* on a heading of one six zero magnetic. Climbing to his feet, Finn leaned out of the gondola, looking for landmarks. He was drifting over a good-sized city. He spotted another town about twenty-five miles to the southwest, and a thin sickle-shaped lake glistening in the morning sunlight beyond it. He checked the map again. The sickle-shaped lake had to be the Rye Patch Reservoir west of Mill City, which meant the city under him was Winnemucca. He made a quick calculation and discovered that he had covered roughly five hundred and fifty miles in twelve hours. He had used up two of his four propane canisters keeping the *Spirit* at five thousand feet so he could ride the underbelly of the jet stream. If he descended, he would find warmer air but slower winds. Since the object of the exercise was to put as much distance as he could between the *Spirit* and Seattle, he decided to hang out at five thousand while there was daylight. When the sun went down, he would too. He removed a glove and inspected his fingernails for the telltale blue that indicated oxygen deficiency, a bit of tradecraft he had picked up from Irish Stu. He checked the altimeter, gave the balloon a ten-second shot of hot air, then curled up on the deck of the gondola with his head on his arm, pulled a blanket over his body and dozed.

The sun was overhead and shining in Finn's face when a sonic shock wave from a high-flying jet slammed into the balloon, jolting him awake. He checked the altimeter, saw he had lost altitude. His heading was holding, but the wind had slowed to fourteen knots. Twenty or so miles dead ahead, Kawich Peak loomed in the *Spirit*'s flight path. Unless he could find a current, he would be sucked onto the rugged slope of the 9,400-foot mountain. He tugged on the cord that opened the maneuvering vent in the top of the envelope, letting a gulp of hot air escape, giving the balloon negative buoyancy. It descended to 4,400 feet, but the north-northwesterly gusts blowing the *Spirit* onto Kawich Peak held steady. Anxiously, Finn pulled on the cord again. The *Spirit* lost more altitude. Leveling off at 3,800 feet, he felt the breath of a different wind on his cheek. Minutes later the balloon was riding a southerly current that swept it past the sun-drenched westerly slope of Kawich, which towered over the tiny balloon, its peak lost in mist.

With the sun staining the clouds on the horizon, Finn made out the flickering tinsel of Las Vegas off to port. He dozed again, waking every hour or so to check the heading and altitude and give the envelope a shot of hot air. Over the Mojave Desert the current appeared to bottom out. The *Spirit* veered, drifting in an easterly direction. At first light, with the Grand Canyon rutting the earth's crust to port and the scab of Flagstaff off the starboard bow, Finn patched into his fourth propane canister. He used the nozzles sparingly, letting the *Spirit* settle lower and lower as it floated lazily across Arizona. Late in the afternoon, with a quarter of a canister left, ground winds carried him into New Mexico. As the sun cut through the clouds toward the horizon behind him, he pulled hard on the cord, opening the maneuvering valve. The altimeter began to unwind as the gondola settled toward the forest. Deer grazing on the flank of a hill caught sight of it and bounded off. By now the balloon was so low that quail nesting in the tops of ponderosa pines beat into the air in fright. Coyotes howled at the *Spirit* sailing over their heads.

Skimming wooded hills that stretched as far as the eye could see, Finn searched desperately for a landing site. As the shadows lengthened, the needle on the pressure gauge of the last propane canister fluttered against the red DANGER zone. Still he could not make out a clearing in the woods. He took a quick look at the map and reckoned he was over an Indian reservation, with no sign of civilization for thirty miles. If he was forced down in the forest, the gondola and the balloon would certainly be wrecked, and he could be killed.

With the pressure gauge showing empty, the *Spirit* skidded over a gushing stream that plunged in a needle-thin fall down sheer chalk cliffs into a small oval mountain lake. Beyond the lake the gondola grazed the top branches of scrub oaks jutting from a rise. Up ahead Finn noticed a trail cutting through the impenetrable forest of scrub oaks toward a murky haze hovering over the next rise. From a distance it looked like an Indian smoke signal.

As the *Spirit* approached, the haze dissipated, revealing a town.

Bare-chested, his face streaked with black and vermilion war paint, Doubting Thomas made a dash for the old town jail, then crawled the length of the drainage ditch and came up behind the tree house from its blind side. He edged his eyes above the ground. Then, drawing the long wooden knife from his waistband, he darted behind a toolshed a stone's throw from the dead tree and the house in its branches.

As usual, it had been difficult getting anyone to be Kit Carson. Everyone wanted to be Geronimo or Cochise or Victorio, and the matter had to be decided by drawing straws. The short straw had fallen to Eskinewah Napas, whose name meant "the Boy with a Scar on His Head." "No tickling, no scalping," Eskinewah Napas had insisted, setting out the conditions under which he would agree to play. "When you shoot you got to aim for the feet, and the raid is over as soon as I surrender."

The attack was going according to a carefully devised plan. Doubting Thomas, who was playing Cochise, could see Victorio and Geronimo, their rifles held over their heads, wade across Rattlesnake Wash, jump the fence and, bending double, race through the chicken yard downfield from the tree house. The chickens scurrying out of their path set up a cackle that could be heard all the way up in the town at the top of the hill. A coal black cock with a streak of bright red in his tail feathers reared back and let fly a barnyard yowl to wake the dead. In the tree house, Eskinewah Napas, drawn to the commotion, leveled his repeater on a sill and pumped a BB into the chamber.

Moving like an evening breeze that barely rustled the leaves on a scrub oak, Doubting Thomas came up behind the tree house. He started to climb the ladder when his eye was distracted by a smudge of color over the Sacred Lake. Eskinewah Napas must have seen it at the same time, because he stood up in the tree house and pointed. "Lookee what we got here!" he called. Victorio and Geronimo, gone to ground next to an old bathtub filled with rainwater, came out from behind their hiding place uncertainly. Victorio plucked the black feather from his hair and used the end of it to scratch at a nostril. "If this is some kind of White Eye trick . . . ," he started to say, and then he too spotted the smudge of color.

"It's a balloon!" Doubting Thomas called, "and it's heading our way."

An instant later the three Apache warriors, whooping wildly, were flying across fields planted with corn toward the footbridges over the river. Stumbling down the ladder, Eskinewah Napas set off after them. "Wait up," he yelled breathlessly. "It might be White Eyes coming to raid the reservation."

Half afraid the hilltop town was a mirage, Finn maneuvered the *Spirit* down toward a field with dozens of pickup trucks parked in neat rows at one end and a smoldering heap of tires at the other. A few feet above the ground he tugged on the red strap attached to the rip panel in the crown, spilling the hot air out of the balloon. He tried to give the envelope a last shot of hot air to soften the landing, but the propane had run out. With a thump the gondola touched down between two te-pees, skipped several times and then, as the air bag collapsed, dragged to a stop through a lush carpet of goldenrod and snakeweed.

Shouting excitedly, a band of thin, half-naked Indian boys tore over the narrow, railless plank footbridges thrown across the river and raced uphill to get a closer look at the balloon. Emaciated dogs, their ribs visible through the skin, their tails curled menacingly between their hind legs, yelped at the gondola. Scores of older Indians hurried over from the town. Stocky squaws pushed elderly Indians in wicker wheelchairs onto a back porch overlooking the field. The Indians in the wheelchairs began drumming their canes on the porch railing.

A lanky one-armed Indian, his long hair twined into dirty braids that brushed his shoulders, raised his right hand. The boys dancing around the air bag, the old Indians drumming on the railing, even the dogs barking at the gondola, simmered down. Several mothers grabbed children and pulled them roughly back.

Finn looked out at the sea of expressionless faces; he felt as welcome as a butterfly in a beehive.

The one-armed Indian kicked at the air bag. "What brings you here?" he asked.

Something in the Indian's tone riveted Finn. He peeled off his desert jacket, climbed out of the gondola and started folding the air out of the yellow-and-black envelope that lay on the ground. "The wind," he replied with a tight smile.

An Indian with a shaved head whooped contemptuously. "If the wind brought you, the wind sure can take you away again."

A dozen young braves, some of them smoking thick hand-rolled cigarettes, began to close in on the gondola. The one-armed Indian drew a long double-edged bone-handled knife from his waistband. "Cut into strips," he told the others, "the nylon will make great banners for our feast day."

The shimmer of the blade caused Finn to catch his breath. The pulse throbbing in his temple sounded like the hooves of the demon kicking up silent storms of sand as it galloped past. In the pit of his stomach, the desire to ride the demon stirred again. He backed up until his back was against the gondola and reached in, feeling for the stock of the shotgun.

A woman with dark, short-cropped hair and a fringed skirt that stirred up dust around the painted toenails of her bare feet appeared at the edge of the circle of Indians. Her head cocked, the barefoot woman took in the gondola with *The Spirit of Saint Louis* written on it, then eyed Finn. "Say hey, Saint Louis," she called, taunting him. "If you don't know where you're goin', why, any wind'll get you there, you bet."

A short, stocky Indian wearing threadbare corduroys and a flannel shirt with the sleeves rolled up and a beaded headband over his long steel gray hair pushed through the crowd. His bare arms and forehead were smudged with the grease stains of a garage mechanic. He was holding the hand of a thin dark-skinned boy in cutoff jeans and streaks of black and vermilion paint on his face. "You got to be real dumb to argue with the wind," the Indian, who looked to be in his late fifties or early sixties, declared gravely, staring down the young braves circling the gondola. "You got to be real stupid to turn away what it brings you." He released the boy's hand and approached Finn. "The sacred winds have carried you to a time warp that goes by the name of Watershed Station," he announced.

On the porch, a toothless old Indian thrust himself out of his wicker wheelchair. Grasping the railing with one hand, brandishing a cane with the other, he called weakly, "Don't give 'im the time of day, Skelt. Loose lips sink ships."

"You tell 'em, Floyd," shouted the Indian woman behind his wheelchair.

Finn turned back to the Indian in corduroys. "I didn't see a Watershed Station on the map."

"Watershed was a ghost town until we evicted the ghosts. It is the geographic heart of the Suma Apache Reservation. I am Eskeltsetle, the Suma headman, which is pretty much the same thing as being mayor of Watershed."

"Name's Finn."

"Finn what? What Finn?"

"Just Finn."

Eskeltsetle searched Finn's face in the fast-fading twilight. The old Indian's eyes narrowed, letting in less light and more information. He remarked the high, chiseled cheekbones, the dark eyes set slightly further apart than usual, the unwavering gaze of someone who could turn extremely violent at the crack of a dry twig.

"You got Indian blood in you," Eskeltsetle said.

"My father was part Navajo."

"The Navajos and Apaches were once a single people," the Indian said. "We spoke the same Athapaskan language, we hunted the same valleys, we prayed to the same Great Spirit."

The Suma headman dipped his thick fingertips into a small beaded buckskin pouch tied to his belt and brought out a pinch of *hoddentin*, a sacred powder made of pollen. Raising his fingers to his lips, he blew the *hoddentin* into the air. A breath of a breeze carried it toward Finn.

"*Metaka Oysin*," Eskeltsetle murmured as the powder, confirming something he suspected, dusted the intruder's feet.

The dark-skinned Apache boy with the streaks of paint on his face and a wooden knife in his belt sidled up behind the Indian, who was his father. "Does he got a name, Skelt?"

"It's Finn."

"Why'd Shenandoah call him Saint Louis?"

Never taking his eyes off Finn, Eskeltsetle spoke to the boy. "Your mother's got a way of coming at things from a different direction than most, Thomas," he observed. "I expect there's no injury done if you was to call him Saint Louis too."

esmerized by the flickering flames, twelve young Suma Apaches, all barefoot, bare-chested, sat cross-legged in two concentric circles inside the wickiup. Shadows danced on the hides and blankets stretched over the bowed branches above their heads. Eskeltsetle, sitting nearest the flap, took a handful of dry sage from an earthenware bowl. Sprinkling it on the fire, he began chanting an Athapaskan death song for Serveriano, the old Suma medicine man whose spirit had crossed the Great Divide the night before. The sage crackled like gunpowder. Fragrant smoke filled the wickiup. Using their palms, the young Apaches bathed in the smoke, purifying their bodies.

The one-armed Indian with dirty braids, whose name was Alchise, leaned forward and extinguished the flame with a patch of cured deer hide, then carefully worked aside the layers of dirt and grass and green leaves to get at the mescal roots that had been cooking in the makeshift oven since noon. Alchise, who was Eskeltsetle's older son and Doubting Thomas's half brother, handed a bit of the sweet, beetlike root to each of the braves. As the young Apaches chewed on the root, Alchise spoke.

"Serveriano, whose sky spirit hovers over the wickiup, used to tell us the *pindah lickoyee*, the White Eye, divided everything they touched. They divided the open range where the buffalo grazed into ranches. They divided the day into hours, the hours into minutes, the minutes into seconds. They ate when the hands on a clock reached a certain position; it didn't matter if they were hungry or not."

"The white man's ways suck," sneered a tall brave with a shaven skull and a deformed ear. His name was Nahkahyen, the Keen Sighted.

"All *right*, my man Nahkahyen," agreed Gianahtah, the Always Ready. "Our ways are purer."

"Talk to us about the *Diné*," Petwawwenin, the Smoker, said to Eskeltsetle.

"Yeah, tell us more about the *People*."

Eskeltsetle nodded gravely. "There is an unbreakable bond between the Apaches and the Earth Mother, a bond nourished by an unquenchable thirst for prophecy. It was predicted the white man would come to our shores long before Columbus discovered America—"

"You left out *supposedly*, man," said Gianahtah, the Always Ready.

"Columbus *supposedly* discovered America," said Alchise.

Nahkahyen, the Keen Sighted, spoke up. "When Columbus *discovered* America, two million of us, more maybe, maybe more, was already here."

Chewing on mescal root, the young Apaches avoided Eskeltsetle's irritated gaze.

Covering his eyes with his bare arm, Nahkahyen, the Keen Sighted, groaned softly. "For too long," he said, his voice choking with rage, "Apaches have been fair game for serial killers called white men. For too long we have been forced into concentration camps called reservations, where our women die in childbirth, our children die of whooping cough and influenza, our braves die of rotting of the liver brought on by alcohol. Serveriano's death at seventy-seven was the exception to the rule. Until I was twelve I didn't know an Apache could die of old age."

Nahkahyen, the Keen Sighted, leaned forward and rubbed his fingertips in the still-hot cinders, then marked his face with three distinct ashgray streaks. The gesture, used from the dawn of time by Apaches about to set out on the warpath, was not lost on the braves in the wickiup. Several of them grunted in respect.

"I have spoken to Mr. Early in New Jerusalem," announced Nahkahyen. "I told him about the man in the green bow tie who comes to our casino to humiliate us." There was a murmur from several of the braves. Eskeltsetle closed his eyes. "Mr. Early has made an appointment for me," Nahkahyen continued, "with a state prosecutor in Santa Fe a week from Wednesday."

Suddenly everyone was talking at once.

"Remember what happened to Klosen, the Hair Rope, when he shot his mouth off . . ."

"Remember what happened to Uclenny, the Rapid Runner, when he threatened to spill everything to the newspapers . . ."

"When Baychendaysan, the Long Nose, set out for New Jerusalem, he disappeared from the face of the earth . . ."

"Remember the stomach cramps," Eskeltsetle said. "It is child's play to poison the drinking water which comes from the Sacred Lake."

From the hills outside the wickiup came the nasal ripple of a bluegrass banjo; furious groundswells of turbulent arpeggios, one bursting on the back of another, broke against a shore. Gianahtah, the Always Ready, turned on Eskeltsetle. "What about the stranger who sails on the wind to Watershed?" he asked.

"How is it you permit him to remain among us?" demanded Alchise.

Eskeltsetle did not respond immediately and no one, not even Alchise, dared to interrupt his silence. Finally Eskeltsetle looked up at the sage smoke swirling under the curved roof of the wickiup. The smoke suddenly thinned, revealing a large black spider, an insect sacred to the Apaches, clinging to the center of a web. "I have read it on the wind that brought the stranger my wife calls Saint Louis," Eskeltsetle said huskily. "The coming of the one with Navajo blood in his veins is clearly an omen. He has been sent to us by Wakantanka, the Great Spirit, to right a wrong."

"I got nothing against the occasional rain dance when there's a drought," Nahkahyen, the Keen Sighted, muttered with a raw laugh. Smiling crookedly, he reached up and crushed the spider between his thumb and forefinger. "But listening to the weather forecast can have a lot to do with its success."

t's ten-thirty," Shenandoah called from the kitchen. "High time Doubting Thomas was hittin' the hay."

"Everyone knows kitchen clocks run fast," the boy complained. He was sprawled on one of the pickup seats set up like couches in a semicircle facing the kiva fireplace. "Besides which, it's still practically light out."

Shenandoah appeared in the doorway carrying a kerosene lamp. She had changed into washed-out jeans and a T-shirt with "Live and Learn" printed across the chest, and "Older and Wiser" printed across the back. A gray cat with thick fur and green eyes stared out from between her bare feet. "If you say it's night, Thomas here'll promise you it's day," Shenandoah warned Finn. "Now you see why we took to callin' him Doubtin' Thomas. Like the saint in question, he won't swallow a resurrection he don't see with his own eyes."

"Who would?" mumbled Eskeltsetle, touching a match to the wick of a second kerosene lamp.

It was the evening of Finn's second day in Watershed. With Eskeltsetle's blessing, he had moved into the abandoned flat over the old mine-company offices next door on Sore Loser Road. His gondola and balloon had been stored in the shed behind the outhouse.

"I don't mind none being called Doubting Thomas," Thomas was telling Finn. "That makes me a saint like you."

"Hell, I'm no saint . . ."

Shenandoah waved at Thomas in a way that left him no room for maneuver. "Haul ass, boy. Get your warm body off to dreamland."

Sliding off the pickup seat, Thomas snatched a flashlight from a table and let Eskeltsetle lead him from the room. "You promised you'd tell me about how your grandfather went to Washington to meet the president," he reminded him.

"Don't go fillin' your son's head with crazy Apache stories," Shenandoah called after them.

"They're not crazy Apache stories," Eskeltsetle retorted from the door. "They're actual history, pure and simple."

Shenandoah began clearing the dinner dishes off the trestle table. "So what is it you do when you're not flyin' balloons to ghost towns that ain't on any map?"

Carrying the empty beer bottles, Finn followed her into the kitchen. "If you mean what do I do for work, I do anything. I wash dishes. I dig fence holes. I split logs. I pick lettuce."

"Just what we needed to make a dent in Watershed's unemployment statistics—another jack-of-no-trades!"

"If things get real tight, I make butter."

When Shenandoah looked quizzically at him, Finn laughed. "I shared a jeep back during the Gulf War with a black second lieutenant from Tennessee. His last name was Pilgrim, I never did learn his first name. I hear he works for some congressman in Washington now. Anyhow, one night while we were batting our arms and legs to keep from freezing to death he told me the story of the two frogs trapped in a bucket of milk. If you heard it, stop me. One frog figured the situation was hopeless and drowned. The other flailed away with his frog's legs and made butter." Finn flashed a sheepish smile. "That's me, flailing away. With my frog's legs. Making butter."

Shenandoah worked the pump, spilling water onto the dishes piled in the deep sink. "Eskeltsetle told me you was in the Gulf War. Did you get to see the desert?"

Finn leaned back against a "Death by Chocolate" poster thumbtacked to the wall, finishing off a bottle of beer. "That's all there is in Saudi Arabia—desert."

"How long you spend there?"

"Five months, fourteen days, twenty-three hours."

"What did you do with yourself? To pass the time, I mean. Me, I get off on watchin' the sun rise in the Painted Desert, but I'd go ballistic if I had to watch it for five months."

"I eventually went ballistic, but that's another story," Finn said. "In the Gulf I was a Special Forces meteorologist. The first thing after the sun rose, the last thing before it set, I'd launch a small helium balloon which gave off radio signals. Then I'd track the balloon with a tiny receiver, something about the size of a Walkman, to map the ground winds. That way the support helicopters and planes could approach targets so the smoke wouldn't hide them."

Finn tilted back his head and swallowed a mouthful of beer. "The Gulf's not on the same planet as Watershed," he went on, wiping his lips on his sleeve. "When I wasn't out on patrol I used to serenade the dunes with my banjo. I counted stars. I counted how many days I had to go before getting my discharge papers." He laughed under his breath. "I turned in squares."

"What's turnin' in squares supposed to mean?"

"Yeah, well, when someone gets lost in the desert, which happens all the time on patrol—the desert has no permanent landmarks, which makes navigation difficult—when someone gets lost they send out search parties. You mark the spot where the missing person was last seen, okay? Then you start turning in squares, each leg longer than the leg before it." Finn shook his head, a faraway look in his eyes. "Sometimes it felt as if I spent the entire war turning in squares. Sometimes I think I've been turning in squares my whole life."

Shenandoah, her back to Finn, asked quietly, "What did you lose back there in the desert?"

Finn raised his eyes and studied the back of her neck. "Polaris."

"Who's Polaris?"

"Polaris is the North Star."

Shenandoah glanced over her shoulder and their eyes met. "You look young but you sure talk old." Wheeling on the heel of a bare foot, skipping nimbly over the sleeping cat, she pushed through the screen door into the night. Returning a few minutes later with a turn of firewood, she deposited it on the floorboards in front of the wood-burning stove and fed a split log into the stove. Cranking up the flame, she filled an old casserole with water and set it to heat.

After a while Finn asked, "So are you Suma Apache?"

"I had a great-grandma who was Suma. My Apache name's the same as hers, Ishkaynay. Turns out that Ishkaynay—try not to smile—means 'boy.' "

"Who tacked that on you?"

"The local warriors took to callin' me Ishkaynay when I came to live in Watershed. It's what comes of bein' flat-chested. Apache men are into

Apache liberation, but they ain't worked up a sweat yet about Apache women's liberation." She tested the water, decided the temperature was right and poured it into an enamel bowl with a bone handle. She carried the bowl into the main room. Finn trailed after her. With a snap of her wrist she closed the curtains over the large plate-glass window with

WATERSHED GENERAL STORE

written across it. "Went an' put them up yesterday," she remarked, fingering the stiff material. "Turnin' the old curtains into slipcovers for the pickup seats. Turnin' the old slipcovers into original Apache miniskirts for our Indian handcraft store."

Finn said, "Everyone's getting promoted."

Shenandoah almost smiled. Fluffing a cushion, she settled down on it with her legs crossed and her back against the wall, added salt crystals to the warm water and began soaking her fingertips.

"What that for?" Finn asked.

"It's what I call wet work," Shenandoah replied. The gray cat, ambling in from the kitchen, sank down next to her and fixed its unblinking eyes on Finn. "I do this twenty minutes a day come hell or high water," Shenandoah allowed. "A girl has got to keep her fingers supple . . ."

Nursing his bottle of beer, Finn wandered around the room. Everything in view—the window curtains, the pickup seats covered with the old curtains, the frayed Navajo scatter rugs—seemed washed out, bleak. The only splashes of color came from bouquets of freshly picked wildflowers—scarlet bugler, yellow clover, purple larkspur, red onion skin, goldenrod—spilling from number-ten cans filled with water. The wide wooden shelves along two walls of the room were heaped with spare pickup parts. Old-fashioned wooden milk boxes filled with more spare parts were piled one on top of the other on either side of the front door.

"There's an order behind all this disorder, a method to all this madness," Shenandoah explained from the floor. "It's like on a ship. You got to know how to look at it. My husband happens to be the used-pickup king of northern New Mexico."

"I saw the pickups lined up in the field when I landed."

"Skelt has got more than forty out there," Shenandoah said with some pride. "He's a certified mechanical genius. Maybe one out of three pickups towed in here—you oughta see some of them, they're ripe for the junk heap—one of three he puts back together and sells off real good. The ones he can't put back on the road he cannibalizes and sells the spare parts off them there shelves."

Finn said something about how the Suma Apaches appeared to have a good thing going in Watershed.

"We got the pickup business," Shenandoah said. "We got Skelt's navy pension—he put in twenty years on destroyers, which is where he learned about machinery. We got the Social Security checks of the twelve Apaches in the Suma old-age home who couldn't get into regular old-age homes because they was Apaches. We got the Indian handcraft store specializing in Apache miniskirts and Apache art printed by driving cars over inked woodblocks. We got the fireworks concession. We also got two hundred and fifty-five mouths to feed, which is all that's left on earth of the Suma Apaches. We're the smallest Indian tribe in America, living on the smallest Indian reservation in America."

"How do you make ends meet?"

"Ain't easy. The big thing we got goin' is the casino we started up weekends and holidays," Shenandoah said. "That's why I soak my fingers; I deal poker. Gamblin's not allowed in New Mexico, but this ain't New Mexico. This is an Indian reservation, which means the federal Indian gamblin' laws apply. When the county gets around to pavin' over the road up from New Jerusalem, why, we're gonna go an' open the casino seven days a week and tap into the tourist trade. We been tryin' to get the state to run power and phone lines up here for years. Hell, we'll run our own lines up here. There'll be no unemployment in Watershed. All our kids'll get to go to Harvard and the reservation'll pick up the tab. The Suma Apaches could become the richest tribe in America, if only . . ."

"If only?"

"I'm glad you asked," Shenandoah said, changing the subject abruptly. "My dad was a professional Texan and a professional gambler and a Baptist and a Democrat, in that order. He hated Catholics even though my mother was one, and Republicans. He almost always won at cards, but he won more from Catholics and Republicans. He began each meal with a prayer. 'Lord, grant that I may always be right, for Thou knowest I am hard to turn.' My father was a question mark to me." She rolled her eyes. "Life is buzzin' with question marks, as opposed to answer marks. How does a thermos know to keep hot liquid hot and cold, cold? How come the cave dudes could paint perfect buffalo, but their drawings of each other look like a child did them? Why does a potato get soft when you boil it and an egg get hard?"

Finn sank onto a pickup seat. "Where did you grow up?"

Shenandoah's eyes focused on a memory. "In a car. I was always on route. My dad was lookin' for the ultimate poker game." She smiled anxiously. "Sometimes I wake up nights thinkin' I'm curled up in the back of one of those old four-door Chevies with the big tail fins."

Finn finished the rest of the beer. "Was Watershed really a ghost town until the Apaches evicted the ghosts?"

Shenandoah concentrated on her soaking fingers, which were incredibly long and delicate. "Watershed's got a hell of a history. Back in the 1870s the off-duty soldiers posted along the Rio Grande used to comb the hills looking for what the Apaches called yellow iron. One fine day some damn fool pony sergeant panned gold out of Rattlesnake Wash, which runs into and out of the lake you passed over. Next thing you know a town sprang up on the crest of the hill above the wash. They went and called it Watershed Station because it was on the watershed line of these hills. The general store here sits smack on a local divide, which makes it just about the highest buildin' in Watershed." Suddenly Shenandoah looked as if she were fighting back tears. "If I was to stand upstairs in my bedroom and cry, which ain't likely as I used up my ration of tears before I came to live in Watershed—but if, I *was* to, cry, the tears, when they hit the ground, would flow west an' wind up in Arizona. If I was to cry in Doubtin' Thomas's room, the tears'd flow east and irrigate Texas."

Finn said, "Texas is hundreds of miles from here."

"Don't matter none. A scientific fact is a scientific fact. Watershed was booming until the twenties," Shenandoah went on. "The Atlantic and Pacific Mining Company operated a general store, a saloon, a Western Union office, a lumberyard, a livery stable, a feed yard, a hotel, also a county jail, also a casino down at the south end of Sore Loser Road. They even had theirselves a whorehouse, which is where the old-age home is today. The upstairs bedrooms have still got mirrors on the ceilin's. When they're not lookin' at satellite television workin' off the generator out back, the old folks stretch out on beds and watch theirselves grow older in the mirror."

Shenandoah lifted her hands from the enamel bowl and shook off the water and dried her fingers on the fur of the purring cat. "What's keepin' Skelt? He's got to be tellin' Thomas the history of the Apaches from the year one, you bet." She took a deck of cards from a sewing box and began to shuffle them with a slow, flowing motion of her fingers and wrists.

"You know any tricks?"

"Hell, yes." Shenandoah held the deck in her left hand and showed Finn the top card. "Queen of hearts." She put the queen of hearts back on top of the deck. Then she dealt Finn the top card and herself the next card.

"Look at your card."

Finn leaned forward and flipped over his card. It was the seven of spades. He turned over her card. It was the queen of hearts.

"I double-dealed you, Saint Louis. I dealt you the second card. I use a technique called the two-card push-off. You could do it if you practiced a few thousand hours and soaked your hands in warm water twenty minutes a day."

"I don't believe I'm seeing what I'm seeing. Show me more."

"You want me to show you more." She set out five hands of five cards faceup on the floor, then began to scoop them up. "When a hand's over with I can scoop up the discards so that, say, the four jacks that was scattered in the discards wind up on the top or bottom of the deck. Okay, watch close. Now I'm gonna give the deck what we call a riffle shuffle." She divided the deck into two packs and begins to riffle them together. "So what I'm really doin' is countin' the cards as they spring off my thumbs and arrangin' the deck so the jacks will all come to yours truly on the next deal. I started with the four jacks on the top, right? When I finish shufflin', the four jacks will be fifth, tenth, fifteenth and twentieth from the top."

Finn shook his head. "That's plain impossible."

Shenandoah was getting a kick out of performing. She laid out five hands of five-card stud. One after another the four jacks fell to her.

"Do you ever lose?" he asked as she flipped over the last of the four jacks.

"Let's just say I got a better chance of winnin' than the next guy."

"Where did you say you did your wheeling and dealing?"

10

A stream of cars and pickups, their headlights flickering through the rain pelting the scrub oaks, made their way up the wide dirt road from New Jerusalem. Across the street from the two-story Rattlesnake Casino at the bitter end of Sore Loser Road, sopping wet Apache boys scurried through the unpaved parking lot hawking spider-web dream catchers and toy tomahawks. An accordion spewed country-western into the moist night air as Finn, dressed in his rumpled once-white three-piece suit, pushed through the swinging door into the casino. Overhead a giant mirrored ball, suspended on a cable from the dome and working off a gasoline generator behind the building, scattered shards of colored light in every direction. Standing next to an elaborate gold-lettered antique sign that said, "Ladies check your lipstick, Gents check your hats and guns," Alchise, the tuxedo sleeve of his missing arm pinned neatly back, fixed his expressionless eyes on Finn.

"How's business?" Finn asked pleasantly.

"Everyone's a winner," Alchise muttered sarcastically, "except us Apaches."

Behind a teller's window, Petwawwenin, the Smoker, deftly topped off stacks of plastic chips and pushed twenty dollars' worth of them under the gold grille. "Don't bet all your chips on one number," he told Finn with a cool smile. "Spread them around. That way you'll take longer to lose your shirt."

"Thanks for the advice."

"Any time."

Finn meandered past rows of slot machines into the main hall. For a while he stood behind a fat man who licked the tip of a knife-sharpened stub of a pencil and noted in a small book the winning numbers at a roulette table. Every once in a while the fat man would lean forward and drop a hundred-dollar chip onto a number, then grimace as the young Apache working the table raked it in. Finn himself lost ten dollars betting the even numbers, and five more when snake eyes turned up at a crap table. He drifted over to a blackjack horseshoe and watched the action for a while. A heavily made-up middle-aged woman wearing a two-tone cowboy shirt and a pink Stetson patted the empty chair next to her. "Bring me luck—set yourself down next to me, young fella," she said with a rasp. A long filter-tipped cigarillo bobbed on her lower lip as she talked. When Finn hesitated, she said, "Honest to God, honey, I don't bite."

Finn slipped into the empty seat and dropped his last five-dollar chip onto the table.

"Handle's Mildred," the woman in the pink Stetson informed him out of the side of her mouth. Across the casino a woman feeding quarters into a one-armed bandit shrieked as a cascade of coins spilled from the slot machine into her plastic cup. Mildred shut one eye and sneaked a look at her closed card with the other eye. "Hit me," she told the dealer. Then: "Once more." Snorting in frustration when she saw the card she had drawn, she slipped off her stool. "My daddy always said, the first thing you got to do if you're in a hole is stop digging."

Finn held his own for a quarter of an hour, then hit a lucky streak that included two back-to-back blackjacks and quit while he was ahead. Collecting his chips, he headed for the bar, treated himself to a whiskey, then threaded his way past the tables and gamblers to the double green doors on one side of the casino. A small silver plaque over them read, "High Roller Heaven." Clinking the ice cubes in his glass against each other, he pushed through into the green room.

Nahtanh, the Cornflower, sidled up to him. "This here section of the casino is for the heavy hitters," he said. He flexed his sinewy shoulder inside his tuxedo. "You don't appear to me to be a heavy hitter."

"Looks can be deceiving," Finn said. He wandered over to the poker table and watched Shenandoah deal five-card stud to four heavy hitters. She was dressed in black trousers, a white-on-white shirt without pockets or cuffs and a black string bow tie. Distributing the cards, she let her eyes flick over Finn without a glint of recognition. A few minutes later a short, muscular, balding middle-aged man wearing a green bow tie joined the game. He set out half a dozen thousand-dollar chips on the table.

Shenandoah never looked up at him. She dealt everyone a closed card, then started setting out the open cards. After each round of open cards, the players bet.

"Cost you five hundred," an Indian Finn recognized as a Watershed Station Apache announced after Shenandoah dealt him an open king.

"Up five hundred," said the man in the green bow tie, who had a queen showing. His voice had a pompous guttural quality, as if the possibility of losing never crossed his mind.

Two of the heavy hitters stayed; the fourth dropped out. Shenandoah dealt everyone a second open card. The Apache had a king nine showing. Pushing hundred-dollar chips forward, he bet five hundred again. Green Bow Tie barely glanced at his queen seven, both spades. "Back at you," he said, raising the bet to one thousand. One of the other players, with a jack four showing, turned over his cards and dropped out. The heavy hitter next to him pursed his lips, studied the king nine in front of the Apache and the two spades in front of Green Bow Tie, then saw the bet.

Shenandoah set out a new round of cards. The heavy hitter still in the game smiled as she dealt him a six, giving him a pair of sixes. "Sixes talk," Shenandoah announced.

"Sixes say two thousand," the heavy hitter said, pushing forward a fistful of chips.

His face expressionless, the Apache raised a thousand. Green Bow Tie, who had three spades showing, raised another thousand. The pair of sixes and the Apache called.

Shenandoah dealt the last round. The Apache drew a second nine, Green Bow Tie a fourth spade, the heavy hitter an ace.

"Nines talk," Shenandoah said.

"You want to see my hole card," said the Apache with the nines showing, "it's going to cost you." He pushed forward five thousand-dollar chips.

Green Bow Tie didn't bat an eye. "Up five thousand," he said.

Looking worried for the first time, the heavy hitter with the pair of sixes peeked at his hole card again. "You're bluffing," he announced. "Five more."

The Apache, betting into a possible flush on one side and aces over on the other, thought a moment, then raised another five thousand.

"Three raises is the limit," Shenandoah announced.

Green Bow Tie and the hitter with the sixes showing called.

"Kings over," the Apache said, turning over a king in the hole.

"Aces over," the heavy hitter said, turning over an ace in the hole.

Green Bow Tie flipped over his hole card. It was a low spade. "I'm afraid I caught the flush, gentlemen," he said.

The heavy hitter with the aces over pocketed the few chips he had left. "I'm afraid I caught cold," he said, sliding off his chair.

A young man in designer jeans, a Texan judging from the string tie and the gold buffalo clasp on it, took his place. "You-all sure got yourself beautiful fingers, babe," he told Shenandoah. "When did you say you got off work?"

"Past your bedtime."

"I'd sure be willing to hang out to the crack a dawn for you, babe."

Shenandoah said very quietly, "Simmer down, midnight cowboy, or one of my Apache brothers will scalp you."

Behind her, Gianahtah, the Always Ready, bared his teeth in a wintry smile.

Shenandoah set out closed cards, then dealt each player an open card. As the game progressed, a mountain of chips accumulated in front of the man in the green bow tie. The big loser was the Apache. Word spread that there was a heavy winner. People drifted over from the roulette table. "There are nights when the gods smile down on people in bow ties," Green Bow Tie announced when Shenandoah dealt him a second eight. "This has to be one of them."

Finn noticed Eskeltsetle standing off to one side, his heavy-lidded eyes fixed on the game. Shenandoah seemed to glance in his direction. Eskeltsetle nodded imperceptibly.

Her hands moving over the deck in a blur, Shenandoah dealt another round of open cards. The Apache, with a pair of jacks showing, pushed forward the last of his chips. "I'm in for four thousand."

"I figure the Indian for three jacks," the woman next to Finn whispered. "Else he wouldn't raise."

With only a pair of eights showing, Green Bow Tie matched the bet. The Apache turned over a seven in the hole. "All I got is the jacks," he said.

Green Bow Tie turned over his hole card. It was a third eight. "Gotcha," he said, reaching for the chips.

Nahtanh materialized at his elbow with a plastic bucket. Green Bow Tie raked the chips into it and headed for the teller's window to cash them in. Trailing after him, Finn watched from behind a slot machine as Petwawwenin, the Smoker, counted the chips, then filled a leather attaché case with cash and handed it over the grille. Turning toward the exit, Green Bow Tie pushed through the swinging doors and disappeared into the night.

"Looks like you quit while you were ahead," Petwawwenin commented when Finn cashed in his chips.

"I was following the lead of the dude in the green bow tie," Finn retorted. "Does he play here often?"

Petwawwenin slid one hundred and twenty dollars in crisp twenty-dollar bills under the grille to Finn. Each bill was folded lengthwise down the spine as if someone had started to turn it into a paper glider. "You obviously ain't heard about curiosity killing the pussycat," Petwawwenin remarked, and he brought up from the pit of his Apache soul the iciest smile Finn had ever seen.

11

Over the years Watershed Station had lost dozens of cats to coyotes, which was why Shenandoah wasn't about to let her new cat stay out all night. Armed with a flashlight, she padded barefoot around the yard behind the general store, searching under the porch, peering into the crawl space where the bottles of gas were stored. She was wearing two gauzelike sheaths, one over the other, that kept slipping off her shoulders, obliging her to shrug them back on from time to time. The night was alive with the sound of owls cooing in the shadowy foliage of trees and dogs barking in the distance. Making her way downhill to Rattlesnake Wash, its dark water foaming white over volcanic boulders, she peered under the footbridges, which the town strays often used for shelter. "Here, pussy," she called in an undertone, poking through the Nissan pickup that Eskeltsetle was in the process of cannibalizing. "Memememe, memememe."

The mournful strains of a banjo reached Shenandoah's ears. Drawn to the sound, she followed it across the yard outside the Atlantic and Pacific Mining Company office. "Pussy, pussy, pussy," she called. "Where the fuck are you, pussy?" The twanging of the banjo grew louder as she made her way up the narrow wooden steps clinging to the side of the building. On the landing she cupped her hands and peered through a pane of the door.

"Son of a bitch!" she exclaimed.

Inside, the cat could be seen lapping milk from a saucer on the floor. The flames of candles set in wine bottles sent shadows dancing around the room. Sitting on a broken chair facing the cat, Finn was serenading her with his banjo.

The music broke off in mid-riff as Shenandoah came barreling through the door. "Round here we're careful 'bout kickin' fresh turds on a hot day," she said angrily. "What the hell, I'll make an exception for you."

"What are you steamed about?"

"I been lookin' everywhere for that damn cat."

"She was the one who came to me."

Shenandoah took a deep breath, shook her head and simmered down. "The next thing you're gonna tell me is she opened the goddamn door."

"I opened the door." He tried not to smile. "I didn't want to be rude. What do you call your cat?"

"I call the cat Geronimo."

Finn leaned the banjo against a wall. "Could I interest you in a saucer of milk?" he asked quietly.

There was a sudden stillness in the room.

Eyeing him warily, Shenandoah chewed on the inside of a cheek. "Let's get things real straight between us, Saint Louis. I'm hitched till death do us part to Eskeltsetle, and glad to be. He's one beautiful Apache even if he is old enough to be my father." She stared unblinkingly into Finn's eyes. "Here's the deal: I like you real fine, but like is the limit of my possibilities."

He looked away. "You're giving me more than I got a right to, but less than I need."

"I'm givin' you as much as I can give you. You can take it, you can leave it."

Finn looked back. "I'll take it. Let's drink to friendship."

"I don't mind, long as we're talkin' the same language." She nudged the saucer of milk with her big toe. "Do you have somethin' with more alcohol content than milk?"

Finn spilled some cheap whiskey into two tumblers. "I'd offer you ice if there was electricity and I had a fridge. Do you want water?"

"An Apache never dilutes whiskey with water unless he's runnin' outa whiskey."

Finn handed her a tumbler. They clicked glasses. "Cheers, I guess," she said without enthusiasm. She tilted back her head and downed a shot. The whiskey burned her throat. She opened her mouth and breathed out. "This here ain't whiskey, this here is pure unadulterated Suma firewater. I need to ventilate my lungs."

Shenandoah curled up on a corner of Finn's army cot, her sheaths riding up her thighs, her back against a pillow, the pillow against the wall. Geronimo leaped up next to her and she absently ran her long fine fingers against the grain through the fur on the cat's arched back. Finn settled down on the floor facing the cot, his legs stretched out in front of him, his back against the brick-and-wood bookcase he'd built for the books he was going to buy when he got some money. Sipping his whiskey, he tried to keep his eyes off Shenandoah's bare thighs.

Shenandoah picked up the two frayed paperbacks lying on the cot and started leafing through them. "You read books?"

"Sometimes."

"So who collected the *Collected Works?* Who's Robert Frost?"

"He wrote poems," Finn said. "All the poems he ever wrote in his entire life are collected in that one book."

She worked the ball of her thumb down the spine of the other paperback. "What makes Gatsby great?"

Finn thought about that for a moment. "When he thinks, he thinks big. When he loves, he loves big. When he loses, he loses everything."

"That's a fair description of Skelt. He's as great as this Gatsby fella, only Apache style."

"How did you guys get together?"

"I was wonderin' when you'd get around to that," Shenandoah said, flashing a faint self-mocking smile. "Everyone always does." He started to take back the question, but she cut him off with an impatient wave of the hand. "Hell, I don't mind."

She began talking so softly that Finn had to strain to hear her. "Emotionally speakin'," she said, "I'd gone and dug myself into a hole. I was hangin' out in Santa Fe, but I was fed up with the white guys I was datin', I was fed up with the white world. I was livin' with a white dude at the time, one day we saw this hombre ridin' a bi-cycle with a blond-haired kid balanced on the handlebars, they was both grinnin' awful ear-to-ear grins. 'So did you see that, Shenan!' my dude says. 'Why, it makes me regret we never had a bi-cycle together,' he says. *A bi-cycle together!* Truth is I woulda married the first Apache that happened along. Thanks God it was Eskeltsetle. He was on the short side but strong as an ox and one hunk of an Indian, with that flat nose of his that starts up above his beautiful eyes and plunges straight down like a ski jump. Skelt saw right off what the problem was: I wasn't sure who I was. In White Eye country they got a fancy name for this; it's called an identity crisis. So Skelt—who is one crazy Apache, right? who claims he talks to the Great Spirit—Skelt went 'n' talked to me. And who's to say what he told me didn't come straight from the horse's mouth? I mean, who's to say God wasn't speakin' to me *through* one crazy Apache named Eskeltsetle?"

Finn was mesmerized by her story. "What did Skelt tell you?"

Shenandoah shrugged a shoulder back into her sheaths. "He wanted me to come back and live with him on the reservation, but I wasn't sure I'd fit in. So Skelt takes me down to the Santa Fe military cemetery and shows me these two old grave markers, they were so faded you had to read them with your fingertips. One said 'Indian Scout—O. Y. Slater—Medal of Honor—Sergeant Company A—Indian Wars—March 29, 1893.' The other said 'Ishkaynay—Apache Woman.' "

"Ishkaynay was the name of your great-grandmother," Finn remembered.

"Seems like O. Y. Slater, maybe his Medal of Honor was rattlin' against his faded blue army tunic, maybe it wasn't, it don't change the story none, O. Y. Slater turned up one winter mornin' when a fresh snow'd blanketed the four tepees in a clearin' in the woods. The women were boilin' roots over a fire. The braves were off huntin', the winter was particularly hard, they was all starvin' from lack of game. Medal of Honor winner O. Y. Slater worked the lever of his Sharp repeater and shot the four old men who were guardin' the women and children, then he scalped them to collect the bounty on Apache scalps. Medal of Honor winner Slater picked out one of the Suma Apache women—she was fifteen at the time, beautiful the way only an Apache can be beautiful, with a long nose and lean body and fire in her eyes—he picked her out and tied her hands and led her on a leash out of the hills and down to Santa Fe. She scrubbed his floors, she cooked his food, she warmed his bed, eventually she gave birth to a daughter, then she fell sick with what they called swamp fever in those days. Medal of Honor winner Slater and Ishkaynay died of swamp fever the same week and was buried next to each other in the cemetery. It was Skelt's grandfather who came and took Ishkaynay's little half-breed daughter back into the hills and raised her with the Suma Apaches, which is how come he knew the story. That little girl was the mother of my mother."

Finn reached out to touch her ankle, but she jerked it back as if she had been burned. "So Skelt shows me these grave markers—that was ten years ago next month—he shows them to me and he says, 'Shenandoah, you are who you think you are. All you got to do is invent yourself over again.' So there I was, with cold Indian-killer blood contaminatin' my hot Apache blood, and Skelt was tellin' me I could be anythin' I wanted to be. And what I wanted to be was female and Apache and a dealer who had some control over the games she played in."

"And here you are . . . ," Finn said carefully.

"Here I am," she agreed.

". . . controlling the games you play in."

"You bet."

For a while neither of them said anything. Then: "I watched you dealing poker in the casino last night."

"What's that supposed to mean?"

"The game was rigged. You were double-dealing everyone. I watched you shuffling; you were counting the cards as they came off your thumbs."

Moon shadows from the branches of scrub oaks outside the window flitted across Shenandoah's face as she leaped from the cot to prowl the room. Startled, Geronimo turned around her ankles, upsetting the saucer of milk. "Fuckin' Saint Louis," Shenandoah muttered. "You oughta mind your own goddamn business." She grabbed the cat and tried to coax her into drinking the milk from the floor. "I don't goddamn believe it," she said, suddenly on the verge of tears. "I'm goin' to fuckin' cry over spilt milk!"

Finn held up his hands. "Peace, huh? I'm sorry I shot my mouth off—"

"Listen up, Saint Louis. I mean, fuck, everyone in that casino cheats at somethin'—the stock market, their expense accounts, their taxes, their wives." She went to the window and stared out into the night, then turned and came at him, her bare feet slapping against the floorboards. "It was only a card game; it's not somethin' you want to work up a sweat over." She blew air through her lips in exasperation. "Jesus, you're so fuckin' innocent it hurts. You got no idea what really goes on in this world."

Finn climbed to his feet and stood with his back against the wall. "What goes on in this world? What do you know that I don't?"

"I know plenty you don't even dream about."

"Like what?"

"Like what goes on in the casino, to name one situation," she spit out in a cold fury. "Like how this dude in the green bow tie strolls into the room they set aside for heavy hitters and waltzes off with the loose change.

Forty thousand here, a hundred thousand there. The Apache who did most of the losin' was playing with casino money."

"The casino tells you to lose that kind of money on purpose?"

"You think I lose it by accident?"

"Who's the joker in the green bow tie? Who sends him?"

Shenandoah heaved a shoulder.

"You got to have an idea."

Shenandoah was sorry she had raised the subject. "I have an idea, but they'd tickle me to death if I passed it on to you."

Finn asked quietly, "Who'd tickle you to death?"

At Shenandoah's feet Geronimo started lapping up the milk on the floorboards. Shenandoah shook her head in disbelief. "Crying over spilt milk," she said. "I suppose there has got to be a first time for everythin'."

skeltsetle had gone to ground in the womb of the Earth Mother. Sitting cross legged in the hollow darkness of the wickiup, chanting under his breath, he spilled a ladleful of sacred water from the needlelike fall onto the smoldering stones in the pit. The steam scalded his bare chest, stung his closed eyelids. Sweat poured from the pores of his skin, drenching his corduroys. He reached down and touched the cool earth with his fingertips to remind himself that something besides heat existed. Fumbling in the pitch darkness, he found the wickiup flap and turned it back and let a tongue of cool air lick his wounds.

From where he was sitting he could see Shenandoah, the cat tucked under her arm, coming down the steps of the old Atlantic and Pacific Mining Company office.

He let the flap slip back and hurled more water onto the red-hot stones, pushing himself deeper into pain, constructing, like his father and his father's father before him, a working relationship with pain . . . the pain of his people, the pain of the young Apaches who scorned him, the pain of his lost youth and his lost pride and his lost dreams. All that was left to him was his boy Thomas and Shenandoah. He had seen Finn looking at her, he had seen her avoiding his eye . . .

When he thought he couldn't stand more pain, Eskeltsetle reached again for the ladle. The hiss of the water hitting the stones sounded in his ears like the voice of Wakantanka. It seemed to whisper the same words over and over: *Adobe Palace. Adobe Palace. Adobe Palace.*

13

No one could say for sure where Rattlesnake Wash originated. Serveriano, the old Suma medicine man whose sky spirit was now beyond the Great Divide, used to tell the young Suma Apaches that the waters flowed from the eyes of Wakantanka, who was shedding tears for the plight of the Diné. Eskeltsetle claimed the river spurted from the bowels of the earth beyond the mesa crawling with Indian paintbrush and goldenrod, high above the Sacred Lake. Some of the younger Apaches thought that there was no single source; that the runoff trickling out of the mountains formed rivulets, which widened into creeks and streams and eventually merged to form what was known as Rattlesnake Wash. Gathering force as it went, it flowed across the mesa, plunged down the cliffs into the Sacred Lake and appeared again, at the lake's spout, in a turbulent white torrent. It circled the rise on which Watershed Station was built, then disappeared into an almost impenetrable forest of scrub oaks, surfacing eight miles beyond Watershed on a boulder-strewn flat, where the river spread out like the fingers of a hand, each finger angling off in a different direction. Several miles further on, the smallest of the fingers of the river skimmed over water-smoothed shale into what was left of a two-hundred-year-old *acequias*, a man-made irrigation ditch. In turn, the ditch curled through a long narrow gorge with sheer sides and wound up in a box canyon known, because of the eighteenth-century triangular adobe fortress sitting on a rocky saddle atop one of its chalk white cliffs, as the Adobe Palace. Built by the Spanish as an outpost against marauding Apache and Comanche war parties, it had been listed on old Spanish maps as El Palacio Adobe. The fortress walls, stretching fifty yards to a side, were really a series of attached one-story adobe houses with flat roofs and narrow slits for windows. A *torreón*, or watchtower, stood at each of the fortress's three corners. Over the centuries two of the towers, and portions of the houses that formed the walls, had collapsed in ruins. At the center of the fortress, looking like a wind-eroded sand castle, stood the two-story adobe Church of San Antonio de Gracia. On a clear day, from its bell tower it was possible to see as far south as the Sandia Mountains above Albuquerque, as far north as the volcanic San Antonio Mountain at the Colorado border.

To a distant observer, the Adobe Palace would have appeared deserted, a Spanish footprint in the dust of history. Only someone approaching quite close would have noticed signs of life. Where Spanish bells had once tolled in the church's steeple, a small motorized dish antenna, pivoting on gimbals, pointed permanently at a communication satellite orbiting three hundred miles overhead. Beneath the outer adobe walls a juniper coyote fence, entangled with a species of wild thorny roses and coils of razor wire, blocked the steep approaches to the fortress. Below the coyote fence, the floor of the canyon—once a sacred burial ground for the ancestors of the Apaches—was littered with the bleached bones of coyotes, jackrabbits, bobcats, snowshoe hares, mule deer and elks that had strayed into a killing field seeded with small plastic antipersonnel mines.

14

M idway through their final year at the Villa, the KGB training institute that the resident students, tongue in cheek, called the Seminary, the graduates got around to constructing what in espionage circles was referred to as a legend—the pseudonym and pseudoidentity they would use when they were assigned to an overseas station. An aloof young Georgian Marxist named Edouard Cheklachvilli, running his thumb down a typewritten list, selected the code name Parsifal. The image of a knight at a round table appealed to the part of him that could justify anything as long as it was in pursuit of a grail. The twentieth was clearly not Cheklachvilli's favorite century and his eventual posting to the United States only reinforced this prejudice.

Nowadays, when he thought about it, which was curiously often, Parsifal saw himself as a medieval spirit adrift in the modern world. If he had to cirumnavigate planet Earth he would have preferred to do it in eighty days. He liked starch in his collars and women who expected men to open doors for them. He detested body odors and daylight saving time and lady journalists who delivered the evening news with sexy breathlessness. He didn't get a kick out of leaving messages on answering machines at the sound of the beep, he didn't enjoy slipping plastic cards into slots or making love to someone he had just met. And he suspected Sigmund Freud had gotten it all wrong: what was repressed in the twentieth century, like the nineteen that went before it, was not sexuality but death.

Death was Parsifal's Pale, a realm he reigned over with the aplomb of Arthur chairing the Round Table. How had he described himself to the Russian woman who had crossed herself before receiving the communion bullet? *I am the rider of the pale horse: death.*

During his almost sixteen years in America Parsifal had been sent off on his pale horse eighteen times, eliminating people who, for one reason or another, had offended his Soviet masters. All of the killings had been made to look like accidents or natural deaths or random murders. Once, in a masterpiece of wetwork tradecraft, he made it appear as if the victim, an Indian, had been electrocuted by lightning while talking on the telephone during a thunderstorm. It occurred to Parsifal that writers, poets and painters might put on a good show, but deep down they were unsure of themselves; unsure of how good they really were. Plumbers, eye surgeons and professional killers, on the other hand, were the real artists. They were able to measure themselves against the results of their handiwork.

Which was why plumbers, eye surgeons and professional killers suffered from an occupational disorder that Parsifal associated with an innocent arrogance peculiar to knights at a round table: a delicate sniffing of the air in the presence of a challenge, a faint smile of contempt for those who shrank from it. "I am in history's mainstream, albeit a century or two behind," Parsifal once confided to a center psychiatrist during a debriefing at a Soviet R & R dacha. It was the only time in memory that he had even come close to dissecting what he did. "Face reality: wetwork has been with us since *Homo erectus* staggered onto his hind legs and gripped a club in what became known as his hands. We are still at it, climbing onto our hind legs, killing each other by inches, torturing each other toward death."

Downtown Santa Fe turned out to be as appropriate a place as any to entertain these thoughts, for Parsifal was stalking his nineteenth victim, a tall Indian with a shaven skull and a deformed ear. Le Juif had provided a description of the target, along with the day and hour the Indian would turn up in Santa Fe. An early evening breeze stirred odors from a freshly tarred stretch of pavement. The Indian, dressed in a flannel shirt, worn jeans and worn sneakers, strode down the street heading for the main entrance of the capitol.

A yellow school bus swung in toward the curb. A hoard of teenagers spilled from its doors and crowded onto the walkway leading to the building. Parsifal edged into the group behind the tall Indian. In the crush of bodies Parsifal managed to jostle the Indian, who felt a slight pinprick in his thigh, something like the sting of an insect, as Parsifal's briefcase scraped against him.

The Indian glanced over his shoulder, annoyed. "Watch where you're going," he growled, his dark eyes flashing.

"Hey, sorry."

The Indian nodded moodily and continued on toward the doors. Parsifal let the students push past him. Just inside the capitol, the teenagers piled up, gaping at something on the ground. Several adults were bending over someone who had slumped to the floor.

"The only good Injun is a dead Injun," Parsifal muttered to himself. Tucking the briefcase under his arm so as not to scratch anyone else, he set off at a brisk pace down the street.

He had prepared the briefcase the night before, prying away a brass corner at one of the exterior edges, sharpening it with a file, coating the jagged edge with a film of ricin, a highly toxic poison made from castor-oil seed that works its way through the bloodstream to the heart and brings on a deadly coma. By the time an autopsy could be performed, the ricin would have decomposed, and there would be no trace of it left in the blood. As for the tiny insect bite on the body's thigh, if it was noticed at all it would take a very talented coroner to link it to the collapse and death of the victim.

Eight minutes later Parsifal was punching a Houston number into a public telephone. When someone finally answered, he said, "Is this ——?" and gave Le Juif the number of the booth.

Le Juif snickered under his breath; over the phone line it sounded as if a mole was gnawing on the coaxial cable. "You have dialed the wrong number," he announced, and hung up.

Parsifal had cracked once the way old porcelain cracks; paper-thin fault lines, easily overlooked unless you had reason to suspect their presence, appeared on the glaze. The first hint that something was very wrong came when he started dreaming in English; when his dreams slipped into nightmares; when the nightmares were filled with nauseating odors of decaying corpses; when he woke up at the first trace of first light trembling like the last dry leaf clinging to an autumn tree. Le Juif had detected the tremor in Parsifal's voice when he called in to report the completion of his most recent assignment, the elimination of a hard-line middle-level diplomat who was due to take over Foggy Bottom's Soviet desk.

"Are you all right?" asked Le Juif, uncharacteristically solicitous.

"No."

"Is the problem physical or mental?"

"All of the above. I am mentally exhausted, a state which has implications for the body. I have difficulty getting out of bed in the morning. I have difficulty getting into bed at night. I drink cognac until I can no longer remember how long I have been in the business of collecting rare firearms."

"It's been nine years and three months. Don't do anything rash. Sit tight. I will get back to you," Le Juif promised. He dispatched an emergency signal to Moscow Center, which took the form of a discreet ad telegraphed to an English monthly, *The Antiquarian Gun Collector*. "New Mexico–based rare-arms dealer seeks Restoration flintlock pistols manufactured by Maubeuge for the Gardes du Corps du Roi." Twenty-four hours later Parsifal discovered a letter in his mailbox. An English gentleman owned an impeccable brace of Maubeuge pistols, circa 1814. The blued barrels bore the inscription in gold, *Gardes du Corps du Roi*. The locks were inscribed *Maubeuge Manuf.* The trigger guards were engraved with fleurs-de-lys finials numbered E.22 and E.23. The Englishman would make the pistols available for inspection if O. O. Howard, whom the seller knew by reputation, was willing to come to London. Asking price: $25,500. A date, an hour, a Belgravia address were suggested. If Mr. Howard would send word of what flight he was on he would find a private limousine waiting for him at the airport.

Parsifal discovered a thin man with a dreary face and a disgusting after-shave lotion holding up a card with "O. O. Howard" hand-lettered on it at the Gatwick arrivals hall. Without a word the chauffeur led the way to a Daimler and took a roundabout route toward the city; in espionage jargon this was called dry cleaning. He stopped once for gas, a second time to check the pressure in his tires, then drove twice into cul-de-sacs before making a high-speed U-turn and heading for Heathrow Airport, where he handed Parsifal a plane ticket to Stockholm and a passport identifying him as a Canadian national. In Stockholm another sweeper provided him with a Soviet passport and identity card, and passage on a tourist cruise ship departing on the evening tide for Leningrad.

In the Soviet Union, Parsifal was treated as a hero back from the war zone. "You have earned a promotion. From this date you will wear the rank of lieutenant colonel in the KGB. You have also earned a sabbatical," the head of the North American department of the First Chief Directorate (foreign intelligence) said. He could not avoid noticing his agent's haunted eyes. "Buying and selling guns would take a toll on anyone," he added soothingly.

Parsifal was hustled off to the KGB sanatorium at Semvonovskoye, once Stalin's second dacha, a hundred kilometers south of Moscow, where he spent six weeks in a private suite. The daily routine included regular doses of herbal potions, eucalyptus inhalations, hot paraffin wraps, acupuncture, massages, saunas, workouts in a gymnasium, spartan lunches, sumptuous dinners with attractive women who bathed regularly, wore no perfume and took it for granted they would be spending the night. There were also long rambling discussions with two psychiatrists attached to the directorate's Intelligence Institute, and the inevitable debriefings by a team made up of representatives of the various technical departments servicing the First Chief Directorate's overseas operations.

"What opinion do you have of the new first secretary?" Parsifal asked the chief of the North American department one afternoon. They were strolling along an embankment that ran parallel to the river flowing past the dacha. Parsifal's companion carried a small imitation leather satchel containing an iced bottle of Dom Pérignon and two long-stemmed glasses.

"Gorbachev? Ha! If the West thinks he is a serious reformer," said Parsifal's immediate chief, "they are in for a surprise. He will tinker with the system to eliminate some of its more glaring inconsistencies. The nomenklatura has grown fat. He will put it on a diet. There will be the usual cries of pain from the usual bureaucrats. But our intelligence agency will survive intact. After all, Gorbachev at heart is a Communist. He is committed, as we all are, to preserving the system, not destroying it."

Reaching the edge of a sprawling village, they made their way single file on planks that had been set out on the wide muddy main street. Smoke curled up from brick chimneys. In a field behind a factory that converted animal carcasses into fertilizer, and smelled from it, children threw stones at a three-legged dog. Parsifal and his companion passed the village dispensary, a dilapidated two-story brick building with broken windowpanes through which a framed photograph of Lenin was visible. They passed the local Communist Party headquarters with the inevitable hammer and sickle on the point of the roof and a tiny fenced flower garden in front. Sweaty peasant women wearing long smocks and identical black plastic boots trudged by in the mud, their feet producing sucking sounds with each step. Several of the women carried *avoski* filled with spring onions slung over their shoulders.

"What if you are misreading Gorbachev?" Parsifal asked as they hiked through a fallow field on the far side of the village. "What if he is misreading himself?"

They sat down on a fallen tree above a bend in the river. The head of the North American department clamped the bottle of champagne between his thighs and popped the cork, which arced like a mortar shell into the river, then carefully filled the two glasses and handed one to Parsifal.

Parsifal seemed mesmerized by the rippling of the river. "What if Gorbachev opens the floodgate a crack and the river, once it starts to flood, tears the gate off its hinges?"

The head of the North American department tugged at an embarrassingly large earlobe. "In the worst-case scenario we will have to tighten our belts. Ha! We will be reduced to toasting our heroes with Russian champagne. But the services we render to the Party and to the State will not go out of style." He rolled the long stem of his glass between his thumb and forefinger, then leaned toward Parsifal to indicate he was about to share classified information. "Trust me, there are contingency plans," he said cryptically. He raised his glass. "*Nasha z'dravia.*"

"*Nasha z'dravia.*"

Parsifal slipped back into America as effortlessly as he had slipped out of it. In the months that followed he watched as the floodgate in Russia opened wider and wider. Poland allowed its Communists to be voted out of office, and the Red Army didn't plunge across the frontier. The wall dividing Berlin came down, chipped away in part by tourists eager for souvenirs of the Cold War. In Rumania, Ceauşescu and his wife were put up against another wall and executed. In Moscow, the statue of the KGB's founder, Felix Dzerzhinski, was dragged from its pedestal. Newspapers began acting as if they were no longer constrained by a Party line. Communists began turning in their Party cards. The Union of Soviet Socialist Republics splintered.

And then *The New York Times* reported that the KGB had been disbanded and replaced by the MBRF, the Ministry for Security of the Russian Federation. That same day Parsifal, buying and selling rare guns out of his mobile home in Truth or Consequences, New Mexico, received a cryptic message from Le Juif: Parsifal was to be at a public telephone on the ground floor of a shopping mall in Las Cruces at noon on the following day.

At the appointed hour the phone rang. Holding a handkerchief over his nose to filter the stale odors, Parsifal closed himself into the booth. He heard Le Juif's distinctive high-pitched metallic voice in his ear—a Russian Jew speaking Texas English with an electronically enhanced nasal twang. "To dine with the devil," Le Juif exclaimed—the words seemed to ride on undertones of bewilderment—"use a long spoon."

Parsifal didn't trust his ears. "A long spoon?"

"Right. A long spoon. To dine with the devil."

"This is some kind of joke."

"Read the newspapers," snapped Le Juif.

Parsifal controlled his voice with an effort. "What are you telling me?" he whispered harshly.

"I am telling you that it is all ending with a whimper instead of a bang. I am telling you to slip like a spider back into your crack in the wall. I am telling you to use a long spoon if and when you decide to engage in social intercourse with Satan."

Le Juif started to say something else, then changed his mind. The dial tone pounded in Parsifal's ear.

"To dine with the devil use a long spoon" had been the last in a long list of cryptograms Parsifal had committed to memory before he squirmed through the rusted barbed wire blocking the river in Goritzia a lifetime ago. It meant "Go to ground and wait." It meant "Hibernate." It meant the situation back home was more chaotic than it appeared to be even in the newspapers. It meant that the KGB was too busy saving the furniture to run agents.

Parsifal went into a hibernating mode. He collected his one-time cipher pads (matchbooks hidden under the seed in a bird feeder) and burned them. He flushed his stock of ricin down the toilet in a public rest room. He coated his homemade silencer with thick industrial grease and wrapped it in tinfoil and put the tinfoil in a metal cookie box and buried the box in a vacant lot behind the gas station around the corner. He stashed in the crawl space under the linoleum floor the seemingly ancient Motorola AM-FM clock radio that could pick up coded signals from Moscow.

And he waited.

Two years went by without a word from Le Juif. Then two more. In Russia the situation continued to deteriorate. The Communist Party's right to exist was challenged in the courts. Gorbachev was almost overthrown in an attempted coup from which Boris Yeltsin, the apparatchik turned democrat, emerged more powerful than the master whose skin he had saved. In short order Yeltsin did what the plotters couldn't: he dethroned Gorbachev in a palace coup.

In Truth or Consequences, Parsifal's life grew flat, like beer that has been opened and forgotten on a counter. He bought the lot that sloped down to the Rio Grande behind his mobile home and a John Deere mower and cut the grass so often that his neighbor joked he was going to open a miniature golf course. He installed air conditioning in his bedroom and then never used it because it gave off a disagreeable odor. He had a brief affair with a woman half his age who showered before and after every act of sexual intercourse and thought the way he made love was perfectly normal (in the sense that everything under the sun was normal). He roamed the western states searching for rare firearms. In a junk shop in

Arizona he came across an 1880 Belgian pinfire pepperbox nine-millimeter revolver with a polished hammer, folding trigger and ebonized grips, which he bought for a song. As the months slipped by he began to think the unthinkable: that King Arthur had abandoned Parsifal; that the KGB, if there still was a KGB, had forgotten he existed; that he would grow old on his bank of the Rio Grande and die in Truth or Consequences without riding his pale horse again.

The possibility left him feeling distinctly relieved—and vaguely disappointed.

Just when he had abandoned all hope of hearing again from Le Juif, Parsifal discovered the message, printed in a child's scrawl of large block letters, inside the wrapper of his local newsletter. "Talk shop," Le Juif murmured when Parsifal met him in the reading room of the Albuquerque Public Library. "Admit it—you thought they had forgotten we existed, misplaced the files, stranded us in this godforsaken country, but they haven't. We have got ourselves a new Resident."

Which is how Parsifal came to dig up the silencer buried in the vacant lot behind the gas station and get back into the business of wetwork.

16

W hat about the Jogger?" Le Juif demanded after he rang Parsifal back in Santa Fe and learned of the death of the Indian. "Have you come up with a scenario?"

"Wherever he goes, the Jogger jogs," Parsifal said. "I found the bar where the local jocks hang out. I told them I ran every morning. I asked them where joggers went to avoid traffic and car fumes. They gave me the most popular route; you head out of town on Canyon Road, hang a right on Camino Cabra, then run uphill past the university to the museum complex, then around the complex and back downhill on Camino del Monte Sol to Canyon Road and the center of town."

"You have scouted the route?"

"I drove it, yes. From a security point of view, it seems like a logical choice—no high-rises once you leave the downtown wart, wide streets with buildings set back from the roadway, almost no wooded areas, few cars parked along the way."

"Every chain has a weak link. Have you identified it yet?"

"I had business to attend to first," Parsifal explained. "If I want to do something well, I can only do one thing at a time."

"Consider the possibility that if something is worth doing," Le Juif said with an electronically enhanced cackle, "it may be worth doing badly."

Parsifal changed the subject. "Have the people we work for declared war on the American Indians?"

"Everything we do," Le Juif answered, "is a tiny piece that fits into a vast puzzle. Strive on."

Parsifal lost his temper. "That kind of answer went out of style with Joseph Stalin," he said in a fierce whisper.

Le Juif seemed to enjoy Parsifal's frustration. "Beating your head against a wall is more likely to produce a headache than a hole in the wall," he said.

Parsifal, furious, severed the connection.

17

D riving one of Eskeltsetle's Toyota pickups with a rebored engine purring under the hood, Nissan suspension and a faded bumper sticker that read, "I spend my money on women and beer—the rest I just waste," Finn headed down the wide dirt road that meandered through the hills and dropped, in a dizzying series of S-curves, onto the flat near New Jerusalem. Forty minutes out of Watershed Station he crossed the old wooden bridge spanning Apache Arroyo, skirted the small airstrip that according to local legend had been laid out by Charles Lindbergh, passed the abandoned turn-of-the-century yucca rope-fiber factory and the Little League field and swung onto the broad, maple-lined main street. He drove past a 1920s brick office building with a sign over the door that read: "The Occasional Chronicle." Underneath, in smaller print, it said: "Published three or four times a week, depending on how much news there is and whether the fish are biting." He turned right at the light and pulled into a shopping complex and parked behind Hind's Hardware, which had an ad for propane tanks in the window. With the money he had earned helping Eskeltsetle cannibalize pickups, he bought a paper bag full of army surplus equipment and two propane tanks in the basement of Hind's.

He was hefting the second tank into the back of his pickup when four Indians emerged from the supermarket next to the hardware store. Two of them, big men with bloated faces and red eyes, were pushing shopping carts in which two other Indians were riding. Both shopping carts were filled with gallon jugs of California Dreaming. Before Finn knew what was happening, the two shopping carts were hemming him in. He backpedaled through a light rain to the garbage bins as the shopping carts and the Indians closed in on him. "Hold on, fellas," Finn said pleasantly, raising a hand, palm out.

"You wouldn't got change for a fifty-dollar bill?" demanded a particularly heavy Indian pushing one of the shopping carts.

The Indian riding in his cart belched. "Course we don't got a fifty-dollar bill," he remarked. "But how would you get access to that kind of information?"

"Yeah, how?" agreed the third Indian with a belly laugh. "Answer the man."

Finn's hand dropped to his side. His dark eyes hardened. "You don't really want to push it," he said softly.

"White man thinks we don't want to push it," sneered the Indian in the second shopping cart. He motioned for his friend to wheel him closer. "What makes you think we don't want to push it?" he asked, squinting up into Finn's face.

"You don't want to push it unless you have paid-up hospital insurance," Finn said. He wasn't boasting; he was just stating facts. " 'Cause two of you are going to come down with real bad headaches, one of you will get stomach cramps the result of busted balls, and it'll come down to the last joker and me, man on man, and chances are good he'll wind up in traction."

The Indians must have noticed the slight hunching of Finn's shoulders, the infinitesimal tightening of the muscles around his eyes, the faint flexing of his knees as he shifted his weight onto the balls of his sneakers.

Suddenly sober, smiling nervously, the heavy Indian rocked back his shopping cart. "Hell, we was only testing the water," he said with an unnatural laugh. "Ain't that the situation, Dell?"

"Let's burn him," the Indian named Dell murmured. He started to climb out of the shopping cart, but his companions had lost the scent. Seeing which way the wind was blowing, Dell settled back into the cart.

"What's this world coming to?" grumbled the heavy Indian as he duckstepped backward with the shopping cart. "A full-blooded Navajo can't go an' ask the white man to change a fifty no more."

18

A week later the rain petered out and summer set in with a vengeance. With Eskeltsetle at the wheel, Doubting Thomas sandwiched between his mother and Finn on the shabby vinyl seat, and *The Spirit of Saint Louis* loaded into the back of a four-wheel-drive pickup, the four of them set out along a rutted firebreak that snaked through the scrub oaks and emerged above the Suma Apache's sacred oval mountain lake. Using equipment he had picked up at Hind's Hardware, Finn inflated a small balloon, fitted it with a cheap battery-powered transmitter, released it into the air and tracked it visually for a few minutes. When it was lost to view, he picked up the signal on his miniature receiver and tracked it for another twenty minutes. Checking the signal against an army compass, he plotted the prevailing winds on Eskeltsetle's logging map. Once he figured out the winds, he would be able to launch the *Spirit* so that it landed on the field filled with Eskeltsetle's used pickups behind the Watershed general store.

"We have to launch four or five miles more to the east," Finn told Eskeltsetle.

"I don't want to land," Doubting Thomas called from a boulder overlooking the gushing stream. "I want to drift with the wind forever."

Sitting on a rocky outcrop, soaking her feet in the icy water upstream from the needlelike fall that spilled down the face of a chalk cliff into the lake, Shenandoah watched Finn track the wind. "You need to land," she shouted back. "You got school tomorrow, you bet."

Climbing into the pickup, they continued up the firebreak until they came to a mesa filled with Indian paintbrush and goldenrod. Anasazi ruins were tucked into an overhang of a low cliff. "Our ancestors lived here centuries before Jesus was born," Eskeltsetle explained over the throb of the motor. "Apaches say, when you walk you leave your breath hanging in the air. If you breathe deeply you can breathe in the breath of the Ancient Ones who lived here before us."

Eskeltsetle pulled up in the shadow of the cliff. While Doubting Thomas scurried after butterflies, Finn fitted another small balloon with a transmitter and released it into the air. He picked up the signal on his receiver and tracked it until the signal faded. "If we start here," Finn announced as he studied the logging map, "we'll finish up smack on the watershed of Watershed Station."

With everyone pitching in, Finn unrolled the balloon on the ground. Eskeltsetle rigged up a giant fan to the car battery and started to blow air through the hooped crown into the hollow of the envelope. Finn lashed two propane canisters to the aluminum frame of the gondola and hooked up the fuel lines. As the skin of the balloon stirred restlessly on the bed of goldenrod, he lit off the burners, aimed the nozzles and dispatched a bubble of hot air into the balloon. Doubting Thomas whooped excitedly as *The Spirit of Saint Louis* billowed, then slowly righted itself. The gondola strained against the mooring lines. Doubting Thomas and Shenandoah clambered into it alongside Finn. Eskeltsetle circled them, slipping the mooring lines.

"Ooooooooooh," Doubting Thomas shrieked as the balloon plucked the gondola off the ground.

In her mind's eye Shenandoah saw the earth slide away, then slowly rotate under the gondola like a globe spinning on its poles. It was the first time she had detached herself from planet Earth, the first time she had felt lighter than air. Her head swam with exhilaration. "Why, we're standin' dead still," she called to Doubting Thomas. "It's the world that's backin' away from us."

"Come off it," the boy scolded her. He waved wildly to Eskeltsetle, who had climbed onto the hood of the pickup. "I'm innocent, okay, but I'm not stupid."

"What do you know?" Shenandoah shot back. "The sun durin' the day, the stars at night, they all spin round the earth." She smiled at Finn, drawing him into her little conspiracy. "Imagination is everythin'."

Below them the world unfolded like a map. First came the field filled with Indian paintbrush and goldenrod and Eskeltsetle waving from the hood of the pickup, then the slope of the ridge with the firebreak cutting through it, then as far as the eye could see groundswells covered with scrub oak and ponderosa pine and fir. Finn leveled the balloon off at six hundred feet. Shenandoah spotted a herd of mule deer darting through a stand of aspens and two hawks circling over a canyon. "You was right," she told Doubting Thomas, shaking her head in awe. "Forget the goddamn school. You oughta drift with the wind forever."

Smiling anxiously, she added, as if she were just discovering it, as if the discovery were an original sin, "If you're gonna go hog, hell, you might as well go whole hog!"

19

Shirtless, his forearms smudged with grease, Finn worked the tackle, slowly winching the engine out of the battered Ford pickup until Eskeltsetle signaled for him to stop. Together they wrestled the engine to one side. Finn lowered it onto the chocks and unhooked the chains. Eskeltsetle took a set of wrenches from his work chest, tossed one to Finn, and they began dismantling the engine, cleaning the pieces with gasoline and sorting them on a square of plastic.

Struggling to free a rusted bolt, Finn asked, "Is it true about your grandfather going to Washington to meet the president?"

"Who told you that?"

"Doubting Thomas, that time you were putting him to bed."

"It's gospel," Eskeltsetle said. "The Great White Father in Washington wanted to wow the Apaches with how big the country was and how many White Eyes lived in it, so he invited us to send a delegation to the White House." Holding a spark plug up to the sunlight and squinting at it, Eskeltsetle laughed under his breath. "My grandfather was a member of the delegation. When they set out, he decided he'd count all the White Eyes he came across between the New Mexico territory and Washington. After a few hours on the train he saw there were too many, so he decided to count houses instead."

"Pretty soon he saw there were too many houses," Finn guessed.

"Right. So he gave that up and tried to count towns. In the end he gave that up too."

"He was wowed by the size of the country."

"Right again. But things didn't work out the way the Great White Father thought they would. When my grandfather got back to the reser-

vation and told the story, no one believed him." Eskeltsetle cleared his
throat. "Me too, when I tell them what I see, they don't believe me."

Finn, soaking gaskets in a can filled with gasoline, looked up. Something in Eskeltsetle's tone riveted him. "What do you see?" When Eskeltsetle didn't answer, he added, "It has got to do with the casino, doesn't it?"

"What makes you say that?"

"Something's going on there. I watched Shenandoah dealing some
joker with a green bow tie a while back—I could see she was double-
dealing everyone and letting him win. She admitted as much when I put
it to her."

Eskeltsetle peered at Finn over what was left of the engine. "What else
did she tell you?"

"She said they'd tickle her to death if she told me any more." Finn
came around to Eskeltsetle's side of the engine. At the far end of the field,
a pack of Apache boys, half naked and painted for war, scampered downhill toward Rattlesnake Wash, whooping as they ran. "The joker with the
bow tie turned up again last weekend," Finn went on quietly. "Shenandoah double-dealed him again. This time he waltzed off with forty thousand bucks. I followed him out to the parking lot. He was driving a white
Suzuki jeep. It had a Taos E-Z Mart privileged-parking sticker on the rear
window. The joker in the green bow tie shouldn't be hard to find."

Eskeltsetle settled cross-legged onto the ground and started to breathe
deeply through his nostrils. He reminded himself that Finn had been sent
on the wind by Wakantanka to right a wrong. Why this sudden loss of
nerve? When he had calmed down he said, "I guess, hanging around Watershed Station, you were bound to find out."

Finn sat cross-legged facing Eskeltsetle. "Who's shaking down the
casino, Skelt? Is it the Mafia?"

Eskeltsetle raised his eyes to stare at the sky. It was easy to see he was
aching to answer the question but was afraid to take the plunge.

"Why don't you tell me?" Finn asked.

"It's risky, knowing."

"It's my skin."

Eskeltsetle fingered the beaded buckskin pouch tied to his belt. "Not
yet. I need to check it out."

"With who?"

"With the guy who runs the show."

20

P ushing through thickets that all but hid the footpaths he had used as a child, Eskeltsetle made his way into the mountains. As the air thinned his breathing became labored. At one point he waded into a cloud that veiled the stands of fir and muffled the wild carping of the bluebirds. Several snowshoe hares scurried from under his moccasins. Burrs attached themselves like leeches to his buckskin leggings. Pulling himself from tree to tree, Eskeltsetle continued to climb until he came to the clearing the Suma Apaches thought of as the roof of the world, and to the great Anasazi ceremonial altar at its heart. Scrambling up the worn steps onto the altar chiseled out of a giant stone a thousand years before, he settled down cross-legged at the top, trying to catch his breath.

Off to his right, where the clearing sloped away and leveled off, he could make out the Suma Apache burial ground. Around him, at every point of the compass, clouds shrouded the land. A feeling of being in harmony with the universe filled Eskeltsetle; he imagined that the earth had ceased to exist, that he had finally arrived at the threshold of Wakantanka's heaven. He raised his eyes and his hands and called out, "Oh Wakantanka, who threw the earth on a potter's wheel and fired it in a kiln heated by a thousand suns, send me a sign. Guide your servant Eskeltsetle to the hunting ground where there are so many buffalo it takes three days for a herd to pass."

Above Eskeltsetle's head the billowing mist was suddenly saturated with light. For an instant the cloud took the form of a face that resembled an Apache war mask, with three distinct ash-gray streaks. A moment later shafts of sunlight stabbed through the cloud. One beam struck the altar inches from Eskeltsetle's moccasin. He jerked back his foot as if it had been branded. His lungs filled with sweet oxygen, his heart filled with sweet bliss. He started to laugh out loud. He laughed until his voice was hoarse, he laughed until his laughter echoed through the cloud, he laughed until the tears streamed down his leathery cheeks.

In the history of the world, had anyone other than Moses looked on the face of Wakantanka and lived? It could only be a sign that the Great Spirit was pleased with his servant Eskeltsetle; that his messenger, who had come to Watershed on the wind, would deliver the Apaches from their enemies; that the time was fast approaching when the white man's civilization would rot away; that the sacred valleys and sacred hills and sacred rivers and sacred lakes would soon be restored to the Diné.

21

After the sweat, the Apache women prepared the communal meal in the kitchen of the general store, then carried the paper plates filled with chili and fruit salad into the main room and offered them to the men. In the corner near the fireplace Eskeltsetle, wearing basketball sneakers, baggy black trousers and a high-necked Apache shirt, was deep in conversation with an old Apache who parted his hair in the middle. Eskeltsetle waved away the food when Shenandoah offered them plates. The old Apache shook his head stubbornly. Gripping his elbow, Eskeltsetle leaned forward and sent arguments spinning into his ear. The old man listened with his eyes fixed on the floorboards. Every time he shrugged, Eskeltsetle tightened the grip on his elbow and talked some more. Finally, nodding as if something had been decided, he pulled the old Apache out the back door and across the yard to Finn, who was leaning against a tree and eating off a paper plate.

"This is Tooahyaysay, the Strong Swimmer," Eskeltsetle announced. "He is a trained accountant and keeps the casino books. I have convinced him to give you answers to the questions you are not smart enough to ask."

Tooahyaysay grunted. Over Eskeltsetle's shoulder Finn caught a glimpse of Shenandoah peering into the night from the kitchen door. She seemed to be looking for ghosts. Eskeltsetle nudged the old Apache. "Nobody is going to know where his information comes from."

His lips barely moving, Tooahyaysay spoke in a crusty whisper. Finn leaned toward him so as not to miss a word. "I get a telephone call maybe once, maybe twice a month saying to expect the man wearing the green bow tie, saying also how much he is going to win."

"Who phones you?" Finn asked.

Tooahyaysay glanced at Eskeltsetle, who nodded encouragement. Reluctantly, the old Apache turned back to Finn.

"A year and a half back . . ." He cleared a frog of nervousness from his throat. "A year and a half back, Baychendaysan, the Long Nose, talked the tribe into getting into the casino business. He didn't invent the idea, it was the brainstorm of Mr. Early over in New Jerusalem, who was so hot on it he personally walked the dossier through the state offices in Santa Fe. Eight months ago, right after the casino opened, a white man turned up in Watershed. He wore tinted eyeglasses even though it was raining. He was driving a jet black Cadillac with New Mexico plates and tinted windows. He sat in the car eating a wedge of pizza and listening to opera on a tape deck. He did not get out of the car until the aria was over. When the music ended he strolled across the casino to my small office. The door was not marked but he seemed to know exactly where it was. He entered without knocking. His small feet were fitted into soft leather shoes that came to a point. He asked for me by name. He told me his name was Dewey, but he did not say whether Dewey was his given name or his family name. He told me I should think of him as the representative of an international organization with Sicilian roots. He said something about how the people he worked for would provide protection for the Rattlesnake Casino, in return for which they would expect periodic payments in unmarked funds."

"What kind of protection?"

"Against cars being stolen from the parking lot. Against the casino burning to the ground. Against the poisoning of the Sacred Lake, which is the reservoir from which we draw our drinking water."

"He could have been bluffing," Finn said. "You could have told him to get lost."

"At first we did refuse," Eskeltsetle said.

Tooahyaysay said, "The man who called himself Dewey narrowed his eyes and shook his head very slowly and left without a word."

"Two days later," Eskeltsetle picked up the story, "everyone in Watershed came down with stomach cramps and the runs—everyone except the twenty or so who'd been drinking beer instead of the water that's piped down to us from the Sacred Lake."

"A week later Dewey turned up again," Tooahyaysay said. "He told us the next time they spiked the water they would do it with a thimbleful of cholera microbes."

Eskeltsetle continued in an urgent whisper. "We had a big tribal pow-wow. I counseled caution. I suggested that we give them the money and buy time. Everyone more or less agreed. But a few weeks after we started paying protection, Baychendaysan, the Long Nose, cracked. He climbed onto a chair and said it was blackmail, pure and simple. He said no way would the Apaches let some white honchos milk the casino. Next day he got into his pickup and roared off toward New Jerusalem to blast the story all over the front page of *The Occasional Chronicle*. But he never turned up in New Jerusalem, he never spoke to Mr. Early. His pickup was found in a ditch off the S-curves between here and New Jerusalem. It was empty. Baychendaysan, the Long Nose, disappeared from the face of the earth."

"The Long Nose was not the only one to disappear," Tooahyaysay said. "Klosen, the Hair Rope, announced he was going to see the county sher-iff. A week later his body was found slumped over a telephone in his girl-friend's mobile home in a trailer park outside New Jerusalem. The county coroner ruled he had been electrocuted by lightning while talking on the telephone during a thunderstorm. A few months later Uclenny, the Rapid Runner, said he was going to follow the man in the green bow tie and turn him in to the state cops."

"Uclenny was found hanging from the rafters of a barn outside of Taos," Eskeltsetle said. "The county coroner ruled it was a suicide."

"This is what Shenandoah calls tickling someone to death," Finn re-marked.

Recounting what had happened to Apaches who had tried to put an end to the blackmail made Tooahyaysay perspire. He pulled a bandanna from his hip pocket and mopped his brow. "Last month," he said, whis-pering now, "Nahkahyen, the Keen Sighted, made an appointment with the state prosecutor in Santa Fe. He died inside the building before he could see the state prosecutor."

"What killed him?" Finn wanted to know.

"A heart attack," Tooahyaysay said.

Eskeltsetle kept his hooded eyes fixed on Finn. "Nahkahyen was twenty-seven."

For several moments the only sound came from Rattlesnake Wash mur-muring over volcanic boulders. Eskeltsetle's Apache nostrils flared. A wild look came into his bloodshot eyes. "I read it on the wind that brought you to Watershed Station, I read it in the shaft of sunlight that struck the altar inches from my foot. You are the messenger of Wakantanka. You have been sent to us by the Great Spirit to ride the wild horse."

Finn wasn't enthusiastic. "Last time I rode a wild horse, it ended badly for the horse." He shrugged. "Look, I'm willing to try, but I wouldn't know where to start."

"The Suma Apaches have a guardian angel," Eskeltsetle told Finn. "Begin with him."

22

P ushing through the heavy glass door into the *Occasional Chronicle* building, riding to the fourth floor in a noisy elevator, Finn approached the receptionist holding fort at the entrance to a glass-enclosed city room with three reporters typing away on old Remingtons.

"I'd sure like to see the editor," he announced.

"Whom shall I say wants him?"

Finn produced the introduction Eskeltsetle had printed out on the back of an envelope. Snatching the envelope, the receptionist, a middle-aged woman with a sour face and penciled eyebrows, disappeared without a word through a door with "Editor" engraved on a polished brass plaque. She returned a moment later to wave Finn impatiently into a large corner office filled with drifts of bound newspapers. Dozens of fishing rods were stacked against walls covered with framed front pages. Walking down an aisle formed by the bound newspapers, Finn found himself confronting an overweight man with little eyes, unkempt hair and a scruffy beard slumped in a wooden swivel chair behind an enormous glass-covered desk. A fat cigar jutted from his soft lips; a haze of bluish smoke hovered like hoarfrost over the desk. A plaque on the desk identified the bearded man: "G. D. Early, owner & editor."

Early raised his eyes from Eskeltsetle's note and studied Finn over the silver rims of his half glasses. "You're standing on hallowed ground," he growled, batting away the cigar smoke with the back of a hand. "It was T. Thaddeus Fargo, a Boston typesetter, who braved the eight hundred Hostile-infested miles of the Santa Fe Trail and founded the *Chronicle*. That was back in 'eighty eight. The paper was occasional in the sense that it was published when Fargo wasn't casting for trout in Apache Arroyo or another of the streams we got here'bouts, which is a tradition I more or less kept up when I bought the *Chronicle*. Do you fish, Mr. Finn? Do you make your own flies or do you use store-bought? Not that it tells me much about you that Mr. Sigmund Freud couldn't have figured out shrinking you on one of those leather couches of his for six months."

Chuckling at his own joke, Early reread the back of the envelope. "Skelt here has a sixth sense about lots of things, including when the fish are running and where. He wants me to give you five minutes of my precious time." Early cracked a fat knuckle; the sound reverberated through the room. "I'm all ears."

Squinting over the rims of his glasses, sucking absently on his cigar, he heard Finn out. Then he swiveled in his chair and stared out the window so that Finn would not notice how rattled he was. Who had been feeding Finn fairy tales about the Mafia shaking down the Apache casino? That old fart Eskeltsetle, who thought he had a special line to God? Or the asshole accountant Tooahyaysay, the one they called the Strong Swimmer? Or one of the hothead braves who sat around moaning about how the white man had cheated and murdered Apaches a hundred years ago as if it had happened yesterday?

Early stared down at the traffic on Main Street. Leaning forward, he felt the strength drain from his legs, but he forced himself to keep his eyes on the street. Years before, some thirty pounds lighter and running Treasury agents out of Thailand, Early had been initiated by a Cambodian gunrunner delivering AK-47s to the Khmer Rouge into the mysteries of *chod*, a Buddhist concept that encouraged you to embrace the thing you feared most. Early's gunrunning friend had practiced what he preached; since death was the thing he feared most, he had slept in the same bed with his dead mother for a week before burying her. The exercise hopefully stood him in good stead the day the Khmer Rouge, discovering rust on the AK-47 firing pins, beheaded him with a dull sword. The thing Early feared most was heights, so in tight situations he fortified himself by practicing *chod*. Now, gazing down, a cold sweat formed on his upper lip as the street, four floors below, swam in and out of focus. His breath coming in short gasps, he swiveled back to face Finn, loosened his tie and ran a thick forefinger between his starched collar and thick neck.

"You all right?" Finn asked.

Early ignored the question. "What brings you to our corner of New Mexico, Mr. Finn?"

"If I told you you wouldn't believe me."

Early sucked on his cigar. "Try me."

"The wind. Literally." Finn explained how he had set out from the Pacific Rim and sailed on the jet stream until his propane ran out.

"How did you stumble across the green-bow-tie story?"

Finn didn't want to bring Tooahyaysay into the conversation if he could avoid it, so he said, "I was hanging around the casino. I recognized the guy wearing the green bow tie. Each time he drops a handful of thousand-dollar chips on the table and starts betting as if it's never crossed his mind he could lose. I've seen him do it twice now. The first time he walked off with a hundred and ten thousand, the second time forty thousand."

"How can you be sure he's not just someone with a knack for five-card stud?"

Finn said, "Someone phones up the casino before Green Bow Tie turns up. The someone tells them how much the casino is supposed to lose."

"Assuming the man in the bow tie is milking the casino, who's he working for?"

"It's got to be the Mafia; everyone knows they shake down casinos."

Early's little eyes receded into his fleshy face. "Sounds to me like the Apache accountant Tooahyaysay has been feeding you a cock-and-bull story. Maybe he's embezzling the money and trying to cover up the loss. Maybe he's letting one of the Apaches milk the casino to bring the profits down in the ledger."

"I don't know anyone named Tooahyaysay."

Early grunted.

"The last time Green Bow Tie showed up," Finn said, "I followed him out to the parking lot across from the casino. He was driving a white Suzuki jeep. There was a Taos E-Z Mart privileged-parking sticker pasted on the rear window. It ought to be child's play to track this joker down and check out the story."

"You willing to repeat all this to the FBI?" Early asked.

Finn shrugged. "I got nothing to lose."

"When you're young, life is like a long slow ocean voyage and death is like the horizon; no matter how much you sail toward it, it's always a comfortable distance out there ahead of you."

"Are you trying to tell me I could get in trouble?"

Early leaned back in his swivel chair, which creaked under his weight. "The year *The Occasional Chronicle* came out with its first issue, Mark Twain said something about how the difference between the right word and the nearly right word is the same as the difference between lightning and a lightning bug. If there's a grain of truth to what you're saying, *trouble*, Mr. Finn, is the *nearly* right word." He snickered in appreciation at his turn of phrase. "Tell you what—I'll lay your story on the Feds and get back to you."

23

A s usual, Le Juif didn't beat around the bush when he phoned back. "Are you equipped with pencil and paper?" he demanded in his metallic drawl. "I have what American baseball fans call a doubleheader for you."

Suffocating in a booth on the edge of the highway, Parsifal quipped, "Two for the price of one."

"If you love you don't count," Le Juif shot back. His voice sounded as if it were dredging a river as he gave Parsifal the details of the assignment. "Any questions?" he asked.

"Lots of questions," Parsifal remarked. "Like: given what's happening in the world, why am I still in this business? Like: who has decided that my work is useful? Like: what do they hope to accomplish?"

"Yours is not to reason why, yours is but to do and die."

"Do *or* die," Parsifal corrected him.

Le Juif coughed up a mocking laugh. "And, or; either, or."

The line went dead.

ooahyaysay, the Strong Swimmer, folded his clothes carefully on the ledge of shale and slipped naked into the Sacred Lake. Swimming with long easy strokes, breathing occasionally through the side of his mouth, barely creating a ripple as he knifed through the icy water, he crossed to the large flat shelf not far from where Rattlesnake Wash spilled out of the lake and down toward Watershed Station. Holding on to the shelf to catch his breath, he let his head angle back into the water and gazed up at the Milky Way, cutting like the wake of a giant comet across the vast expanse of stars. As a young boy he had clung to this same shelf and stared up at the same swarm of stars. In all these years of swimming the Sacred Lake, he had never tired of the sight. He remembered reading somewhere that the pinprick of light could have quit the fiery star a million years before it reached the pupil of his eye. Which meant he might be looking at the dawn of time, when the ancestors of the earliest Indians crossed over from Siberia on ice floes and migrated down to the fertile mountains, when dinosaurs roamed the earth and giant birds soared above it.

Tooahyaysay bent his head forward and watched the pinpricks of light dancing in the dark still water. The mystery, the magic of the Sacred Lake never failed to purify his body and his soul.

Slipping into the water, the Strong Swimmer headed back across the lake toward the ledge of shale. He was reaching up to the ledge when a viselike grip closed over his right ankle and wrenched his thin body underwater. Opening his eyes wide, staring into the murky depths, he could make out a dark creature with gogglelike eyes clinging to his leg. He kicked at the creature with his free foot and flailed at the water with his arms, but he couldn't free himself from the clutch of the monster. Inch by inch he was dragged deeper into the lake. Looking up as his breath ran out, he thought he saw the pinpricks from the dawn of time exploding as they struck the surface of the mystical lake.

25

High mountain thunderstorms lashed northern New Mexico for days on end, filling the dry canyons and the arroyos and the man-made irrigation ditches with angry torrents. When the sun finally rose over the scrub oaks, the water quickly receded. In Watershed Station, young men laid down planks so Apaches could cross the muddy streets without soiling their running sneakers. Women pushed the old Apaches in wheelchairs onto the back porch, where they sat for hours basking in the sun's warmth. Doubting Thomas waded into Rattlesnake Wash and stood stock-still where the white water gushed between black boulders, his feet planted and spread, trying to snare trout with his bare hands the way Eskeltsetle had taught him. The old man's hand had always been faster than the young boy's eye; no matter how still Doubting Thomas stood, no matter how swiftly his hand snaked through the water, the silvery blue trout always managed to dart away. All Doubting Thomas's fingers closed over was water.

He was still thigh-deep in the river when the Apaches appeared on the hill, coming from the Sacred Lake. He waded to the bank and watched them for a moment, then scurried up the slope and burst through the screen door into the general store. Eskeltsetle, who was cataloging pickup parts stocked on the shelves, looked up expecting to see a fish in the boy's hands and pride in the pupils of his eyes. Instead he saw terror. Shenandoah appeared in the kitchen door.

Gasping for breath, Doubting Thomas choked on words he couldn't spit out fast enough. "Some . . . body . . . is . . . killed."

Eskeltsetle and Shenandoah pushed past the boy onto the porch. A crowd of young Sumas was making its way down Sore Loser Road. Four of them carried a makeshift stretcher, from which water still dripped. On the stretcher was a body covered by a tattered Navajo blanket. The group stopped in front of the porch. Alchise looked up at his father. "We found him floating facedown in the Sacred Lake," he said. He wiped sweat or tears away from his eyes with the sleeve of his only arm. Then he drew back the blanket so Eskeltsetle could see the dead man's face. "Someone's trying to make it look like the Strong Swimmer went and drowned," Alchise said with a bitter sneer.

Tears spilled from Shenandoah's eyes. "Where will it end?" she whispered harshly.

Finn came around the side of the general store and joined them on the porch. "It could have been an accident," he insisted. "He was an old man. He could have been fishing and fallen in. Where the chalk cliffs come down to the water's edge it's impossible to climb out."

Shenandoah turned on him furiously. "Why do you think they called him the Strong Swimmer? Even at his age he could have swum across the lake and back ten times."

"Tooahyaysay," Eskeltsetle murmured. "Wakantanka forgive me for what I have done to you."

Shenandoah reached for Finn's arm and drew him to her and breathed into his ear. "If I'm right about Tooahyaysay," she said, "if he *was* murdered, you're next on the Mafia's hit list. You know things you shouldn't know." She murmured a prayer. "Oh, Sweet Jesus, who looks after the birds of the air, the fish of the sea, look after Saint Louis and Doubting Thomas and Skelt and your suffering servant, me."

Hugging herself to control the trembling, she added by way of amen, "You bet."

26

O ne of the Suma boys who regularly hawked dream catchers in the casino parking lot rapped his knuckles on Finn's door. Someone wanted to speak to him on Watershed Station's only telephone outside the casino, in the booth on Sore Loser Road across from the Indian handcraft store. Finn pulled on jeans, a shirt and a pair of worn sneakers and followed the boy through the backyards to the booth. The phone was dangling on its cord. He picked it up and listened for a moment. Finally he said, "Yeah?"

"That you, Finn?"

Finn recognized the voice of G. D. Early, owner and editor of *The Occasional Chronicle*, but he said, "Who's asking for him?"

A belly laugh came over the line. "Don't play games with me, Finn. Listen up. I laid your story on an FBI agent I know in Albuquerque. He hears this kind of shit all the time. People come out of the woodwork and swear the Mafia is shaking down the Laundromat or the bowling alley or whatever. Most of the time they're chasing shadows. Still, he's willing to hear you out."

Finn glanced up and down the street. Several Apaches were shoveling gravel from the back of a pickup to fill a pothole in front of the casino. The boy who hawked dream catchers sat cross-legged near the phone booth, singing to himself as he played jacks in the dirt. Finn said into the phone, "He doesn't sound thrilled."

The voice on the other end of the line turned irritable. "You came to me with the story. I went to a lot of pain to set up the meeting."

"Where? When?"

"My agent friend says we need to be discreet. His kid's team is coming up to New Jerusalem tomorrow night for a Little League play-off. There's a doubleheader. The Albuquerque team plays second. He says he'll slip across the fields and meet you in the abandoned yucca rope factory behind the stadium at ten."

"You figuring on being there?"

"My agent friend says three's a crowd."

"Ten tomorrow. At the yucca rope factory. Right."

"Right as rain."

f I was in your sneakers," Shenandoah was saying, "I'd tell Mr. Early where he could shove his meetin'." She glanced quickly at Finn to see if he was still listening; his body was on the pickup seat in front of the kiva fireplace, but his head was somewhere else. "I'd be very precise when it came to describin' his anatomy," she added.

Sitting with her back to the wall, dressed in her black casino trousers and white-on-white shirt, Shenandoah removed her hands from the enamel bowl filled with warm water and salt crystals and waved them in the air to dry them. Flexing her fingers, she picked up a deck of cards and began shuffling. "Here's the deal: if somethin' was to happen to you . . ." She left the sentence hanging.

Finn caught his breath. "If something happened to me?"

They could hear Eskeltsetle puttering around in the kitchen. Shenandoah looked away. "It would break Thomas's heart," she said quietly. "Stay put, Saint Louis. Don't go meetin' anyone in any abandoned factory."

"Do you believe in God?" Finn asked out of the blue. "Do you believe in an afterlife and all the rest?"

She looked up at him curiously. "My mother raised me Roman Catholic. I believe what the Bible says. In the beginnin' Wakantanka created the heaven and the earth, and the earth was without form, and darkness was upon the face of the deep, and the Spirit of Wakantanka moved upon the face of the waters."

"I didn't know Catholics believed in Wakantanka."

"Catholics believe in God. Apaches believe in God. What's the big deal what you call him?"

Finn stretched out on the pickup seat. He was wearing dirty sneakers. Shenandoah eyed them trying to figure out how she could get him to take his sneakers off her new seat covers without hurting his feelings.

Somewhere in the woods a coyote yowled at the half moon threading through lace-thin clouds. "And this heaven that Wakantanka created," Finn asked after a while. "How do you see it in your imagination?"

Shenandoah absently practiced a two-card push-off, repeating the sleight-of-hand gesture over and over. "The way I picture heaven, there's this big trunk at the entrance, the kind my father used to have in the back of his Chevy when he was crisscrossin' Texas lookin' for the ultimate poker game. I see my Indian name stenciled on the side of the trunk in faded red letters. Ish-kay-nay. In the trunk is everythin' I ever lost in my whole entire life: the raggedy doll with the Oriental eyes that actually shed tears if you remembered to fill the plastic bottle in her back, the silver ankle bracelet with the tiny silver buffalos, the yellow silk ribbons my mother used to twine into my braids, the Mamas and the Papas LP that I got on my tenth birthday, the red scarf my mother knitted me when I was twelve, the gold earrin' I lost at seven-card stud before I mastered the two-card push-off, the seven-speed bicycle my father won for me at poker but lost back the day after, my innocence the first time I climbed into the rack with a man." She checked her wristwatch and jumped to her feet. "I got to go. Casino opens in ten minutes. Hey, will you do me two personal favors, Saint Louis? One: don't keep that appointment at the rope factory. If I ever get to heaven, assumin' of course that I'm headin' for heaven, I don't want to find you in the goddamn trunk too."

"What's the second favor?"

"Take your goddamn sneakers off when you stretch out on my goddamn seat covers."

skeltsetle spooned cooked rice into a small wooden bowl. Holding it aloft with both hands, he murmured a prayer to Wakantanka in the Apache dialect. Then he pushed through the screen door and, reaching up, lodged the bowl in a fork of a branch of a dead oak. Returning to the kitchen, he filled two wooden bowls with rice and vegetables, and seasoned the mixture with shredded roots he had painstakingly unearthed with the blade of his knife that morning and which tasted like raw sweet potato. He handed one bowl to Finn and led the way into the other room. The two men sat across from each other at the trestle table and ate in silence.

When they finished they set the bowls aside. Eskeltsetle worked tobacco onto a rectangle of paper and rolled a thick cigarette. He lit it with a wooden match, took a long drag on the cigarette and passed it to Finn, who smoked in order not to offend his host.

From the bank of Rattlesnake Wash below the town came the hooting of an owl. Eskeltsetle cocked his head. "Our fathers," he said, "taught us that the ghosts of the dead rise from their graves and install themselves in the bodies of owls. They taught us that if you listen carefully, you can hear in the hooting of an owl the voices of ghosts speaking Athapaskan."

"We're knocking at the door of the twenty-first century," Finn said. "You don't really believe all that stuff about owls and ghosts, do you?"

"Death has been much on my mind lately," Eskeltsetle said, ignoring Finn's remark. A faint smile worked its way onto his lips. He studied Finn, trying to see him as Shenandoah might see him. He could tell that Shenandoah, who was something of a loner, felt comfortable with him. He wondered if she was holding back out of loyalty—or love. Reaching out, he accepted the cigarette from Finn. "When an Apache dies," he continued, "he's buried with everything he owns. This is done to prevent his ghost from returning to retrieve his worldly possessions, which could bring what we call ghost sickness, and death, to the dead man's village. The wickiup in which the dead Apache lived is burned to the ground. The handful of relatives and close friends who attend the burial burn their clothes afterward, and then bathe in sage smoke to purify their bodies. They change their names and the names of their children so that they will no longer be called by the names the dead man used."

"Why do we talk of death?" Finn wanted to know, but Eskeltsetle rambled on as if he hadn't interrupted.

"Few outsiders understand Apaches. It is not so much that we turn our backs on death, it is more a matter of moving forward into life." Eskeltsetle came to the point. "You wanted my advice, here it is: you must keep the appointment at the rope factory, for it is only by meeting your destiny that you embrace life."

Finn was not enthusiastic. "I came here looking for a backwater where I could rise above the demon."

Eskeltsetle shook his head. "Your demon is never farther from you than your shadow." Then he closed his eyes and said something that startled Finn. "Your shadow darkens my door." The old Apache opened his eyes and raised his chin. "Us Apaches," he went on, cutting off Finn's question before he could ask it, "don't believe the world will last forever. We say that the rocks and the mountains will be around a long time, but even they will disappear. And when they have all gone—the rocks and the mountains and the Apaches and the white man—what will be left?"

Eskeltsetle offered Finn a turn at the cigarette. "What will be left," he said softly, "are our deeds."

29

His twelve-gauge pump-action shotgun wrapped in newspaper and slung under an arm, Finn turned around the abandoned yucca rope factory looking for an open window or an open door. A bloated moon floated in the pale rose-gray sky over New Jerusalem. High school band music and the excited shrieks of children drifted across the fields from the brightly lit Little League stadium. Somewhere inside the vast brick factory a cat in heat wailed plaintively.

Near the loading ports at the rear of the building, Finn discovered a door ajar. It creaked on its rusted hinges as he eased it open with the barrel of the shotgun.

Releasing the safety on the gun, feeling for the trigger through the newspaper, moving as if an instinct for hand-to-hand combat was second nature, he slipped inside and flattened himself against the wall; became part of the wall. Overhead, silvery shafts of moonlight filtered through the sooty panes in the skylights, strewing the cement floor with stunted shadows. In the loading room immense wooden spools piled on top of each other formed columns, the columns formed aisles. Turning into one aisle, walking soundlessly on the balls of his feet, listening with darting eyes that took in every shadow and tested it to see if it could be human, Finn started into the heart of the yucca rope factory.

Off to the sides, giant crates with rotted yucca fibers spilling out of them slumped against the walls. Finn scrambled over a conveyor belt, then ducked through a low opening, following the belt into a vast empty cavern of a hangar with giant hunks of equipment floating overhead on the ends of cables dangling from the high ceiling. Narrowing his eyes, peering into the hangar, he tried to pierce the darkness and distinguish a human form. If an FBI agent was going to meet him here, he sure was being discreet about it, he thought.

Off to his right he made out a metal staircase spiraling up to a walkway that had been used to service the suspended machinery. Backing up the first few steps, Finn turned and climbed to the walkway, then made his way across it, all the while probing the shadows below him. At the far end of the hangar he stood with his back against the wall and listened. The building seemed to creak like a sailing ship. From somewhere below came a scraping sound—or had he imagined it? Staked out on perimeter patrol in the Gulf, Finn had spent a lifetime of nights staring at shadows until they took on human forms; once he had emptied the clip of an M16 at what he took to be a bearded, turbaned monster of a man lurching toward him across the sand only to discover, when Lieutenant Pilgrim illuminated the area with a flare, that he had slaughtered a stray goat.

Now, on the catwalk, he spotted the glint of a doorknob off to his left. He edged sideways and turned it. A door opened in the bulkhead. Removing the newspaper from his shotgun, fingering the trigger, resting the tip of the barrel on his right shoulder, he slipped through the door into what turned out to be a narrow corridor that ran the length of the factory. On both sides were cubicles that contained the paraphernalia of rope making—crates of chemicals, barrels of glues and lubricants, jars of dyes, spare parts for the machinery. In one cubicle, records and manifests spilled out of torn cartons piled up on the linoleum floor. In the dim light seeping through a paneless window, the mass of paper looked like shallow drifts of snow. Finn kicked at the paper, then wheeled back toward the corridor—and felt the business end of a very cold pistol pressing into his solar plexus. He heard a distinct click as the gun was cocked.

"The weapon aimed at you," a shadowy figure instructed him in a bored voice, "is an 1880 Belgian pinfire pepperbox nine-millimeter revolver. It is a sweet shooting gun with almost no recoil. In its heyday the pepperbox was the last word in firearms, with a polished hammer and folding trigger and ebonized grips. The ammunition is difficult to come by, so I don't waste it on target practice. I only shoot to kill. If you remain absolutely motionless, it won't go off."

Finn froze.

"You must be Finn," the voice continued conversationally. The owner of the voice sniffed delicately at the air, like a dog memorizing the smell of a garment before tracking its owner.

"Don't know anyone named Finn," Finn said.

Laughing under his breath, the shadow reached up and lightly fingered the silver earring in Finn's left lobe, then reached further back to touch the short ponytail.

The fist holding the pistol never wavered. "You *are* Finn," the voice announced.

"You wouldn't be FBI?" Finn asked hopefully.

The shadow snickered playfully.

"I didn't think you were," Finn said.

The man holding the pistol removed the shotgun from Finn's hand. "Weapons can be dangerous for your health," he noted.

Finn felt light-headed, as if he had been smoking some Kuwaiti hashish. The moment had the weightless quality of a dream sequence. "What happens now?" he asked. He thought he knew the answer: embracing life had brought him to the door of death.

The figure in the shadows raised the shotgun until the barrel was inches from Finn's teeth. "What happens now," he announced in a voice devoid of tone, of texture, "is you commit suicide."

A crooked smile deformed Finn's lips. He was frightened but not surprised; he had always been sure that death would catch up with him before love. Words over which he had no control surged like bile from the back of his throat. "You can go to hell," he told his executioner.

"Tch tch," the shadow said. "*No eto ne vremya iskat vragov.*"

A vague memory stirred in Finn's brain. "You're talking Russian," he said huskily.

Something in Finn's intonation caught Parsifal's attention. "How would you know it is Russian?"

Instinctively Finn understood that conversation was a straw to clutch at. "I had a roommate in college who was Russian," he said quickly. "He used to talk Russian with his father on the phone. I recognize Russian when I hear it. I thought the person sent to kill me would talk Italian."

Parsifal was intrigued. "Why Italian?"

Finn could actually feel his heart pumping blood. "People who work for the Mafia are supposed to talk Italian, not Russian."

With infinite slowness Parsifal retracted the barrel of the shotgun. "What makes you think I work for the Mafia?"

Finn wasn't sure where the conversation was going—not that it mattered. "It's the Mafia that wants me out of the way."

"Why?"

"Because of the casino. Because of Green Bow Tie."

Finn could hear the executioner inhaling and exhaling as his eyes searched the face of his victim. Finally Parsifal gestured with the shotgun toward a carton. "Sit."

His thoughts racing incoherently, Finn backed up to the carton and settled down on it. It dawned on him that he had gotten a reprieve; how long it would last depended on his giving the right answers to the killer's questions.

But which answers were the right answers?

Parsifal sat down on a carton facing Finn. He rested the shotgun across his knees but kept the Belgium pepperbox pointed at Finn's chest. His gun arm never wavered. "Start at the start," he ordered. "Tell me about the casino. Tell me about Green Bow Tie."

Finn said very slowly, "If you don't work for the Mafia, who do you work for?"

Parsifal raised the pepperbox until it was aimed directly between Finn's eyes; he was asking the questions, not answering them. Finn held up a hand, palm outward; he had gotten the message. "Eight months ago," he began, talking to save his life, hoping that what he was saying would mean something to the man sent to kill him, "the Suma Apaches opened a casino in Watershed Station. Someone named Dewey turned up in a shiny black Cadillac. He was eating a wedge of pizza and listening to opera on the car tape deck. He told the Apache keeping the casino books that he worked for an international organization with Sicilian roots. He said he would be sending around someone in a green bow tie now and then to skim off the cream—fifty thousand one night, a hundred thousand another."

Finn went on to explain how one by one the Apaches who complained about the scheme had disappeared: Baychendaysan, the Long Nose, had vanished without a trace; Klosen, the Hair Rope, had been electrocuted while talking on the telephone during a thunderstorm; Uclenny, the Rapid Runner, had been found hanging from a rafter in a barn; Nahkahyen, the Keen Sighted, had died of a heart attack moments before keeping an appointment with a state prosecutor; the previous week, the casino bookkeeper, Tooahyaysay, the Strong Swimmer, had drowned in the Sacred Lake after telling Finn about the Mafia milking the casino. "And now you were about to"—Finn's mouth, suddenly chalk dry, could barely pronounce the words—"kill me."

Parsifal listened without interrupting. His eyes grew darker as the story unfolded. Seven and a half months before—executing his second assignment for the new Resident—he had killed an Indian with a prominent nose; he had forced his pickup off the road halfway down the S-curves a few miles out of New Jerusalem, had put a bullet between the driver's eyes, had chained a discarded radiator to the victim's ankle before throwing him off a cliff into a deep mountain lake fed by a needle-thin waterfall. Several months later he had orchestrated the death of another Indian so it would appear as if he had been electrocuted while talking on the phone during a thunderstorm. The suicide in the barn, the heart attack in Santa Fe, the drowning of the old Indian in the mountain lake—they had all been stamped with Parsifal's trademark: murders that went onto police blotters as suicides or accidental deaths. Parsifal had become curious at the batch of Indian victims; had even raised the subject with Le Juif after phoning him with word of the death of the young Indian in Santa Fe.

"Have the people we work for declared war on the American Indians?"

"Everything we do is a tiny piece that fits into a vast puzzle. Strive on."

"That kind of answer went out of style with Joseph Stalin."

"Beating your head against a wall is more likely to produce a headache than a hole in the wall."

For once Parsifal had been the one to sever the connection.

And then there had been the intriguing matter of the man who went by the name of Dewey. Someone named Dewey—it could have been a first name or a surname—had debriefed the Russian woman barricaded in the small apartment in Dallas; had brought her pizza and crisply folded twenty-dollar bills and the tape of an opera to play while they talked shop. According to Finn, someone named Dewey had sat in a shiny black Cadillac outside the Apache casino eating a wedge of pizza and listening to an opera on the car stereo before shaking down the Apaches in the name of an international organization with Sicilian roots. Assuming, as seemed likely, that the two Deweys were one and the same man, what connection did the Russian woman barricaded in a Dallas apartment have with Apaches running a casino in the wilds of northern New Mexico? Had Le Juif sold out to the Mafia and knowingly become its agent? Had he been duped into taking orders from the Mafia in the mistaken belief that he was still working for a rejuvenated KGB? Was Parsifal redux nothing more than a Mafia hit man?

Parsifal remembered the conversation with Le Juif in the library reading room. "There is a cutout in place between me and the Resident," Le Juif had explained. "It is the woman with the code name of La Gioconda."

Parsifal recalled having doubts. "How can you be sure the new Resident is genuine?"

Le Juif, normally a meticulous handler of wetwork agents, had seemed so sure of himself. "La Gioconda conveyed his bona fides. She passed on an identifying cryptogram known only to me and our masters in Moscow Center."

Was it within the realm of possibility that the Mafia had gotten its sticky hands on the identifying cryptogram?

Parsifal shook his head; the idea was too far-fetched. "You are feeding me what Americans call a cock-and-bull story," he told Finn.

"Every word is true," Finn whispered.

Moving between shafts of moonlight, Parsifal crossed the room. In one easy motion he twirled the shotgun on the trigger guard and pressed the tip of the barrel into Finn's forehead.

Finn closed his eyes and waited for the explosion to drown out the roar of the pulse pounding in his ears.

30

Parsifal dialed the unlisted Houston number on a pay phone in the parking lot behind Hind's Hardware. When a voice answered he fed quarters into the slot. "I'm trying to call ——." He read off the number of the booth.

"You have dialed a wrong number," a familiar voice shot back, and hung up.

Ten minutes later the phone rang. Parsifal plucked it off the hook. "I have the brace of pistols you sent me for," he said. "I purchased two for the price of one. You can tell Prince Igor that he is the proud owner of a pair of gold-mounted 1905 numbered Mannlicher semiautomatic pistols with 'H. Faure Le Page, 8 Rue Richelieu, Paris' inscribed on the interior of the rosewood case."

"Did the negotiations go smoothly?" Le Juif wanted to know.

"Absolutely," Parsifal said. "There were two owners. The first decided to celebrate the sale by abandoning his job and family and going fishing. The second owner is using his share of the proceeds to finance a trip around the world—to disappear from public view for a while."

Le Juif snorted in satisfaction. "There is no predicting what people will do when they come into money," he remarked. A moment later the dial tone throbbed in Parsifal's ear.

Parsifal turned away from the hooded public phone and looked at Finn, who was leaning against the fender of his pickup. "What would you give to know who ordered me to kill you?" he called across the deserted lot.

Finn could feel the demon stirring in the pit of his stomach. "My right arm," he called back.

Parsifal nodded. "The question intrigues me too. The Americans who work for the Central Intelligence Agency have an expression. When they go over an operation to see where it went wrong, they say they are walking back the cat. How about it, Mr. Finn? What do you say you and I pool our violence and walk back the cat together? What do you say we start at the start?"

"There's this joker name of Frost has a line that stuck in my head—something about how the best way out is through. I say . . . let's do it."

31

Concealed in the Indian paintbrush on either side of the dirt road, crickets sucked at the airless night. In the dark cabin of the Toyota, Finn sat behind the wheel chewing on sunflower seeds, Parsifal slouched in the death seat nursing a long filter-tipped cigarette. The pickup's windows were wide open, but it didn't help much. From Mary Magdalene's two-story clapboard whorehouse, in a clearing off the dirt road fifty yards down from the parked Toyota, came the musical tinkle of a bottle splintering. In a ground-floor room a player piano started up. Several men sang along with it. "Swanee, how I love you, how I love you, my dear old Swanee." The piano and the men broke off abruptly. A woman giggled into the night. "So did you dudes come all the way out here to sing," she asked in exasperation, "or screw?"

"You must have a handle," Finn was saying to the figure lost in the shadows next to him.

"My name is Howard."

"Howard what?"

"Howard is my last name."

"So where did you learn to speak Russian, Mr. Howard?"

Parsifal held his cigarette out the window and flicked off the ash. "I'll answer your question," he said, eyeing Finn in the darkness, "when I can tell you without having to kill you."

A tall man stumbled down the porch steps of the whorehouse and staggered past the cars parked bumper to bumper at the side of the dirt road until he found his own. He slid into the driver's seat and frisked his pockets for the key. Then, gunning the motor, backing and filling to make a U-turn, he headed slowly down the dirt road toward Santa Fe, twelve miles due north of Mary Magdalene's.

The car's headlights skimmed across Finn's face. Parsifal studied his companion. He wondered if it had been smart to team up with him. It was never to late to correct a mistake.

Ten minutes past midnight the silhouette of a stocky man materialized in the doorway of the whorehouse. Finn spit a sunflower seed out the window and leaned into the wheel. "That's him."

Without a word Parsifal grabbed the old blanket that had been thrown over the torn vinyl seat, eased open the door, slipped out of the pickup and disappeared into the brush at the side of the road. On the porch of the house, the stocky man patted his pockets, came up with a lighter and a cigar and sucked the cigar into life. Behind him the screen door banged gently closed. A man could be heard reciting Hamlet's "To be or not to be" soliloquy in a drunken growl. A half-naked girl appeared at one of the second-floor windows and fanned her small pointed breasts with a magazine.

Urinating at the side of the road, his legs spread wide, the stocky man waved his straw hat at her.

"You-all come back real quick now, darlin'," the girl called down in a whiny child's voice. "Ah got tricks up mah sleeve you-all never dreamed-a."

"You do know how to gratify a client, Jo-Ellen, honey," the man declared. Whistling through his teeth, he produced car keys from a trouser pocket and started down the line of parked cars and pickups, trying to recall where he had abandoned his four-door Chrysler. Watching from the cabin of his pickup, Finn could make out the stocky man crouching and stabbing a key into a lock. Then he dropped from sight. Finn heard what sounded like a brief scuffle, then the muted rasp of someone gasping for air.

"You-all being sick again, darlin'?" Jo-Ellen called in a disgruntled voice. Someone must have spoken to her inside the room because Finn could hear her say, "If a threesome'd tickle your fancy, darlin', ah don't mind a-toll," and she too disappeared from view.

Moments later Finn heard a body being dragged along the side of the road, then something wrapped in a blanket was hefted into the back of the pickup. Parsifal drummed his knuckles on a rear fender. Finn gave him time to get back to the Chrysler, then released the emergency brake. The

Toyota coasted slowly down the dirt road. When it rounded a bend and Mary Magdalene's clapboard whorehouse dropped from sight, Finn jump-started the pickup, switched on the headlights and stepped on the gas. He glanced in the rearview mirror. The Chrysler was right behind him.

32

W hat makes you suspect Early?" Parsifal had asked when they started at the start in the lot behind Hind's Hardware.

"It was Mr. Early, the self-appointed guardian angel to the Indians at Watershed Station, who talked the Apaches into opening a casino in the first place," Finn said. "It was Mr. Early who walked the dossier through the state bureaucracy in Santa Fe."

"You will have to do better than that," Parsifal remarked.

"Baychendaysan, the Long Nose, was on his way to New Jerusalem to see Early when he disappeared from the face of the earth. Nahkahyen, the Keen Sighted, went to Early with the story about the casino being shaken down by the Mafia. Early made an appointment for him with the state prosecutor. Nahkahyen died before he could keep the appointment. Hold your water, there's more. The day I told Early about Green Bow Tie shaking down the Apache casino, he guessed I'd been talking to the casino's bookkeeper, Tooahyaysay, the Strong Swimmer. Two days later the Strong Swimmer's body was found floating in the Sacred Lake." Finn was persuading himself as he persuaded Parsifal. "It's as plain as the nose on your face—all roads lead to Early."

Parsifal shrugged; he wasn't convinced. "Early had close ties with the Apaches. It was only natural they'd go to him with their troubles—"

"You're forgetting that it was Early who set up the appointment at the yucca rope factory," Finn went on. "He said he'd arranged for an FBI agent to meet me, but there was no FBI agent. You were there instead because Early arranged for you to be there."

Parsifal nodded slowly. "Bingo!" he murmured. "What did you say you did for a living?"

Finn remembered Shenandoah putting the same question to him a lifetime ago. "I do anything," he told Parsifal. "I wash dishes. I dig fence holes. I split logs. I pick lettuce."

"You're wasting your talent," Parsifal said. "You ought to work for an intelligence agency."

"Like you?" Finn asked, but Parsifal only flashed a tired smile that could have been taken either way; he wasn't ready to cross that Rubicon yet.

It had been child's play to track Early down; everybody in New Jerusalem seemed to know where the editor of *The Occasional Chronicle* spent Tuesday and Friday evenings. After kidnapping him, they ditched his Chrysler behind a mountain of stone near an abandoned quarry off Route 14, north of Madrid, and drove north across the state to Watershed Station, arriving at three in the morning. Finn roused Eskeltsetle and explained the situation without going into detail: he and another guy had joined forces to abduct someone who held the secret of who was shaking down the casino. They needed a place to stash him while they questioned him.

Eskeltsetle didn't waste breath posing questions that weren't going to be answered. Rummaging in a shoe box, he came up with a large skeleton key, which he said opened the front door of the out-of-the-way building that had once served Watershed Station as a town jail to keep sore losers and drunken Indians out of circulation and out of earshot; the river gushing under its windows, Eskeltsetle explained, his face as impassive as ever but his eyes bright with laughter, tended to drown out cries for help and declarations of innocence. The keys to the manacles and cells were hanging on a peg just inside the jail's front door.

Now, daylight streamed through a high barred window as Early drifted slowly back to consciousness. He was stretched out on a straw mat on the dirt floor of a cell, with a thin chain manacled to his right ankle and attached to an iron loop embedded in the adobe wall. Early brought a fleshy hand up and shaded his eyes. Two men stood over him. The one he recognized, Finn, dragged over a three-legged stool. "Sit down," he ordered.

Early gripped the thin chain in both hands and yanked at it, but it didn't give. Using the chain for leverage, he pulled himself up and settled groggily on the stool, which sank into the ground under his weight. From time to time he massaged the back of his neck, which ached from Parsifal's precise karate chop that had pitched him into a stupor back at Mary Magdalene's.

"Where am I?" he asked. "What the hell you think you're doing, shanghaiing me like this?" Blinking hard to bring Finn's face into focus, absently cracking a knuckle, Early concentrated on him. "Aiding and abetting, kidnapping, assault, battery, holding someone prisoner against his will—you'll get thirty years if you get a day."

Parsifal kicked with the toe of a shoe at the chain manacling Early to the wall. "You can always make a citizen's arrest," he said dryly.

His humor was lost on Early. "Pull out before it's too late," he advised Finn. "Mary Magdalene's bound to start asking questions when she sees my Chrysler out in front of her place."

"We ditched the Chrysler," Finn explained. "It'll be a miracle if anyone comes across it this century."

Early tried another tack. "When the *Chronicle* doesn't appear on the newsstands, folks back in New Jerusalem will notice my absence. Sheriff's probably combing the countryside for me right now."

Finn recognized the instinct to clutch at straws; he had been there himself recently. "They'll think you're off fishing," he said. "Nobody will miss you for days."

Early cracked a knuckle. "What do you want?"

"Answers," Parsifal said. He sniffed at the air. Judging from the expression on his face, he didn't like what he smelled.

Early looked directly at Parsifal for the first time. "Who's your friend?" he asked Finn, suddenly less sure of himself.

"He's a professional killer. He's the pistol you sent to murder me."

The blood appeared to drain from Early's already pale cheeks. He produced an oversized handkerchief from a hip pocket and mopped the back of his neck. "I don't know what you're talking about," he protested hoarsely.

Parsifal circled behind Early and talked to the back of his head. "You can save yourself a lot of grief by coming clean. When you learned that my young friend here was asking questions about the Mafia and the casino, you—acting on orders from someone you work for, someone you report to—lured him to the yucca rope factory. You or this same someone arranged for me to be there instead of an FBI agent. One way or another you're going to give us the identity of this someone." He wound up in front of the prisoner. "Who do you report to? Is it Green Bow Tie himself, or someone higher up the chain of command?"

Early shook his head; his jowls quivered in his cheeks. "You're barking up the wrong tr—"

Without warning Parsifal slapped him hard across the face, sending Early's silver-rimmed half glasses flying and almost knocking him off the stool. "Do you want me to repeat the question," he asked softly, "or do you remember it?"

"Repeat it as many times as you like," Early muttered sullenly, his fingers caressing the side of his cheek, which had turned beet red. "I can't tell you something I don't know."

33

Raising his head warily above the railing of the tree house, Doubting Thomas snapped open the old telescope and surveyed the other side of the river. He spotted Eskinewah Napas, the Boy with a Scar on His Head, a quiver filled with rubber-tipped arrows strung across his naked back, crawling through a stand of bamboo toward one of the footbridges. Swinging around to the south, Thomas inspected the drainage ditch and the old jail beyond it, built on an out-of-the-way rise above a curve in Rattlesnake Wash. The eye glued to the telescope widened when the jail door opened and a white man Thomas had never seen before emerged into the bright sunlight. Producing a pair of aviator's sunglasses from the breast pocket of his jacket, the man hooked them over one ear and then the other and looked around. Satisfied that the coast was clear, he reached back and pulled a stocky man with disheveled clothing out of the jailhouse. "Phewwwwwwww," Thomas gasped when he noticed that the man's hands were tied behind his back.

What were two white men doing on the Apache reservation? How did they get into the old jailhouse, which in Thomas's experience had always been padlocked? Were grown men playing at cops and robbers the way he and his friends played at cowboys and Indians?

Followed closely by the stranger, the stocky man stumbled down the narrow footpath to the river. Then the stranger did a very peculiar thing, something totally out of Thomas's experience: he reached down, unzipped the man's fly and actually took his penis out for him. When the man finished peeing, the stranger poked the penis back into his trousers and zipped closed his fly. Stooping, he rinsed his hand in the river, then prodded the stocky man back up the hill. A moment later the two disappeared inside the jail.

Closing the telescope with a snap, Thomas leaped from the tree house and raced toward the nearest footbridge. He was halfway through the cornfield when the two Apache boys playing Victorio and Geronimo materialized out of nowhere. "Surrender or face the consequences," they yelled triumphantly, their air guns leveled as Thomas tore past them.

Thomas had recognized the stocky man with his hands tied behind his back. Something real funny was going on in Watershed Station and Eskeltsetle ought to be told about it.

34

During one short break, Parsifal confided in Finn, "I can smell fear every time I walk in there, but it isn't me he's afraid of."

"Who's he afraid of then?"

"The organization he works for. The people he reports to."

"How can you be so sure?"

Parsifal tapped the side of a nostril with a finger. "I have a nose for this kind of thing."

For two days and two nights they took turns grilling Early, one of them questioning him while the other catnapped on a cot in the next room. Slumped on the three-legged stool, his thick lids drooping over his eyes, his breath coming in short rasps, Early insisted he was innocent. "I have nothing but respect for the Apaches," he repeated over and over. "As God is my witness, I don't know anything about any scheme to shake down their casino.

"I left word with this FBI agent I know in Albuquerque to meet Finn," he remarked during a predawn session with Parsifal. "I got a message back suggesting the yucca rope factory. If he didn't show up, it wasn't my fault."

"We're getting nowhere fast," Finn admitted to Eskeltsetle when the Apache chief scrambled down the steep footpath from the town carrying a straw basket filled with food for the prisoner and his two interrogators. "My pal thinks our prisoner is more afraid of the people he works for than he is of us."

"Mr. Early is afraid of something besides you and the people he works for," Eskeltsetle said matter-of-factly.

Finn regarded Eskeltsetle. "What makes you think it's Early's who's in there?"

Eskeltsetle shrugged. "Doubting Thomas saw him yesterday when you let him out to piss. Thomas recognized him from when the three of us was off fishing in Rattlesnake Wash where it narrows and falls into the Sacred Lake. Funny thing happened that day. Thomas and me, we was lying flat on an overhang looking straight down at the falls. We tried to talk Mr. Early into joining us, but he refused. He hung back upstream shouting about how he suffered from something called vertigo. Thomas didn't know what vertigo meant, so I had to explain it. Mr. Early is terrified of heights."

"I should have thought of it before," Finn told Parsifal when he recounted what Eskeltsetle had said. "Of course—Early is scared of heights. The day I went to his office to tell him about how Green Bow Tie was walking off with the casino's cash, he swiveled in his chair and looked down at the street, four floors below. When he swiveled back he was sweating like a stuck pig. I thought for a moment he was going to pass out."

Parsifal's eyes, normally expressionless, danced. "This opens up all sorts of interesting possibilities."

35

On the mesa above the Sacred Lake, near the Anasazi ruins tucked into the overhang of the low cliff, Eskeltsetle worked the fan off the pickup battery until the balloon, stretched out on a bed of Indian paintbrush and goldenrod, stirred. Finn aimed the nozzles and gave the yellow-and-black striped envelope a long shot of hot air. Slowly righting itself, the balloon strained to pull the gondola off the ground. Finn waved to Eskeltsetle, who slipped the mooring lines. The gondola drifted up past the Anasazi ruins. Below, at Eskeltsetle's feet, yucca rope uncoiled from a straw basket. It was attached to the gondola at one end and the axle of Eskeltsetle's pickup on the other. In the gondola, Parsifal sniffed at the warm updraft that was carrying them above the cliff. "This is as near to an odorless environment as I've ever experienced," he remarked.

At seventy yards there was a gentle tug on the gondola; the long leash attached to the pickup's axle had run out. Parsifal prodded Early to his feet, then removed the gag and the blindfold. Gasping, Early shook his head violently. His hands, bound behind his back, strained at the rope, which bit into the soft pink skin of his wrists. He tried to twist back and away from the side of the gondola, but Parsifal pushed him forward again and forced his head around until he was looking down. Eskeltsetle's pickup on the mesa seventy yards below swam in and out of focus. Early's knees buckled under him. Parsifal slapped him twice across the face and held him up.

"I don't . . . oh . . . going to be sick . . ."

"If you absolutely have to throw up," Parsifal said, forcing Early's head over the side, "kindly do it outside the gondola. I can't speak for my young friend, but I personally couldn't deal with the odor."

Working the nozzles, Finn gave the envelope another shot of hot air to keep the balloon aloft. Early made a stab at practicing *chod*, but he didn't get very far with it. Parsifal took a good grip on the ropes binding Early's wrists and ankles and started to shove him up and out of the gondola. "If he won't tell us what we want to know," he said, straining to lift the stocky man, "we might as well get rid of him."

A wild animal scream emerged from the back of Early's throat. Half over the gondola railing, he gagged on words. "Oh God . . . talk . . . tell you what you want . . ."

Parsifal wrestled him back into the gondola. Whimpering, Early collapsed onto the deck, his head angled back against a propane canister, his mouth gaping open, his Adam's apple throbbing as his breath came in short rattling spurts.

Parsifal crouched next to him. "Let's begin with who you work for."

Early managed to say, ". . . a freelancer." He swallowed several times. ". . . renewable one-year contract . . . the Defense Intelligence Agency . . . specialty is laundering money . . . offshore companies . . . Caribbean casinos . . . private banks in Liechtenstein, in Guernsey." He was starting to catch his breath now. Once he began talking, the information seemed to cascade out. "From time to time Harry would ask me to moonlight—"

"Who's Harry?"

"Harry Lahr, the one you call Green Bow Tie. He was under contract to the Agency—"

"The Central Intelligence Agency?"

Early nodded weakly. "I never knew exactly what he did for them—he was attached to something called Special Projects, which could have meant anything, either on the operations side or the intelligence and estimates side."

Parsifal said menacingly, "Pin it down for us."

"I used to think Harry had to be involved with the Soviet section, because he was always running off at the mouth about the Communist menace, the need to maintain our military edge, the usual shit. But he kept me at arm's length—I never got close enough to know for sure."

"Did he ever talk about the Mafia?" Parsifal asked.

Early shook his head. "Never."

"He could have been working for the Mafia without knowing it," Finn put in.

Early said, "He could have been fronting for the Mafia, sure, but who knows who the Mafia was fronting for? In this business you never know where the buck stops."

"It never stops where you think it stops," Parsifal informed Finn. He crouched in front of Early. "How did you meet this Harry Lahr?"

"We knew each other from when we were both running Treasury agents in Thailand in the seventies, putting arms smugglers out of business, tracing dope back upcountry into Cambodia, setting up black market kingpins for a fall. Harry was the same back then, always wearing fancy bow ties, always talking like he was a heavy hitter, distributing fistfuls of greenbacks, dropping names of station chiefs he'd partied with, dropping names of ambassadors' wives he'd gone down on. Later on, in Washington, he'd call me in from time to time on one-shot contracts—Special Projects needed to slip a million or two to a Haitian general or a Cambodian prince or a Japanese politician, but it had to look like it came from a legitimate source. I'd launder the money until you couldn't see the green in the bills, and pass it on."

Early ran out of steam and sagged back against the propane canister. Parsifal grabbed a handful of shirt and started to pull him to his feet. Early cried, "No, please, no." His chest heaved as he drew several deep breaths. "Harry takes me out to lunch about three years ago," he began, closing his eyes, reliving the event, "he orders fancy French wine, he pays the check in cash and leaves a big tip, he says he's quit the Agency, he says he represents a consortium, they're going into business out west, they need someone with laundering expertise on staff. So I think, What the hell, I'm forty-nine, it's time I put the intelligence rat race behind me, besides which the job pays well—the salary, the perks are supposed to come from a newspaper the consortium's going to purchase through a dummy corporation. What could be more tidy? It's the golden parachute I always dreamed about. So I sign on the dotted line, I set up the dummy corporation, I organize the purchase of the newspaper. I draw a monthly check as editor and publisher, on the side I take care of the dry cleaning for the consortium."

"Which is where the casino comes in," Finn guessed.

"I was instructed to establish contacts with the Apaches, and later on, when I'd won their confidence, to point out the advantages of going into the casino business."

Parsifal looked puzzled. "This consortium—what business is it in?"

Early whispered the answer because he was terrified they wouldn't believe him. "It was not something I needed to know, so Harry never told me."

"Who is Dewey?" Parsifal demanded.

"Dewey is the next rung on the ladder, the man Harry reports to. Harry dropped his name once or twice, he said something about him being a nut for opera, but I never met him, I never personally talked to him. The consortium was compartmented like a submarine. I was brought in by Harry, I reported to Harry, I complained to Harry, I kissed Harry's ass, I got my marching orders from Harry."

Parsifal was in his element now, accumulating details the way some men collect lint in their trouser cuffs. "Assuming what you say is true, assuming Dewey is the next rung on the ladder, how many rungs are there?"

Early was on the verge of losing control; his chest heaved, tears streamed down his puffy cheeks. "I don't know. Dear God, you need to believe me. Harry was my horizon, I never got to see past him."

"How do we find Harry Lahr?"

"There's an unlisted phone with an answering machine which he interrogates from a distance. I leave messages, he gets back to me."

Parsifal pulled Early to his feet, spun him around so that he was looking out of the gondola and pulled up hard on the rope binding his wrists. "You have a safety signal, a code that says you're not being manipulated." It was a statement, not a question.

"I describe the weather—"

"I can't hear you."

"I describe the weather, but I get it wrong. If it's snowing, I say something about how hot it is."

"If you're lying to me I'll take you up for another ride in *The Spirit of Saint Louis* and throw you out."

"God is my witness. I'm not lying."

Glancing at Finn, Parsifal tapped the side of his nostril again. "You can take her down," he told him. "I enjoyed the ride. When we're back on planet Earth, we'll arrange for the publisher of *The Occasional Chronicle* to leave a message for his friend in the green bow tie complaining about the rain."

36

He had driven over the route half a dozen times—out of town on Canyon Road, right on Camino Cabra, uphill past the university to the museum complex, around the complex and back downhill on Camino del Monte Sol to Canyon Road and the heart of Santa Fe. He had jogged it twice, sweating bullets as he turned around the museum complex the way a moth turns around a flame. He knew the pieces would fall into place if he kept at it long enough; given his genius for the delicacies of wetwork, they always did.

"The clock is ticking," Le Juif snapped when, in response to a coded signal, he rang Parsifal back at a pay phone in a gas station between Santa Fe and Truth or Consequences. "I hope you've been doing your homework."

"I always do."

"So what do I tell our lord and master, Prince Igor? Is the enterprise he has his heart set on within the realm of possibility?"

"It is what the Americans call a piece of cake," Parsifal informed Le Juif. "There are wooded hills on three sides of the museum complex. They're too far away for any snapshots, even using a zoom lens, so the people who look after the Jogger's health won't waste manpower colonizing them."

"If the hills are that far away, what good are they to you?"

"If you were equipped with a good pair of binoculars, one of the hills affords an excellent view of the road as it winds around the various museum buildings. Someone with dishonorable intentions could fill the space under the backseat of an automobile with plastic and ditch the automobile on the road. From the hill, that same someone could use the transmitter you gave me to send a radio signal to the car and detonate the plastic as the Jogger passes. The hill backs onto the parking lot of a shopping mall. Disappearing into the woodwork after the fireworks would be relatively easy."

"Plastic stinks. Literally. The people responsible for the Jogger's health will sniff the route with dogs—"

"I heard about a technique of neutralizing man's best friend. You boil *Lophophora williamsii*, which is a hallucinogenic cactus better known as peyote, and spill the broth over the road near the parked car. The odor of the peyote temporarily clouds the olfactory lobes of animals. Forget plastic. The dogs won't be able to smell another dog in heat."

"Assuming you are correct about the odor, a stray automobile parked along the Jogger's route, as opposed to the parking lot near the museum, would certainly be towed away."

"That's the one question that still needs an answer," Parsifal admitted. "I'm working on it."

"Get back to me when you have solved it."

The line was cut.

37

You can pass word on to Prince Igor that he is halfway there," Le Juif told La Gioconda. "Knowing Parsifal, knowing the skills he brings to wetwork, he will discover a solution to the problem."

"Where will it end?"

"Did you receive the postal card I sent?"

"I loathe getting out of bed in the morning."

"Do you need anything? Is your leg causing you pain?"

"I have grown ancient before I have grown old. I am certain we will die without seeing each other again."

Le Juif slipped two more quarters into the pay phone. "What is the weather like in Santa Fe?" he asked.

"It has been twenty-eight years. I can no longer do what I do well."

Le Juif coughed up a cryptic laugh. "If something is worth doing—"

She completed the line. "—it is worth doing badly. I am not convinced you are right. I read in the paper that Yeltsin is an alcoholic. Do you think there is any truth to it? Do you think Russia's dreams rest on the shoulders of an alcoholic?"

"I saw a second doctor, a specialist," Le Juif said. "He told me exactly what the first doctor told me—that it is too late for an operation."

Le Juif could hear La Gioconda breathing into her end of the phone line.

"I . . . I hold you in high esteem," he murmured. He bit his lip, then, gently, so as not to frighten the bird from the nest, hung up on her.

he Rio Grande was cresting, and muddier than anyone remembered seeing it at this time of year, but that didn't discourage the
old Pueblo who delivered firewood in the back of his pickup from
fishing off the concrete breakwater at the foot of Parsifal's property. From
the narrow sliding window over the sink of Parsifal's mobile home in
Truth or Consequences, Finn watched the Indian cast with a deft flick of
the wrist, then slowly reel in, check the bait and cast again; the intensity
with which he went through the motions led Finn to suspect that catching fish was one of the more trivial objects of the exercise. The Indian
reeled in again. Squatting, he selected a worm from a coffee can punched
with airholes and skewered it onto the hook. Rising to his feet, he surveyed the sky, which was the color of pearl and almost cloudless, then,
with another flick of the wrist, sent the line spinning again.

"How about that water?" Parsifal called from the other end of the mobile home.

Finn filled a tumbler with tap water and carried it over to where Early,
his hands and feet bound with duct tape, slumped on the bunk bed. On a
shelf above his head, a small windup clock, set two hours ahead, loudly
ticked off the seconds. There was an air-conditioning unit installed in the
wall, but despite the heat it wasn't running. The partition separating the
bedroom from the rest of the mobile home was filled with weapons, each
one nestled in a felt-lined slot. There was a German Schmeisser MP 40, a
Heckler & Koch HK 33, a British Lanchester Mark 1, a Sten Mark 2, a
Russian PPSh 41, a Kalashnikov AK-47 and an American Thompson M
1928 A1. Boxes of ammunition were stacked on the shelf above the
weapons.

Parsifal took the glass from Finn and sniffed at the water. "They're putting in more chlorine than usual this week," he said as he tilted the glass to Early's mouth. Water slopped down the front of his shirt as his flabby throat worked. Handing the empty glass back to Finn, Parsifal reached for the telephone and dialed a number. He listened as the call went through. There was no recorded message, only a beep. Parsifal held the phone to Early's lips and nodded once.

Early swallowed hard. "It's me," he began. "It sure doesn't look as if the damn rain's ever going to let up, but I need to see you all the same. It's about that kid who came to see me—the one who spotted you playing poker in the casino. When the Apaches over in Watershed figure out he's missing, the police are bound to come sniffing around *The Occasional Chronicle*. Could be he left a trail. I could use some guidance. Thought I'd mosey on out to that abandoned quarry off Route 14 on the Santa Fe side of Madrid—"

Parsifal pointed to an hour on his wristwatch.

"Let's say about eleven tonight. That way everyone'll think I'm living it up at Mary Magdalene's."

The heel of Parsifal's hand sliced down, cutting the connection. "You did real well," he informed Early. "Keep up the good work and you may die in bed."

n the steeple of the Church of San Antonio de Gracia, at the old Spanish fortress known as the Adobe Palace, the dish antenna scanned the sky, then locked on to the satellite orbiting overhead. Two stories below, a man wearing Ray-Ban sunglasses and a khaki baseball cap over his short-cropped steely gray hair put his head into the communications room. He was what the French referred to as *fin de race*: tall, thin, with a pasty complexion, sucked in cheeks and large ears. "Any word on Early?" he called to the duty officer, whose name was Miss Abescat.

"Dewey checked in twenty minutes ago. Seems like Harry Lahr found a message from Early on his answering machine."

"What's Dewey's take on the situation?" inquired the man in the baseball cap.

"He thinks Early was probably off fishing."

"Or boozing it up at Mary Magdalene's," remarked the station's computer whiz, a long-haired workaholic named Larry Lefler. He offered up a raunchy laugh from his swivel chair at the next console. "Fishing or cutting bait at the Magdalene's, it ain't the first time he's dropped from sight."

"Dewey says Early's requesting a meeting with Harry for tonight," reported Miss Abescat. "He wants to talk over what to say if and when the police come sucking around re the late lamented Mr. Finn. Dewey's all for telling Harry to go ahead."

The tall man at the door strode into the room. "Okay. Give him the green light."

Miss Abescat, a handsome woman in her mid-thirties who tended to sulk when she didn't feel needed, smiled brightly as she switched on the speakerphone and dialed Dewey's unlisted number. A man answered.

"I'm trying to reach ——." Miss Abescat made up a number.

"You dialed a wrong number," a man said, and hung up. Six minutes later the phone on Miss Abescat's console buzzed. She switched on the speaker.

"It's me," a voice said.

"Re setting up a meeting between the early bird and your man in the bow tie, the answer is affirmative."

The voice on the other end, all business, said, "Roger, understand affirmative." Then the line went dead.

The man in the khaki baseball cap strolled over to the window and stared out at the killing ground strewn with the bleached bones of animals blown up by mines. He pulled a set of large silver worry beads from the pocket of his khaki windbreaker and absently threaded them through his fingers. It was a habit he had picked up during his first posting to Moscow Station, when he ran Muslim agents into the Soviet Union's Central Asian republics from Afghanistan. He was still uneasy about Lahr's friend Early; he would have to speak to Dewey about terminating his contract. Now that the consortium had the Apaches on the hook, it really didn't need a professional launderer on the payroll, especially one who dropped from sight every time the fish were running.

Lefler looked up from his computer. "Did you get a chance to read the report I left on your desk? It's a hell of an idea—boiling peyote and spilling the broth near the car to throw off the dogs."

The man in the khaki baseball cap turned back to the room. "I ran agents into Uzbekistan from Afghanistan who used to urinate on the trail to confuse the dogs. I never heard of boiling peyote. It's certainly imaginative, but I'll want an opinion from the science-and-technology people before we buy into this."

40

His finger curling around the trigger of the shotgun, Finn crouched behind the foreman's shack on the flat above the quarry. Above his head the moon flitted through wisps of clouds, dispatching lacelike patterns across the stone face of the large oval pit. Sitting next to him with his back against the shack, Parsifal sucked morosely on one of his filter-tipped cigarettes.

"It's ten after," Finn whispered. "Maybe he smelled a rat."

"Live rats are relatively odorless," Parsifal said. "It's the dead rats that smell. He'll show. He's a professional. Professionals are like guests at a dinner party; they always turn up fashionably late."

"You seem to know an awful lot about professionals."

Parsifal let the comment pass.

Finn tried another tack. "Why's the clock above your bed running two hours fast?"

"You have a hell of an eye for detail. Someday it may get you into hot water." The end of Parsifal's cigarette glowed in the night. "The clock's not two hours fast. It's ten hours slow."

"You want to spell that out?"

"The clock is set to the time in the town where my mother raised me, where she died of old age when she was forty-two."

Finn understood that his relationship with this professional killer was moving onto a new plateau. "Where do you come from?" he asked.

Parsifal decided this was as good a moment as any to cross this Rubicon. "I was born, I grew up in Akhmeta, which is a flea-bitten town off the beaten track in what used to be called the Soviet Socialist Republic of Georgia. We used to roller-skate in front of the local Communist

Party headquarters because that was the only street in town that was paved. My mother was a German Communist who fled Germany before what we call the Great Patriotic War. She always referred to Leningrad as *Sankt* Petersburg. My father was Georgian. When I think of him, I think of his fingernails, black with soot—he was a miner, you see. He worked himself to death trying to fulfill quotas set by apparatchiks in three-piece suits drinking ersatz coffee in overheated offices in Moscow. But until his dying day, my father *believed* in the thing we call Communism. He believed there was a better world out there only waiting to be constructed."

"Soviet Socialist Republic of Georgia! You're a Russian spy! It's not possible. You speak English as if you were born here."

"I studied your American English in the best school in the world—the KGB language school in Moscow. The course lasted three years. My teacher was an American defector, a Negro soldier who had been stealing walkie-talkies in West Germany and slipped over the Wall before he could be arrested. We'd sit around watching old *I Love Lucy* tapes until I could talk like Lucille Ball. I watched baseball and football to learn the rules and jargon of these impossibly complicated games. For homework I read Hemingway and *Rolling Stone* and *The Village Voice,* for on-the-job training the KGB filled my pockets with dollars and sent me off to hotels to seduce American tourists."

Finn strained to make out Parsifal's expression in the silvery darkness. "You were fighting for a lousy idea."

"In the Gulf you were fighting for oil. That's a better idea?" Parsifal lifted a shoulder in a tired shrug. "I was one of those hybrids created by fifty years of cold war. If you look behind the woodwork, you can find them on either side of what we used to call the Iron Curtain. They wind us up, point us in the right direction and we blunder forward. It's the only thing we know how to do, so we do it. I was wound up sixteen years ago. I'm still blundering forward."

Finn whistled through his teeth. "Jesus, am I in over my head!" Above the shack the moon drifted behind a cloud. "When you came to kill me, you thought the KGB had sent you, right?"

Parsifal snickered into the darkness. "How did you put it—the best way out is through."

"If you didn't kill me it's because you think someone besides the KGB wants me dead."

"Keep going."

"If that's the case, if someone besides the KGB wants my hide, that means the people who wind you up and point you are being wound up, are being pointed—knowingly or unknowingly—by someone other than the KGB. Which brings us back to Early's consortium. Who or what is behind the consortium?"

"The Mafia is the obvious front-runner," Parsifal said, thinking out loud. "But Early worked for the Defense Intelligence Agency, so that has to be another possibility. Green Bow Tie worked for something called Special Projects at the CIA. That's possibility number three."

The moon reappeared from behind the cloud. Parsifal reached down and traced something in the dirt with the tip of a finger.

Early ⟶ Green Bow Tie ⟶ Dewey ⟶ ?

"We won't know where the buck stops until we've walked the cat back as far as it will go," he added.

Finn asked, "Did you ever hear of an Apache called Baychendaysan, the Long Nose? Or Klosen, the Hair Rope? Or Uclenny, the Rapid Runner? Or Nahkahyen, the Keen Sighted? How about Tooahyaysay, the Strong Swimmer?"

Parsifal glanced at Finn. "What makes you ask?"

"A hunch."

"They're all dead and buried and gone to Apache heaven, casualties of the Cold War."

There was a flicker of headlights rounding a curve a mile up the dirt road. Parsifal took a deep breath and climbed to his feet. "What a coincidence," he said. "Here comes someone who can help us with our inquiries, as the British like to say." Casually he jammed a fifty-bullet clip into the Lanchester Mark 1 and worked the bolt, which locked into place with a muffled click. "This is a connoisseur's gun," he murmured as the headlights swung into the parking lot. "It was more or less handmade in 1940, before British industry went on a war footing and started mass-producing weapons, so the finish is high quality. You don't see many submachine guns with wooden stocks."

Still crouching, Finn peered around the side of the shack. The headlights of what looked like a white jeep were trained on Early's Chrysler, which was parked behind a small mountain of stone. After a moment the jeep's door swung open and the figure of a short muscular man appeared. "Early," a voice called. "You out there?"

Finn turned to ask the Russian spy what they should do next, but he had disappeared into the night.

In the clearing the driver of the jeep looked around nervously, then tugged a firearm from a shoulder holster and crouched behind the open door. "You playing games with me?" he called. He said, "Shit." Then he plunged back into the jeep, threw it into reverse and gunned the motor. At that instant Finn's pickup truck screamed around a rise and squealed to a stop thirty yards from the jeep, blocking the road. The pickup's headlights snapped on, illuminating the jeep. A shadow leaped from the pickup, ducked behind a barrel and emptied half a clip into the jeep's left rear tire.

The jeep settled down like a wounded bird.

"Your money or your life," Parsifal called with a savage laugh.

"It's a fucking holdup!" the driver of the jeep shouted. "Early, where the fuck are you?"

Parsifal emptied the other half of the clip into the back of the jeep. A flame licked at its underbelly, then began to spread as gasoline seeped onto the roadway.

His weapon extended and gripped in both hands, the jeep's driver backed away from the flames spurting across the road. He looked around desperately, spotted the foreman's shack over his shoulder and, crouching, made a run for it.

In the darkness he almost impaled himself on the barrel of Finn's shotgun.

On the road, Parsifal, laughing wildly into the night, extinguished the flames with fistfuls of sand.

"Who's your friend?" the driver of the jeep asked as Finn relieved him of his pistol.

"When you find out, you'll wish you hadn't."

C ircling the prisoner tied to the old wooden chair in the foreman's shack, Parsifal sniffed at the air over his head. "It's enough to turn your stomach," he announced. "He splashes his face with cheap aftershave and slicks back the little hair he has with a revolting gel."

Finn finished taping the man's wrists together behind the chair. Coming around to the front, he flicked a finger against the green bow tie askew at the neck button of the prisoner's soiled white-on-white shirt. "Do you wear green all the time or only when you play poker?" he asked.

"Fuck you," Harry Lahr retorted.

"I am going to ask you some questions," Parsifal informed the prisoner; there was a distinct chill to his voice. "You are going to answer them."

"I answer nothing," Harry spat out. He twisted in the chair and stared up at Parsifal through the one eye that hadn't swelled shut after the beating. "I don't have a name, I don't have a rank, I don't have a serial number. Pull out nails, break bones, put out cigarettes on my skin if it gives you a hard-on. I am someone who enjoys pain. From me you don't even get the fucking time of the fucking day."

Parsifal tilted back the chair to a forty-five-degree angle, then let go of it. Harry's head hit the floor, but he only smirked. "You're buying into something you're better off not owning," he said with a sneer. "Trust me, you'll live longer if you don't know the answers to your questions."

Parsifal righted the chair and circled around in front of it. "Your name, at least the one you currently go by, is Harry Lahr. You worked for something called Special Projects at the Central Intelligence Agency until you received an offer of employment from a consortium. You are the second rung on the ladder—Early is one rung under you, Dewey is one rung above you. We want to climb the ladder."

Harry's cut lips curled into a snarl. "You clowns got past Early, big deal. Don't let it swell your heads."

Parsifal reached for his Lanchester Mark 1 and crushed the muzzle into Harry's forehead. "I'll blow you away if you don't tell me what I want to know. Who is Dewey? Is he a cutout between you and someone else? Who do you all work for? Who runs the consortium?"

"Blow me away," Harry managed to mutter, "you blow away any possibility of getting answers to your questions."

Parsifal retracted the Lanchester and studied the reddish ring the barrel had branded on Harry's forehead. "You're hard," he acknowledged, one professional complimenting another.

"I been around," Harry replied huskily.

"You haven't been around me."

Parsifal set the Lanchester down against a wall. From a jacket pocket he produced a thick transparent plastic bag and two thick rubber bands. "I hope you have a strong stomach," he told Finn. "You'll need it."

Finn leaned back against the wall. "Wherever you're going, I've been there."

Parsifal glanced at Finn with interest. "I'll bet you have." He circled around behind Harry and deftly slipped the plastic bag over his head. "When you're ready to answer my questions," he instructed him, "all you have to do is open your fists."

Inside the transparent bag, Harry's good eye darted in terror as Parsifal worked the two rubber bands over his head and down around his neck, sealing the plastic against the skin above his shirt collar and the green bow tie.

Finn watched from the wall. If he felt any emotion, it didn't show on his face.

Harry was using up the air in the sack with short frightened gasps; with each gasp the plastic came closer to sealing his mouth. "The folks who taught me this trick," Parsifal yelled into Harry's ear, "said there was enough air for roughly two minutes. After that you start to suffocate, a process that can last for another three or four minutes before you lose consciousness. You're going to drown, Harry, if you don't tell me what I want to know."

Parsifal kept his eyes on the hands taped together behind the chair; the knuckles turned white as Harry strained to keep them clenched. Inside the sack, the vapor-coated plastic glued itself to his lips.

"He had a point," Finn called across the room. "If he stops breathing, he'll have trouble answering your questions."

Caught up in the contest of wills, Parsifal laughed wildly.

Harry's head was jerking from side to side now as he struggled to suck in the last of the air in the sack. His open eye bulged in its socket, his shoulders shuddered. Then his fists sprang open behind his back.

In one quick motion Parsifal hooked a finger over the rubber bands and yanked the plastic sack off his head.

Harry sucked in a tremendous gulp of air, then a second. His chest heaved. Drained, his body slumped forward in the chair. When he was breathing more or less normally, Parsifal grabbed his chin and pulled his head back. "I'm ready if you are," he said. "Or do we cover your head with plastic again?"

"What do you need to know?"

"Let's start at the start. Who is Dewey?"

Harry's voice was almost inaudible. "He was my lord and master at Special Projects."

"What was Special Projects?"

"It was a world within a world within a world." When Harry hesitated, Parsifal jerked his head back. "Okay, okay. On the surface it was an administrative vehicle for the odd project that needed a home phone, a mailing address. Special Projects had an office, it had a staff, it had a safe filled with one-time pads and laundered money."

"What happened in the back rooms of this world within a world within a world?"

"Dewey wheeled and dealed; he was the CIA's point man with the Mafia clans. Special Projects was the halfway house in which the two worlds, the CIA and the Mafia, came together to discuss matters of mutual interest."

"Congress lets the CIA sleep with the Mafia?" Finn asked from the wall.

"Congress doesn't know about it," Harry said. "Dewey ran the Mafia account out of his hip pocket so there'd be no paper trail if the congressional oversight dilettantes started dealing subpoenas to Company players."

Parsifal rustled the plastic bag next to Harry's ear. "So far you're only skimming the surface."

Harry swallowed hard. "Dewey's real name, at least the one I know him by, is Egidio de Wey. De Wey is where the Dewey alias comes from. Egidio is Italian down to the spit-shined tips of his Milano shoes. He had contacts in Chicago, he had contacts in Reno, he knew the right people in Sicily, he was always yapping away in Italian with them on the phone. Office scuttlebutt had it that it was Egidio, fresh out of Yale, who talked the Mafia into trying to whack Castro back in the sixties. The in-house handle for Special Projects was Little Italy. If you phoned up and were put on hold, you got an earful of Pavarotti singing "La Donna" something or other."

"Who did Egidio report to? Who supervised Special Projects?"

"That wasn't the kind of information Egidio shared with me."

"Okay, let's come at the problem from another direction. Give me an example of one of Special Projects' special projects."

Harry's body appeared to grow smaller in the chair. "Egidio once organized a briefing for everyone connected with Russian ops. He projected a film produced by one of his freelance teams in a CIA screening room at Langley. Even Egidio's Medici turned up. When the lights went out, the door opened and he slipped in. In the dim light from the emergency exit sign over the door you could tell he was royalty; he had starched cuffs with cuff links that glowed in the dark, he had an entourage, he had a bodyguard, he had a girl Friday with long legs and a short skirt. The heads of sections, Dewey included, acted cool, but you knew they were turned on about him being there. The projectionist obviously'd been waiting for him to arrive to roll the film, which was Egidio's brainchild; it showed how Gorbachev was plotting to convince us the Cold War was ancient history so we would let down our guard. The Russkies couldn't beat us in the military hardware department so they were pulling a Trojan horse number—that was the name of the film, *Trojan Horse II*—and lulling us into disarming. From time to time, Egidio's Medici—he was sitting in the row behind Egidio threading these silver beads through his fingers, you could see the light glinting off them, you could hear the beads clicking against each other—the Medici would lean forward and jab Egidio in the shoulder and whisper something, and the two of them would laugh those loud laughs people who are very rich or very sure of themselves laugh."

"What did Egidio's Medici look like?"

"He arrived after they turned the lights out. He left before they turned them on. Even in the dark he wore Ray-Bans."

"He have a handle?"

"Everyone has a handle, but I was too far back in the pecking order to know what it was."

Parsifal reached down and snapped the rubber bands around Harry's neck. Harry winced. Parsifal whispered directly into his ear, "Don't fuck with me, Harry. Did you ever see Egidio's Medici in a consortium context?"

"You know better than that. I never saw anyone in a consortium context."

"Egidio had to report to someone."

"When Egidio signed me on, he said the consortium was someone's swan song. He also said it was mainstream, which I took to mean it had friends in high places. Who those friends were was not my business."

"How do you set up meetings with Egidio de Wey, alias Dewey?"

"Egidio is the last of the paranoids. When he worked at the Agency we used to joke about how he talked to his mother through a cutout. The consortium's run the same way. We're tightly compartmented. Egidio and me, we never meet. We communicate through cutouts. I don't even have a phone number for him. I got a lifetime supply of dead drops, I phone up an unlisted number in Houston, I activate a dead drop with a code word, I leave off the money I won from the Apache casino. If Egidio needs to contact me, he leaves off a code word on my answering machine and I service the appropriate dead drop for his instructions."

Pieces of the puzzle were beginning to fall into place for Parsifal. "Of course! The money Harry here wins from the casino bankrolls the consortium. It's less traceable and easier to come by than money laundered by Early." He turned back to the prisoner. "What is the consortium's brief? What is it out to accomplish?"

"It was not something I needed to know, so Egidio never told me."

"Funny, those were Early's exact words. You don't work in a vacuum; you have to have an idea. Is the consortium Special Projects gone to ground? Is it Dewey in a new incarnation as Mafia capo? Is it the CIA taking care of its own, a sort of golden parachute for retired agents? Is it a generator of untraceable funds for unauthorized operations?"

A whiff of Harry's old spirit returned. "Go ahead, pull the fucking bag over my head again. I'll open my fists to keep from drowning. But when I can talk, I'll tell you the same thing I'm telling you now. There's no way I can tell you what I don't know."

"Let's talk about your dead drops. Give us examples."

"There's one under a broken manhole cover in the parking lot behind the Indian arts museum in Santa Fe. There's a hollowed-out space behind an old framed map of the New Mexico Territory in the Kit Carson Museum in Taos. There's a pigeonhole in an Anasazi ceremonial cave in Frijoles Canyon near Los Alamos."

"Who selects the drop?"

"The dropper."

"Who services the drop?"

"The droppee—namely the next person up or down in the consortium's pecking order."

"If you drop something off for Dewey, he personally picks it up?"

"That's the way the consortium is structured. I'm the cutout between Egidio and Early. Egidio is the cutout between me and the next rung up. Egidio and me, we're tight. Except for the phone contact, between us there is no cutout."

"What's the code word for the manhole behind the museum?"

"Silkworm."

"How about the map in Taos?"

"Monkey Business."

"And the Anasazi pigeonhole?"

"Clay Pigeon."

"If you're lying to me . . ."

Harry managed a pained smirk. "If I'm lying, I'm dying."

"Which brings us to the unlisted phone in Houston."

Harry's Adam's apple worked above his green bow tie as he came up with the telephone number.

Suddenly Parsifal's eyes narrowed and his breath came in short soundless gasps. "Repeat the number."

Harry repeated the number.

"When you dial it, who answers?"

"A man who speaks English with a funny accent. He talks through one of those speech-altering devices."

Parsifal said softly, "You ask if you've reached a certain number, then you read off the number of the booth you're calling from. The man who answers says you have dialed a wrong number and hangs up. Ten, twelve minutes later, the time it takes for him to get to a public booth, he calls you back at the number you gave him."

"Yeah," Harry said, surprised.

"How did you know that?" Finn asked.

Parsifal walked over to the paneless window and stared out into the night. He felt a current of warm air on his face and got a faint whiff of the fire he'd put out with fistfuls of sand. After a long moment he turned back to Finn. "Sorry. What did you say?"

"I asked how you knew about the business with the phone."

Parsifal's mind was tearing through scenarios. "It's a kind of standard operating procedure among spooks," he said.

42

F inn watched from the pickup as Parsifal prodded Harry into the phone booth at the entrance to the parking lot. The low hangarlike Pueblo Bingo Palace off Route 84 was closed for the night; the neon sign above the door was dark, the parking lot was deserted. Parsifal punched in a number, fed coins into the slot, then held the phone to Harry's face. "I'm trying to reach ——," Harry said. He read off the number printed on the phone. Parsifal hung up. Minutes slipped by. An eighteen-wheeler headed for Santa Fe, its lights blazing, roared past on the highway, drowning out the sound of the phone ringing in the booth. Parsifal, standing next to the phone, obviously heard it. He snatched the receiver off the hook and held it up to Harry's mouth. Harry said, "Clay Pigeon. I repeat, Clay Pigeon." Parsifal held the phone so that both he and Harry could hear the conversation. He listened as the voice on the other end, pitched high and distinctly metallic, asked if everything had gone well. Parsifal nodded at Harry. Harry muttered, "Sure. Everything always goes well."

With a forefinger, Parsifal cut the connection.

inn parked the pickup at the end of the dirt road, which was as close to the Watershed Station town jail as he could get, and delivered G. D. Early and Harry Lahr, both bound and gagged, into the hands of the Apaches. "I sure hope you know what you're doing," Alchise told Eskeltsetle as his father fitted the skeleton key into the door and unlocked it.

"The future is in the past," Eskeltsetle replied cryptically.

Petwawwenin, the Smoker, and Nahtanh, the Cornflower, each with a prisoner flung like a rolled carpet over a shoulder, filed past in the darkness. "We're risking a lot on one throw of the dice," muttered Petwawwenin, straining under the weight of Early.

Finn remembered what Petwawwenin had told him the first time he set foot in the Apache casino. "Don't bet all your chips on one number," Finn whispered. "Spread them around."

"Fuck you," retorted Petwawwenin, but Finn, retreating into the night, only laughed under his breath.

Crossing one of the footbridges over Rattlesnake Wash, Finn paused to gaze at the white water rushing under his feet. He remembered how Shenandoah, riding *The Spirit of Saint Louis* off the mesa crawling with Indian paintbrush and goldenrod, had gotten things ass backwards. "We're standin' dead still," she'd called to Doubting Thomas. "It's the world that's backin' away from us." Now, staring down at the river, Finn imagined that it was standing dead still and he was plunging upstream through the twisting breakers. For the space of several magical seconds the fantasy worked.

Then it gave way to reality.

The fantasy had worked at Wadi Ta'if too; Finn had run the film backwards to where Lieutenant Pilgrim called in the air strike, and had rewritten the script. Then reality had intruded—the stench of burning tires and burning corpses had stung his nostrils, had brought tears to his smarting eyes. It had struck Finn then, it struck him now, how tough it was to superimpose your imagination on reality; to reverse a reality. There were times when you could get away with it, but the effect only lasted the blink of an eye.

He wondered whether his newfound Russian friend who lived by a clock set ten hours behind was more proficient; he wondered whether Mr. Howard was in touch with reality, or creating a convenient reality through an act of imagination.

Was the consortium nothing more than a bunch of retired Washington spooks riding a gravy train, or a sinister plot of some kind?

Was there more to it, or less to it, than met the eye?

Wrestling with the riddle, Finn stole uphill through the fields. At the far edge of Watershed Station, he cut across Sore Loser Road and flitted like a shadow through the yards behind the houses to the general store. He felt over the lintel for the skeleton key, let himself in the kitchen door, peered into the main room, half-expecting—half-hoping!—to see Shenandoah, soaking her long delicate fingers in lukewarm water, look up and greet him with a smile and a whimsical "Say hey, Saint Louis." But the room was dark and still and empty. Taking the steps two at a time, Finn made his way up to the second floor. He noticed light seeping under the door of Doubting Thomas's room, stuck his head in and found the boy hunched over in bed, reading a book by flashlight.

Thomas's face lit up when he saw Finn. "Say hey, Saint Louis," he whispered.

Slipping into the room, Finn spotted the two dream catchers dangling over the bed from fishing line thumbtacked to the ceiling. "What do dream catchers do?" he asked.

Doubting Thomas reached up and twirled one. "Skelt says dreams come from shooting stars," he explained seriously. "The stars scatter dreams over the earth when they enter the atmosphere and burn up. The dream catcher is based on the principle of the spider's web: it traps bad dreams the way spiderwebs trap dew in the morning. The bad dreams burn off the way dew burns off spiderwebs when the sun rises."

"Do you have bad dreams?"

"I used to before Skelt hung up the dream catchers. I used to dream I was in hell for my bad deeds."

"And this hell, what did it look like in your dreams?"

Doubting Thomas pulled a face. "For starters, I was barefoot and there were zillions of frogs squashed on the ground. It was real disgusting! There were flames, of course, like when we clear a cornfield by burning off the old stumps, except the fire was going day and night, and every time you breathed in, it smelled like rotten eggs." The boy closed his left eye and squinted at Finn through his right eye. "Have you ever been to hell in your dreams?"

Finn gave a spin to the other dream catcher. "I've been to hell in real life," he said quietly.

Doubting Thomas's left eye flicked open. "What was it like?" he asked in awe.

"It was awful." Finn stared out an open window, his eyes focused on something much further away than the horizon. "Squashed frogs, rotten eggs, they're nothing compared."

"Oh."

44

Drifts of heat accumulated on the floor of the desert, causing everything in sight to splinter into horizontal fragments—the single Russian-made tank leading the convoy through the wadi, open army trucks, tankers with the face of Saddam Hussein painted on their bloated bellies. Behind them came a comic assortment of commandeered delivery trucks with store logos on their sides, orange school buses, white ambulances, brightly painted Chevrolet pickups and black Mercedes taxis, all stolen from Kuwait City, all crammed with soldiers.

Gone to ground in a shallow crater scooped out of the sand on a dune half a mile from the convoy, Lieutenant Pilgrim and Lance Corporal Finn watched through binoculars as the Iraqi convoy crept slowly across the soft sands of Wadi Ta'if. Returning to the jeep concealed in a dry wadi, Finn inflated a small balloon with helium, fitted it with a battery-powered transmitter and released it into the air. He tracked the balloon visually until it dropped from sight, then picked up its signal on a small receiver and tracked it for another few minutes. While he plotted the prevailing winds on an army map, Lieutenant Pilgrim unleashed the whip antenna, cranked the radio and established contact with the air traffic control center behind the American lines.

"Alpha Tango Charlie Charlie One One Black reporting in from coordinates"—Finn pointed out where they were to Pilgrim—"Xray Oscar Bravo Delta, observing westerly winds on the desert floor of ten knots, shifting to southwesterly and fifteen knots at low altitudes. Weather sunny and clear, with the occasional tuft of black smoke spiraling up from a wrecked Iraqi tank. All things considered, it's a great day for a turkey shoot. Speaking of turkey shoots, request air strike on enemy convoy trying to escape through Wadi Ta'if. Over."

The bored voice of the controller crackled over the radio. "Roger, Alpha Tango Charlie Charlie One One Black. All of our screaming eagles are currently occupied. I can't vector anything your way for ten, twelve minutes. Any chance of you guys slowing down the action until some of our eagles can take on ordnance and arrive?"

"Wilco," Lieutenant Pilgrim said. He fished a TOW shoulder-fired anti-tank missile from under the tarpaulin in the back of the jeep. Taking a coin from a pocket, he flipped it in the air and slapped it onto the back of his wrist. "Winner gets to knock off the tank," he said.

"Heads."

Pilgrim looked at the coin. "Some folks have got all the luck."

Taking the weapon from Pilgrim, crouching low, Finn disappeared into the desert and surfaced at a dune closer to the wadi. Crawling to the top, he armed the TOW, sighted on the Russian tank and fired. The missile streaked in low over the desert and caught the tank on the port beam. It burned through the armor plating and exploded inside the turret. The tank pivoted drunkenly on one tread, blocking the trail through the wadi, then burst into flames. Some of the army trucks behind it attempted U-turns but got mired in the sand. Klaxons screamed. At the rear of the convoy a woman wearing a long black dress and a black lace veil over the lower half of her face pulled an armchair off a moving van and sat down. A coal black bedouin dressed in long flowing robes opened a large golf umbrella and held it over her head. Soldiers in khaki trousers and civilian shirts leaped off the delivery trucks and started to scramble up the steep sides of the wadi. Officers poured out of the Mercedes taxis. Drawing pistols, they shouted for the soldiers to defend the convoy. Shots rang out. Several raglike figures could be seen tumbling back down to the floor of the wadi.

From the top of a dune Pilgrim squeezed off two short bursts from his M16. The woman sitting under the golf umbrella disappeared into the moving van. Iraqi soldiers, tossing away their boots, scurried barefoot back down the wadi or took cover under vehicles. A deathly quiet settled over Wadi Ta'if. Then a young officer wearing knee-length boots strode out in front of the burning tank waving a white flag attached to the end of a crutch.

At that moment a flight of slow-flying Navy Hunter Hawks appeared overhead, peeled off and plunged down the spine of the wadi. From his dune Finn could make out sparks spurting from the Gatling guns on either side of the fuselages, and the bullets kicking up spouts of sand on the floor of the wadi. Several of the Hunter Hawks swooped over the convoy and dropped napalm canisters. In seconds Wadi Ta'if was transformed into an inferno.

Flushed, his eyes feverish with horror, Finn leaped to his feet and waved wildly at the planes. "They've surrendered," he screamed. "Stop attacking." His voice was drowned out by one of the Hunter Hawks roaring low over his head, playfully wagging its wings as it circled back toward the wadi.

Cradling his M16, Lieutenant Pilgrim joined Lance Corporal Finn. The two men stood side by side on the top of a dune watching the flames licking at the cars and buses and trucks in the wadi. The heat from the burning tankers grew so intense it dried the tears forming in the corners of Finn's eyes before they could trickle down his cheeks.

oming out of Thomas's room, Finn saw a door ajar at the end of the hall and light from a candle flickering in the room where, if you believed Shenandoah, tears tended to flow in the general direction of Arizona. Without thinking, drawn like iron filings to a magnet, he went in. The room's two windows were wide open; lace curtains drifted in and out on the night's breath. Wearing a man's sleeveless undershirt, Shenandoah was asleep facedown on the bed, her arms wrapped around the pillow, her face buried in it. Finn's frayed paperback copy of Fitzgerald's *Great Gatsby* lay open, spine up, on the wooden box that served as a night table, next to a candle that had almost burned down to the wine bottle in which it was embedded.

Finn lowered himself into a wicker rocking chair and watched Shenandoah sleep. He imagined running the palm of his hand over the skin of her buttocks, which glistened like quicksilver in the darkness. He could almost feel her skin under his hand, warm to the touch, slightly coarse. She must have felt his gaze on her, because she stirred, rolled over, then sat up with a start. "You got a hell of a nerve sneakin' into my bedroom!" she said, spitting out the words as she pulled the sheet up to her neck. "If Skelt finds you here he'll break your ass."

"I needed to set eyes on you." Breathing deeply, Finn closed his eyes and pressed his thumb and third finger against the lids. "I needed to memorize you."

"Nothin's changed none," Shenandoah said in a fierce whisper. "Like is still the limit of my possibilities." When Finn, nodding, rocked forward and stood up, she sighed and waved impatiently for him to sit down again.

"Hey, you sure frightened me. So where have you been for five days, Saint Louis?"

He sank back into the rocking chair. "I been walking back a cat."

"What cat? Whose cat?" Shenandoah ran a hand through her hair. "Skelt told me you'd turn up. He said you planned to stash Mr. Early and another dude in the old jailhouse down by the river. What's goin' on?"

"Early's part of the problem, as opposed to the solution. He's got ties to the people who have been milking the casino."

"Skelt always said Mr. Early was the Apache's guardian angel . . ."

"That's what Mr. Early wanted Skelt to think."

Shenandoah was suddenly very alert. "Did Mr. Early have anythin' to do with all those deaths—Baychendaysan, the Long Nose? Klosen, the Hair Rope? Uclenny, the Rapid Runner? Nahkahyen, the Keen Sighted? Tooahyaysay, the Strong Swimmer?"

On the night table the wick sputtered, then the flame died. "He set them up," Finn said in the darkness. "Someone else—a professional—pulled the rug out from under them."

Shenandoah felt a stab of pain in her chest. Breathing with her mouth open, she brought a palm up to her breast. When she had calmed down she said quietly, "Son of a bitch Mr. Early! Did the Long Nose, did the others hurt?"

"Given the professional in question, chances are they never knew what hit them."

"What *is* goin' on?"

"I won't know until I've reached the end of the tunnel."

"Are you sure there's an end to the tunnel?"

"Every tunnel has an end. It's a matter of staying on your feet long enough to reach it."

"You're a goddamn optimist, Saint Louis. That's one of the things I liked about you the first time I saw you."

Finn was thankful for a crumb. "I didn't know you liked me the first time you saw me."

She smiled bitterly. "Don't let it go to your head."

"I never thought of myself as an optimist."

She shook her head. "If you get in your balloon and run, it's because you think there's someplace to run to. Me, I believe in God, but I don't believe he's an optimist or a pessimist. I don't believe things systematically turn out good or bad."

"Yeah, I see what you mean," Finn said. He wasn't sure he did, but it didn't matter. He figured that as long as she kept talking, she wouldn't kick him out of her bedroom.

"Do you really see what I mean?" Shenandoah managed a weak smile. "I had a half sister who was an optimist, she was as fat as I was thin, she was always tryin' out new diets—liquid diets, fat-free diets, Slim-Fast diets, thirty-pounds-in-thirty-days diets. Once she ate nothin' but grapes for a solid month. When she bought clothes, which was every time she cashed a paycheck, she always bought them two sizes too small . . ."

Fighting back tears, she stared at the lace curtains fluttering in a window.

Finn prompted her. "Your half sister was buying clothes two sizes too small . . ."

"Yeah. She bought them two sizes too small so she could diet into them. Skelt thought she was ripe for the loony bin. She'd eventually pass the skirt or the sweater on to me, even on me it was tight."

Finn asked, "So what happened to your half sister?"

"She found a diet that worked—it's called bulimia, which is when you eat all you want and then jam a finger down your throat to make yourself throw up. She lost so much weight she started fittin' into the clothes she bought. Trouble was she kept on losin' weight, she couldn't stop. Pretty soon the clothes she bought two sizes too small were too big on her. She looked like one of those people you see in pictures of concentration camps. Then she caught pneumonia. Then she died."

Shenandoah fell silent. After a while she put the question she'd been afraid to ask. "Where you off to now?"

Evasive, Finn told her not to worry if he dropped out of sight.

"Me worry?" she said, irritated. "You got to be high on somethin' besides altitude." She snatched a Kleenex from a box next to the bed and loudly blew her nose into it. "I got a major confession to make to you, Saint Louis. I flunked geometry in high school. The reason I flunked geometry was I hated it. The reason I hated it was I couldn't swallow the business about parallel lines never meetin'." She shivered under the sheet, causing it to fall away from one shoulder. "I mean, if parallel lines can't never meet, where's the sense?"

Finn understood she wasn't talking about geometry. "Where's the sense?" he agreed in a husky voice.

"Like is the limit of my possibilities because I love Skelt," Shenandoah whispered.

"You don't owe me explanations."

"If we'd met sooner . . . if we was to meet in another life . . ." She grabbed the pillow and hugged it to her body. "Oh, we had good moments, Skelt and me, don't think we didn't. They lasted a lifetime. Trouble is, a lifetime's awful short." Staring at Finn in the darkness, she saw the abyss loom and panicked. "Get out of my goddamn bedroom," she breathed. "Get out of my goddamn life. Do yourself and me and Skelt a favor—sail away in that balloon of yours. *Please!*"

46

P eering down from the Anasazi ceremonial cave on a ledge overlooking Frijoles Canyon, Finn had a bird's-eye view of the footpath snaking through the narrow valley. It began at the Park Department building at the mouth of the canyon, skirted the ruins of a circular Anasazi village, then meandered past the smoke-scarred cave dwellings in the cliffs. About a mile into the valley the path dipped down to a narrow wooden bridge spanning a shallow stream, and ended up, below Finn, at the foot of the long ladder lashed to the face of the cliff. During the day tourists trooped down the path and scampered up the ladder to visit the great ceremonial cave where, a thousand years before, Anasazi medicine men dressed in eagle feathers and buffalo hides had burned offerings to their gods. At night the Park Department building was closed, the valley deserted. The only sound to reach Finn's ears came from the silver stream whispering over shelves of shale as it cut through the canyon.

"I got to tell you something you're not going to like," Finn was saying. "I don't see how you can do what you do."

"Ends," Parsifal replied, repeating something he had told himself a thousand times, "justify means." He was sitting on a flat stone that might have served as an altar once, lost in the shadows of the overhang at the back of the cave. "If you don't believe that ends justify means," he went on, "you will be incapable of moving the ball forward. I do what I do in the absolute conviction that others who come after me will not have to do what I do. It is not unlike the quest for the Holy Grail."

"You're jerking yourself off," Finn said softly. He thought of the demon lurking in the pit of his own stomach. "You do what you do because you're addicted to violence — you need a daily fix."

Parsifal's voice, very intense, drifted out of the darkness. "What you say has a grain of truth. I think that we are all prisoners trapped inside our brains, trapped inside our genes. We spend our adult lives trying to become intimate with another human being so that we can break out of this prison; so that we can become someone else. Real intimacy is the work of a lifetime, but there are two shortcuts—through the act we call lovemaking and through the act we call murder."

"You're sick," Finn whispered. "You need help."

"We all need help. The first time I saw you, back in the rope factory, it struck me that looking at you was like looking in a mirror."

"You want to be more specific?"

"You are a very violent person."

"What gives you that impression?"

"The nonchalant way you leaned the shotgun barrel against your shoulder when you were searching the rope factory. The sensual way your finger curled around the trigger, almost as if you were caressing a clitoris. You have carried weapons before, Mr. Finn. You are comfortable with them; you hold them the way I hold them—as if they are an extension of your body, as if they are an erection. Watching you move through the rope factory, I understood that you had been trained in house-to-house, room-to-room combat. When I informed you that you were about to commit suicide, you didn't squirm, you didn't sob, you didn't offer prayers to a God you don't believe in, you didn't offer me money you didn't have."

"Dying was something I didn't look forward to," Finn said. "I wanted to get it over with as quickly as possible."

Parsifal laughed under his breath. "In similar situations I have known people to lose control of their sphincter muscles. I didn't detect a whiff of fear coming from your body." He regarded Finn in the darkness. "If I had to guess, I'd say you didn't feel anything. We are cut from the same cloth," he continued, his voice cold and analytical. "Have you ever killed anyone?"

Finn didn't respond.

Parsifal insisted. "One? Several? Many?"

Again Finn said nothing.

"Where?"

"The Gulf. The war."

Parsifal accepted this with a nod.

"I had a CO, a black man name of Pilgrim, he used to say war doesn't decide who's right, it decides who's left."

"What happened to your CO?"

"He got left. I heard he's hanging out in Washington working for some congressman or other."

At the mouth of the canyon, headlights crept into the deserted parking lot and winked out. "That will be Egidio de Wey, alias Dewey, come in his shiny black Cadillac to service the dead-drop code named Clay Pigeon," Parsifal said. He picked up his Russian PPSh 41, jammed a magazine into it and worked the bolt, levering the first round into the chamber. Gripping his shotgun, curling his finger around the trigger, Finn retreated into the low grotto at the back of the cave.

Minutes later the figure of a man could be seen making his way down the footpath. A three-quarter moon suspended over the cliffs threw his shadow ahead of him. He crossed the narrow footbridge spanning the stream and stopped next to a ponderosa pine. There was the flicker of a match as he lit a cigarette. From time to time the end of his cigarette glowed like a firefly in the night.

"He's taking his sweet time," Finn whispered.

"He's sweeping his trail," Parsifal whispered back. "He's making sure he's not being followed."

Dewey took a last long drag on the cigarette before lobbing it into the stream, then stepped back onto the path and continued up to the ladder leading to the ceremonial cave. Finn sensed more than heard Parsifal slip away to his left as Dewey started up the long ladder. He scampered onto the ledge, brushed dust off his trousers and headed directly for the niche in the face of the cliff behind the flat altar stone. He was reaching into the niche when he heard a scraping behind him. He started to whirl around but froze when he felt the barrel of a gun caressing the nape of his neck.

"There are thirty-five rounds in the clip," a voice said. "The PPSh forty-one is on automatic, and I have filed down the sear pin—the slightest pressure on the trigger will send at least ten of the bullets into your neck. The soft heads of the bullets have been sawed open, which means they tend to expand on impact. Any one of them would be enough to sever your spinal column and tear a gaping hole in your throat. Ten of them will certainly decapitate you. Are you armed?"

Dewey nodded once.

"With what?"

"A revolver. It is tucked into the belt behind my back."

Parsifal reached under Dewey's zippered jacket, extracted the weapon and stuck it in his own belt.

"Is the revolver all you are armed with?"

"No. I am also armed with twenty-seven years of experience dealing with scum like you."

Parsifal laughed quietly. "If you come out of this alive, you will have the benefit of being even more experienced. But that's a big *if*. Spread your feet wide. Place your palms flat on the side of the cliff above your head. Press your forehead against the cliff. Do not move a muscle if you want to remain among the living."

Dewey did as he was told.

Keeping his stubby PPSh pressed against the back of Dewey's neck, Parsifal carefully frisked him. Then he backed off a step. "You have good taste in aftershave lotion, though cold water from a tap would serve just as well. You can turn around now."

Dewey turned slowly to face Parsifal. "I was under the impression that no one could make Harry Lahr talk. How did you swing it?"

Finn emerged from the grotto. "He slipped a plastic sack over his head," he said. "Harry preferred talking to drowning."

Dewey angled his head and squinted into the darkness. "So there are two of you." He looked back at Parsifal. "What did Harry give you besides the unlisted telephone in Houston and this dead drop?"

Parsifal said, "He gave us your pedigree. He said that you had been his lord and master at Special Projects. He said that you had Mafia contacts all over the globe. He said that you left the Agency and signed on to a consortium that was someone's swan song, that was mainstream, that had friends in high places."

Dewey seemed more surprised that he had misjudged an associate than angry at the betrayal. "Fucking Harry!"

Parsifal prodded Dewey with his PPSh. Stooping under the lintel, Dewey backed up until he was inside the low oval grotto at the back of the shelf. Finn came in behind them holding a flashlight, which he played on Dewey's face. "Watch him," Parsifal said. "If he moves, let him have a blast in the knees."

Holding his shotgun in one hand and the flashlight in the other, Finn took a good look at Dewey. He was thin and patrician looking, of medium height, and appeared to be in his early sixties. He wore a zippered suede jacket and oversized tinted eyeglasses with thin tortoiseshell frames. His shoes were made of soft patent leather and black and small and pointed. His cheeks seemed exceptionally flushed.

Circling around behind Dewey, Parsifal bound his wrists with a length of electrical wire. Then he kicked his feet out from under him, sending him sprawling in the chalk dust.

"That's not all we know about you," Parsifal informed his prisoner. "We know you were shaking down the Apache casino to provide operating cash for the consortium. We know you were debriefing a Russian defector, a woman, who was hidden in an apartment in Dallas with stinking corridors."

A shadow of concern flitted over Dewey's face as he squirmed into a sitting position. "Who are you?" he asked in a raspy voice.

Finn said to Parsifal, "You never mentioned a Russian defector."

Parsifal said, "There are a lot of things I haven't mentioned." He kicked Dewey sharply in the shoulder. "What did you hope to get from the Russian lady defector? The Cold War is over."

"Phase One may be over," Dewey shot back. "Phase Two is just starting."

"What's he talking about?" Finn asked.

Parsifal laughed under his breath. "We have snared ourselves a rare bird," he said, "someone who in livelier days was referred to as a cold warrior." He circled Dewey and kicked him in the other shoulder. "My young friend and I are working our way up a ladder," he explained. "We started out on the lowest rung with your money-laundering friend Early. Early was kind enough to direct us to the second rung, the man in the green bow tie named Harry Lahr. Harry, in turn, led us to you. What we want to do is reach the top of the ladder. We want to see the world from the summit. We want to know the identity of the CEO of your mysterious consortium. We would also like to know the raison d'être for the consortium. What does it do besides shake down Apache casinos and debrief Russian defectors?"

"Smoking cigarettes is dangerous for your health," Dewey said. "Possessing this kind of information likewise is dangerous for your health. For your own safety, eventually for mine, it is out of the realm of possibility for me to respond to your questions."

"You will respond to these questions, and to others," Parsifal promised. "You will rack your brain for details to convince me that you are not inventing the answers."

Dewey's thin lips stretched into a mirthless smile. "*Va fa enculo!*"

Parsifal produced Dewey's revolver from his waistband and hefted it in his palm. "If I am not mistaken, this is one of those elegant little French Lebels which were manufactured in the twenties and were still in service during the Second World War."

"I see you are something of an expert on firearms," Dewey said with an unmistakable sneer.

"I am an expert on people," Parsifal retorted. "I know how to make them talk. The Lebel—correct me if I am wrong—has a relatively weak muzzle velocity, but it makes up for this in reliability and accuracy. Where did you acquire it?"

"This particular Lebel was given to me by my godfather, who ran a family property near Palermo in Sicily, on the occasion of my eighteenth birthday."

Parsifal flicked the lever and snapped out the cylinder. He emptied the six bullets into the palm of his hand. Crouching in front of Dewey, he dropped five of the bullets on the ground and inserted the sixth into the cylinder. With a jerk of his wrist he snapped the cylinder back into the revolver, spun the chambers several times and cocked the pistol. Then he jammed the barrel deep into Dewey's mouth and pulled the trigger.

The firing pin clicked against an empty chamber.

Parsifal pulled the gun out of Dewey's mouth and thumbed back the hammer. "I didn't catch what you said. Would you repeat it? What is the name of the CEO who runs your consortium?"

Blinking to clear tears from his eyes, Dewey breathed heavily through his nostrils, afraid to open his mouth.

Behind Parsifal, Finn noted, "He's no good to us dead."

Ignoring Finn, Parsifal told Dewey, "There is only one way for you to come out of this alive: by telling me what I want to know. Who was the Russian defector you were debriefing?"

Dewey kept his mouth clamped shut and regarded Parsifal with fear and loathing.

"What information did you get from her while you ate wedges of pizza and listened to arias on her tape recorder?"

Dewey stopped blinking. "You must be the knight at the Round Table," he breathed. "You must be the Jew's Parsifal—"

Parsifal shoved the Lebel between Dewey's open lips and thrust it down his throat, causing him to gag. Then, with Dewey gaping up at him through wide-open eyes, he pulled the trigger.

Again the firing pin clicked against an empty chamber.

Parsifal pulled back the revolver. "Two down, four to go," he murmured.

Finn came up behind Dewey. "You'd better answer his questions before he blows your brains out."

Suddenly Finn detected a foul odor and retreated to the mouth of the grotto. Parsifal pulled a handkerchief from his pocket and covered his nose. "Egidio de Wey, alias Dewey, has lost control of his sphincter muscles," he announced. "From my point of view that is an auspicious sign. It means he is scared shitless, as they say. It means he may be ready to talk."

Still breathing heavily through his nostrils, Dewey twisted his head away. Parsifal took a deep breath through his handkerchief, then, discarding it, reached over and pinched Dewey's nostrils between his fingers. Dewey's eyes bulged. When he could no longer hold out for lack of air, he opened his mouth and gasped. Parsifal thrust the Lebel down his throat again. "This one may be it," he said, and he pulled the trigger.

The hollow click reverberated through the grotto.

Settling back onto his haunches, Parsifal covered his mouth with the handkerchief. "Three down, three to go," he remarked through the folds.

Dewey's eyes, blinking rapidly, burned into Parsifal's. Gradually the blinking slowed down, then stopped. Articulating very distinctly, he pronounced the words *swan* and *song*. Then he stared at Parsifal through eyes that were totally expressionless. Then he pitched forward and crashed, facedown, onto the chalky floor of the grotto.

"Looks like he's fainted," Finn said.

Parsifal balanced the Lebel on a knee and reached around to Dewey's neck, feeling for his pulse. "The son of a bitch," he muttered. Backing away, he shook his head in disgust. He fished the sixth bullet from his jacket pocket, where he had slipped it when he was trying to convince Dewey that he'd loaded the Lebel for Russian roulette. "The revolver was empty," he told Finn. "His heart gave out."

Parsifal removed the electrical wire from Dewey's wrists, retrieved the five bullets from the ground and dropped the Lebel and the bullets into his pocket. He would wipe his fingerprints off the revolver and dispose of it and the bullets far from the cave before the night was over. All that would be left when the first tourist gave the alarm in the morning would be the body of a man who had died of a heart attack.

Backing out of the grotto, Parsifal squatted near the mouth of the cave and stared into the night. "Don't feel bad," he said when Finn joined him. "He wasn't a virgin when it comes to violence."

"I don't feel bad," Finn said. "I don't feel."

Parsifal glanced sideways at his companion, then snorted. To the south, over the constellation of Orion, a large star throbbed dull red. "Do you see that star?" Parsifal asked. "It's called Betelgeuse—it's what's known as a giant red. It is a dying star, so swollen in its death throes that you could fit our entire solar system into it. Death, whether of a star or a man, is a spectacle."

Finn was following his own thoughts. "Without Dewey we're at a dead end. There's no way we can reach the last rung of the ladder."

Parsifal stretched out a finger and traced two lines in the chalk dust at his feet.

Early ——➤ Green Bow Tie ——➤ Dewey ——➤ Egidio's Medici?

Parsifal ——➤ Le Juif ——➤ La Gioconda ——➤ Prince Igor?

Finn played his flashlight on the chalk dust. "Dewey called you Parsifal . . ."

"I am a knight at King Arthur's Round Table in search of the Holy Grail." He arched his brows thoughtfully. "The two lines are connected in at least four places," he went on. "One: when our friend in the green bow tie, Harry Lahr, and Dewey wanted to get in touch with each other, they planted a marker message with the person known as Le Juif, who served as a cutout. Two: when Dewey finished debriefing his Russian lady defector for the consortium, he decided to wipe the trail clean, at which point it was Le Juif who brought me into the picture. Three: when Green Bow Tie heard that you had talked to Early, he must have gone whining to Dewey, who surely passed the complaint on up to his CEO. The CEO somehow sent instructions down the second line to Le Juif, who brought me in to eliminate you."

"And number four?"

Parsifal nodded grimly. "Four is: how could Dewey know that I was the Jew's Parsifal unless the two lines were connected?"

Parsifal reached down and extended the two lines until they met in a V. "It's as plain as Betelgeuse in the constellation of Orion," he told Finn. "Contrary to the conventional wisdom on the subject, parallel lines sometimes *do* meet."

ieutenant Pilgrim had put on twenty pounds and let a bushy beard flecked with gray drape itself over the lower half of his round face since Finn had last set eyes on him, but he recognized his old CO immediately. There was no mistaking the cool way he thrust out his paw to shake hands, the ironic smile playing on his lips or the devil's fire burning in his laughing eyes; for Pilgrim, life was still one big joke, and laughter was the best defense. "Long time no see," he said, pulling Finn past the uniformed security guard into the conference room, kicking shut the door behind him, waving to a seat at one end of the horseshoe-shaped table. "What brings you to DC?"

Finn didn't beat around the bush. "How private is this conversation?"

Pilgrim unfastened his collar button and loosened his tie. "This joint is really a room floating within a room. It's soundproof, dustproof, waterproof, pollen-free, air-conditioned, ion-saturated—you name it, we have it. It's against house rules to take notes in here. They say even the electricity is filtered to make sure no one bugs the place."

"That's not what I meant," Finn said. "Will what I tell you stop with you?"

Pilgrim eyed his friend from the Gulf. "Fish have got to swim, birds have got to fly, I have got to serve one white congressman until I die. That being said, I also have gut loyalties to my friends, especially the ones who still have sand from the Gulf in their shoes."

Finn glanced at the large map of the world on the wall over the horseshoe table. "When I phoned you, I thought we'd meet in a restaurant."

"You specified right away. I don't mean to sound like a prick, but I have a tight schedule."

Finn gestured to the room. "Where are we?"

Pilgrim laughed. "We're in the holy of holies, Room SH219 in the Hart Office Building. It's where members of the House Permanent Select Committee on Intelligence listen to half-truths from the CIA's mandarins. When my congressman, who is vice chairman of this committee, is busy getting his white ass reelected, which is ninety percent of the time he's awake, I sit in for him."

"You have access to CIA secrets?"

"You asked me that when you called. It wasn't something I could answer on the phone. But I'll answer it now: within limits, yes, I have access to CIA secrets." He nodded toward the computer on the table, toward the bank of colored telephones lined up on a side table. "The red one is a direct line to Langley. Some congressmen use it to get the latest stock market report. So what's up? You in some kind of jam?"

Finn took a deep breath. "What's up is a guy tried to kill me. He stopped at the last second because he wasn't sure who wanted me dead. Me and this guy, we're . . . walking back the cat. We're trying to find out who wants me out of the way."

Pilgrim was intrigued. "Walking back the cat is CIA-speak. Which means the guy who tried to kill you comes from the wide world of spooks. Aside from that, you're not giving me much to nibble on."

"Yeah. So what we discovered so far is a nest of former CIA types working out of New Mexico under the cover of something they call the consortium. I thought maybe if I gave you names, you'd give me ranks and serial numbers."

Pilgrim scratched at his beard. "Let's take a shot at it."

"There's a joker name of G. D. Early. He used to work for something called the Defense Intelligence Agency. On the side he laundered money for another something called Special Projects over at the CIA. Then there's another joker from Special Projects, name of Harry Lahr, who talked Early into retiring from Defense Intelligence and going to work for the consortium being set up in New Mexico. The consortium is compartmented the way a submarine is compartmented. Early reports to Harry Lahr. Lahr reports to someone named Dewey, who was his boss at Special Projects until he quit to join the consortium."

"Is Dewey a first name or a last name?"

"It's a code name. His real name is Egidio de Wey. The Dewey comes from de Wey. Dewey reports to someone at the top rung of the consortium ladder, but we don't know who that is."

"Why don't you ask Dewey?"

"We did. He died of a heart attack before he could answer."

Pilgrim didn't bat an eye. "What does this consortium do?"

"That's something else we don't know. It shakes down an Apache casino for operating funds, but that has to be a sideline. The only other thing we know about it is that Dewey, acting presumably for the consortium, debriefed a Russian defector."

Pilgrim finally raised an eyebrow. "Come again?"

Finn said, "There was a woman stashed in an apartment in Dallas. Dewey used to bring her pizza and an attaché case filled with twenty-dollar bills from the Apache casino. The reason we know the money came from the Apache casino is that the bills were folded down the spines."

Pilgrim scraped his chair closer to Finn's. "A woman was shot to death in Dallas not long ago with an eleven-millimeter bullet fired from a handgun that could only have come from another country and another century. The fillings in the victim's teeth, the watch on her wrist, all came from Russia. The FBI did a routine check on her and discovered she'd been a middle level pencil pusher in the KGB when there still was a KGB and it still had pencils; she was an assistant to the assistant, that kind of thing. The CIA swore on the usual stack of Bibles that they didn't know she was in America, didn't even know she had defected. None of the other intelligence agencies admits to giving her the time of day. The FBI is still tripping over its shoelaces trying to figure out how she got to Dallas, and what secrets she could have given to the person or persons who brought her over in exchange for bringing her over. And now you pop up in DC and tell me she was being debriefed by someone named de Wey, alias Dewey, who used to run a unit called Special Projects for the CIA."

Finn grinned. "Yeah."

Pilgrim swiveled the computer screen around until he could see his reflection in it, then lit it off. The screen blinked through a series of automatic checks, then asked for an identifying number. Pilgrim typed something in on the keyboard that didn't appear on the screen. Apparently satisfied, the computer flashed, "Thank you. Wait one. Going online with computer central," then offered up the time, date and a menu. Pilgrim moved the cursor to "Biography (Short)," and hit Enter. "The first name you mentioned was G. D. Early," he remembered. He typed in the name and clicked Enter again. A moment later a paragraph materialized on the screen.

"Early, Gregory Dorman, bn. April 14, 1943. B.S. in biology, Alfred University, Alfred, NY, 1964. 1965–69: U.S. Army Intelligence stationed in Saigon, Phnom Penh and Taiwan. 1969–77: Resident Treasury Dept. Deputy Chief of Station, Thailand, with responsibilities for running Treasury agents in Thailand, Cambodia, Vietnam. 1977–92: Treasury Dept., Washington, with expertise on drug and arms smuggling and money laundering operations. 1992: Contract terminated at his own request."

Finn, reading over Pilgrim's shoulder, said, "Try Harry Lahr."

"Lahr, Harold, no middle name, bn. October 10, 1949. B.A. in economics, Northwestern University, Evanston, IL, 1970. 1970: Commissioned Ensign USNR after completing four-month Officer Candidate School, Newport, RI 1970–74: Communications Officer aboard USS John R. Pierce (DD753). 1974–75: Traveling Southeast Asia. 1975–79: U.S. Naval Intelligence contract employee based in Thailand, responsible for liaison with Treasury Dept. agents operating in Thailand, Cambodia, Vietnam. 1979: Applied to CIA, vetted, accepted. 1979–92: Central Intelligence Agency contract employee, involved in domestic collection, counterterrorism, assistant to the deputy chief of staff for HUMINT tasking. 1992: Separated at own request."

"They left out Special Projects," Finn noted.

Pilgrim backtracked to the menu and called up the CIA organizational chart. He typed in "Special Projects" and hit Enter. The computer screen went blank for a long moment before printing appeared: "Special Projects is a subunit under the Deputy Director for Science and Technology. It is headed by an A7 and has a staff of twenty-eight. It produces and tests state-of-the-art espionage equipment for eventual use by the Directorate of Operations under field conditions."

"That doesn't sound like what Dewey's Special Projects was doing," Finn said. "It was more along the lines of dealing with the Mafia and laundering money. Early said Harry Lahr called him in to freelance for Special Projects when they had to slip a bundle of bucks to foreign leaders."

"That smells like smoke from the Directorate for Operations," Pilgrim remarked. He punched in "Special Projects" and specified "Directorate for Operations." The answer came back instantly: "There is no record of a Special Projects unit operating under the aegis of the Directorate for Operations."

"If there was no Special Projects, what did de Wey, alias Dewey, do for a living?" Finn asked.

"Let's take a look-see at the gospel according to the CIA," Pilgrim said. He scrolled back to the menu and called up "Biography (Short)" again, then punched in "de Wey." The computer brought up a paragraph.

"de Wey, Egidio Fabio, bn. 1935 in Palermo, Sicily. 1946: Immigrated with parents to America. 1955: Naturalized U.S. citizenship. B.A. in comparative literature, Cornell University, Ithaca, NY, 1956; M.A. in medieval history, Cornell University, 1958. 1958–62: Associate professor, medieval history, CCNY, New York, NY, 1962: Recruited to CIA on CIA initiative, known by operational name of Dewey. 1963–69: Deputy chief of station, Rome. 1969–80: Worked in various departments of Directorate for Operations, Washington (Counterintelligence, Counter-narcotics). 1980–92: Italian desk, officer in charge of liaison with Italian-source assets, domestic and foreign. 1987: Granted a six-month sabbatical after minor cardiac attack. 1992: Separated at own request. January 1994: Drowned in boating accident off Florida Keys (see Cleveland, Rudge)."

Finn whistled under his breath. "Dewey didn't drown in any boating accident."

Pilgrim said, "The plot thickens. 'Liaison with Italian-source assets, domestic and foreign' means de Wey, alias Dewey, was the CIA's point man with the Mafia at a time when the CIA wasn't admitting it had contacts with the Mafia. Then there is the little problem of how he could debrief the Russian pencil pusher in Dallas if he drowned in a boating accident the previous winter. Not to mention how he could die of a heart attack when you questioned him if he was already dead."

Pilgrim turned back to the keyboard, typed in "Cleveland, Rudge" and hit Enter.

"Cleveland, Rudge Blaine, bn. 1939. B.A. in Russian literature, Yale University, New Haven, CT, 1960; M.A. in Russian history, Harvard University, Cambridge, MA, 1962; Ph.D. in Soviet studies, Yale University, 1966. 1966: Recruited to CIA on CIA initiative. 1966–67: Russian-language school. 1967–68: Posted to Soviet Division, Washington. Assistant to the deputy chief of Soviet desk. 1968–71: Posted to Moscow Station. 1971–73: Deputy chief of Soviet desk, Washington. 1973–77: Moscow chief of station. 1977–80: Chief of Soviet desk, Washington. 1980–85: Assistant to deputy director for operations (ADDO), Washington. 1985–92: deputy director for operations (DDO), Washington. December 1992, took early retirement option at the request of director, Central Intelligence (DCI). January 1994: Drowned when his sloop was caught in a storm off the Florida Keys (along with retired CIA colleague de Wey, Egidio; see de Wey, Egidio, alias Dewey)."

Pilgrim snickered. "It's not every day that one of the CIA's Medicis ups and drowns in a boating accident."

Finn grabbed his arm. "What did you say?"

"The CIA doesn't lose many of its top people in boating accidents—"

"Before that. You said something about one of the CIA's Medicis."

"Medici is the in-house nickname for the CIA's four princes—the lords and masters of the Company's four major directorates. Rudge Cleveland was a Medici; he ran Operations. He was a legend in his day. Nobody sneezed in the world of spooks without Rudge Cleveland getting a report on the person's health."

Finn said excitedly, "According to Harry Lahr, when Dewey ran Special Projects, he reported to someone Harry described as 'Egidio's Medici.' "

Pilgrim looked up at Finn. "Your friend de Wey, alias Dewey, ran the CIA's Italian desk during the years that Cleveland was ADDO and then DDO. Desk officers at the Agency report directly to the ADDO, which means that Dewey must have worked for Cleveland before he became a Medici. Which means Dewey and Cleveland already had a working relationship when Cleveland became the deputy director of operations. Then they both retire. Then they both get knocked off in a boating accident."

"Dewey didn't drown in any boating accident off the Florida Keys," Finn said. "He died when his heart stopped beating in an Anasazi ceremonial cave in Frijoles Canyon, New Mexico, two days ago."

"If what you say is true, if de Wey didn't drown, it raises the tantalizing possibility that Cleveland didn't drown either," Pilgrim said. He leaned back in his chair and rubbed his stomach, which spilled over his belt, and stared at the ceiling. "I met Cleveland a bunch of times; he used to sit in the very seat you're sitting in, briefing the select committee on his specialty, which was the Cold War. He was what you'd call a Neanderthal when it came to current events. Which is why the Select Committee on Intelligence eventually pushed the director of Central Intelligence to push Cleveland to accept early retirement."

"What is a Neanderthal on current events?" Finn asked.

"In the early nineties, with twenty-five or so years of Soviet ops under his belt, Cleveland ran smack up against the conventional wisdom touted by the analysts' side of the CIA and almost everybody else in the

Washington establishment—namely that perestroika was genuine; that the Soviet Union was confronting an economic and ultimately a political upheaval of cataclysmic proportions which would oblige the Soviet leadership to look at the world with new eyes. In short, the Cold War was over. Trouble was that Cleveland—who could name every member of the Politburo, who could describe their tastes in wine and women, who knew whose son had married whose daughter, who knew where the bodies were buried and who had buried them—this same Cleveland argued that perestroika was a passing fad, this season's skirt. He made the case that Russian history was littered with the wreckage of reform movements. For him, Russia was and would remain the archenemy of Western democracy. Anyone who didn't see this was blind or, worse, a traitor."

"So he was fired."

"He was eased out. The select committee can live with dissenting views, but the bottom line was that nobody trusted him. It's an old problem at the CIA, almost an occupational disease. Like a lot of folks over at the Agency, Cleveland spent most of his professional life breaking laws in foreign countries. We felt, given his strong views on the subject of Russia, that he'd have no qualms about breaking laws in the U.S."

Pilgrim pushed back his chair, walked over to the bank of telephones, switched the red one to a speakerphone so that Finn could hear the other end of the conversation and hit the button.

The eager voice of a young man came over the speaker. "Federal Bureau of Statistics, demographic section. Duty Officer Stillman speaking. What can we do for you?"

Pilgrim called into the tiny microphone, "This is Pilgrim over at the select committee."

"You don't have to shout," the duty officer said. "I can hear you real fine. You want to enter your identifying code number?"

Pilgrim punched in a series of numbers.

"Thank you, Mr. Pilgrim. How can I help you?"

Pilgrim said, "We want to check out something. You had a Medici name of Cleveland, as in the city of the same name, also a retired desk officer name of de Wey—I'm spelling that with a small d as in delta, then an e, new word, capital W as in whiskey, then an e and a y. Both men were reported to have died in a boating accident about two years ago. Can you dig out the file on the accident?"

"Wait one," the duty officer said. A minute later he came back on the line. "What exactly do you want to know?"

"My short biography says their sailboat was caught in a storm off the Florida Keys. Were their bodies autopsied to confirm the cause of death?"

"There were no bodies to autopsy," the duty officer reported. "A commercial trawler came across the abandoned boat floating upside down. The Coast Guard combed the area for forty-eight hours. All they found was a partially inflated life raft, also floating upside down."

Pilgrim said, "Thanks," and cut the connection. He looked across the room at Finn and laughed. "This story is getting curiouser and curiouser," he said.

Finn gestured toward the computer with his chin. "What other locks can you pick?"

"The sky's the limit."

"If I was to give you an unlisted phone number in Houston, could you come up with the address?"

"Try me."

48

The old warhorse of a nurse who thought that relatives were something you had to put up with but friends were beyond the pale laid down the law. "Five minutes, not the wink of an eye longer," she warned. She lowered her head as if she were about to charge and sized up the visitor through the top halves of her rimless bifocals. "Mind you, don't you let him talk too much—it wears him out."

Parsifal slipped into the intensive-care unit and pulled up a folding chair next to the third bed. Le Juif must have sensed someone was there because his eyes, sunken into his skull, slowly opened. The corners of his lips hinted at a tired smile. His breath came in shallow, almost soundless gasps. The tube inserted in one of his nostrils made talking difficult. "How did you find me?" he rasped.

"It's a matter of knowing the right people," Parsifal replied. "Your unlisted phone number led to an address. Your address led to the widow on the floor below who invites you for gefilte fish on the Jewish holidays. The widow led to the private ambulance service she called when you collapsed. The ambulance service led here."

Parsifal reached over the low bed rail and rested the tips of his fingers on the back of Le Juif's wrist, next to the bandage covering the intravenous needle inserted into a vein. The skin on the wrist was almost translucent, and incredibly soft to the touch. From under the sheet covering Le Juif's cadaverous body came the fetid odor that a man emits when his intestines have ceased to function.

"We have come a long way together," Parsifal said carefully.

Le Juif closed his eyes. "Made mistakes," he mumbled. His lips worked as if he were chewing cud. Then he coughed up a sardonic laugh. "Mistakes don't matter. If something worth doing, worth doing badly."

"There is still a stretch of road ahead of us."

"Strive on alone," Le Juif said. "For me, quest ends here."

Parsifal glanced around to make sure nobody could overhear them. The old woman in the next bed appeared to be unconscious. In a windowed cubicle off the intensive-care unit, a nurse filed her nails as she monitored heartbeats on a computer screen. Parsifal bent over the rail. "We have been betrayed," he whispered.

Le Juif's eyes twitched open in their dark sockets.

Talking rapidly, Parsifal made his pitch. "Me, you, La Gioconda—we all toil for Prince Igor. But Prince Igor does not toil for the cause of Marx, of Engels, of Lenin, of Bukharin. He does not share our dream. If Prince Igor gets his way, greed will smother justice and generosity."

A wild look appeared in Le Juif's gaping eyes. He tried to raise his head off the pillow, but fell back weakly. "Let me die in peace," he muttered.

"Prince Igor is not one of us. Somewhere along the way he managed to take control of our cell. There's a nest of ex-CIA agents working out of New Mexico. They are organized into something they call the consortium. It is highly compartmented. When one of the agents wanted to get in touch with another, he planted a message with a cutout. You were the cutout. You passed it on."

"La Gioconda said they were subcontractors—"

"One of the middle-level consortium agents who goes by the name of Dewey debriefed a Russian woman defector hidden in a safe house in Dallas. When he had squeezed the lemon dry, he decided to get rid of her. Someone in the consortium passed the assignment on to you. You passed it on to me."

Le Juif gasped for words. "If she was Russian defector, logical Igor would want to silence her—"

"You passed on orders for me to eliminate a young man who lived on an Apache reservation near New Jerusalem. He had stepped on the consortium's toes; he had stumbled on how they got their hands on operating funds. It was the consortium, staffed by former CIA agents, that was annoyed with him, that wanted him out of the way. It was our network, staffed by KGB agents, that was called in to execute the death sentence."

White spittle appeared at the corner of Le Juif's mouth. "A life's work . . . *ne vozmozhna!*"

"It *is* possible," Parsifal hissed under his breath. He stood up and leaned over the bed rail until his face was hovering above Le Juif's. "I interrogated the man who goes by the name of Dewey. He used to run a unit called Special Projects at the CIA before he signed on with the consortium. Special Projects was rabidly anti-Russian; it took the line that Moscow was the eternal enemy, that the Cold War was only beginning. While I was questioning Dewey, it suddenly dawned on him who I was. 'You must be the Jew's Parsifal,' he said. How could he know I was the Jew's Parsifal unless he and his CIA friends had penetrated our cell?"

The head nurse appeared at the door. "One more minute," she called. "Your friend needs peace and quiet."

Parsifal stared down at Le Juif. "Either La Gioconda or Prince Igor is a double agent."

"*Ne vozmozhna*," Le Juif repeated. "La Gioconda I have known my whole life. As for Prince Igor, La Gioconda passed on the identifying cryptogram known only to me and our masters in Moscow."

"The consortium had a Russian defector," Parsifal reminded Le Juif. "Dewey debriefed her for four months. She told me so herself. The time frame fits; four months after they installed her in the Dallas apartment, Prince Igor turned up to reactivate La Gioconda and you and me. And you handed me Prince Igor's first wetwork assignment; he wanted me to eliminate the woman in the Dallas apartment."

Le Juif's hand came up to his gaunt neck. "I feel death . . . in my throat. What . . . taking him so long?"

Parsifal realized he was squeezing Le Juif's shoulder. Letting go, he saw that he had bruised his skin. "Who is Prince Igor?" he asked.

Le Juif shook his head. "Don't know . . ."

"How do I contact him?"

"The way I do . . . through Gioconda."

"How do I contact La Gioconda?"

"Against all rules . . ."

"You have to tell me." When Le Juif didn't respond, Parsifal grasped his bony shoulders and pulled him into a sitting position. "*Mozhna minya gavorit.*"

The nurse monitoring the computer screen looked up from her fingernails. "Hey, what's going on?" she called through the window.

"*Gavorit!*" Parsifal cried.

Le Juif started to say something. Cradling the old man in his arms, Parsifal put his ear next to Le Juif's mouth and listened.

The head nurse came charging into the ward. "What in God's name do you think you're doing?" she shouted.

Gently Parsifal lowered Le Juif back onto the bed. "Die in peace, old man," he murmured. "I'll set things right."

The nurse grabbed Parsifal's sleeve and pulled him roughly toward the door. "Get out of here," she said through clenched teeth. She turned back to the bed and felt for Le Juif's pulse.

Le Juif could make out Parsifal gazing at him for a long moment from the door before disappearing down the corridor. Then he pressed his eyes closed. Tears, squeezed out from under his lids, trickled down the furrows of his cheeks. The head nurse fluffed the pillow under his head and stroked his hair, which was damp with sweat and sticking to his scalp. "Rest now," she said soothingly. "Sleep."

When she had gone, Le Juif reached over and worked the intravenous tube out of the socket of the needle piercing his vein. He twisted his head and watched the syrupy liquid fall, drop by drop, onto the sheet whose whiteness dazzled his eyes. After a while objects blurred, a phenomenon he attributed to the onset of snow blindness. Then, with his eyes wide open, he ceased to see. At that instant everything became crystal clear, as if it had been brought into sharp focus with a sudden twist of a knob. Le Juif, stark naked, was standing on a shore washed by waves that tickled the sand out from under his toes when they receded. He could hear the wind whispering past his ear. He could feel the cool wetness of the sand under his bare feet and the warmth of the sun on his erect penis. He could make out the balloon soaring into the stratosphere, growing smaller and smaller until it was lost from sight.

His caked lips moving imperceptibly, Le Juif mouthed the last words generated by his dying brain. "Hang on to the dream . . ."

49

On the second floor of the adobe Church of San Antonio de Gracia overlooking the decaying Spanish fortress known as the Adobe Palace, the feces (as the chief of station delicately put it) had hit the fan.

Using her primmest voice and a Justice Department access code, Miss Abescat had opened a direct line to the Los Alamos police department re the body that had been discovered at the site of one of Dewey's dead drops with Harry Lahr. According to the coroner's report, preliminary autopsy findings showed that a male Caucasian, believed to be in his late fifties or early sixties, of medium height and weight, without distinguishing marks, so far unidentified, had died of a heart attack in Frijoles Canyon. The chief of station, an eternal worrywart who went by the code name Swan Song, was not convinced; he personally knew of a dozen ways to kill someone so that it would look as if he had died of natural causes. "I don't believe in leprechauns or coincidences," he announced to the hands mustered at battle stations. "I do believe in alarm bells and wake-up calls."

His suspicions took root when the Cuban named Gonzales, who was listed on the Adobe Palace roster as a perimeter guard but doubled as a driver, returned from the quarry north of Madrid with word that he had found Lahr's jeep; judging from the shredded tire and the bullet holes in the vehicle, Lahr had been involved in a shoot-out. Gonzales also reported finding Early's four-door Chrysler parked behind a mountain of stone at the quarry. There was no sign of either Early or Lahr. Had they stumbled into a gang of drug runners or a nest of illegal immigrants from Mexico? Or had they been lured to the quarry by someone who, twenty-four hours later, lured Dewey to the dead drop in Frijoles Canyon?

Swan Song presided over the controlled panic of the war room with his habitual coolness. "We need to look past the trees in order to see the woods," he said. "We need to perceive *a pattern*." He pulled his silver worry beads from the pocket of his windbreaker and began working them through his fingers. Click, click. "We appear to have lost three agents." Click, click. "One of them, Dewey, is known to have died servicing a dead drop he used with Harry Lahr. According to our logs, Dewey was servicing the dead drop at Lahr's initiative." Click, click. "But Lahr couldn't have summoned him there, at least not of his own free will, because he himself had previously been summoned to a rendezvous with Early from which neither man returned." Click, click. "From these slender threads we can construct a worst-case scenario: it is beginning to look as if someone is walking back the cat on the consortium."

"This someone, God knows how, became suspicious of Early," Miss Abescat said breathlessly.

"He talked Early into luring Lahr to the quarry," proposed Lefler, the long-haired computer whiz. "After which he prevailed upon Lahr to lure Dewey to the Anasazi ceremonial cave."

"He was hoping Dewey would lead him to you," said J. J. Knopf, the Adobe Palace's burly security chief. He absently ran a finger under the strap of his holster where it chafed the skin on his shoulder. "But Dewey died on him."

"Which brings us to the sixty-four-thousand-dollar question," said Swan Song. Click, click. "Did Dewey die *before* talking about the Adobe Palace, or after?"

"Clearly *before*," suggested Miss Abescat hopefully, "or else we would have had a big bad wolf knocking on our door by now."

Lefler swiveled three hundred and sixty degrees in his chair. "It could be the Apaches," he said.

J. J. Knopf agreed. "They knew Early. They also knew Lahr. Somehow they must have put two and two together."

"In which case," said Miss Abescat, "they'd have reason to be pissed re the situation, since it's the profits from their casino that's paying our phone bill."

"The Apaches are certainly prime suspects," Swan Song said thoughtfully. "The next logical step is take a careful look at Watershed Station."

He walked over to the window and watched the six off-duty contract employees playing volleyball on a makeshift court. There was a burst of gleeful bantering every time one of them spiked the ball. Near the Adobe Palace's great arched double doors, Gonzales could be seen topping off the Jeep from a jerry can. Swan Song caught his attention with a wave. "How soon can you put the show on the road?" he called down.

"Ready when you are, Boss," Gonzales shouted back.

Making his way through the station's barracks to a small office that doubled as a bedroom, Swan Song laced on a pair of lightweight hiking boots, then took the night binoculars and a shoulder holster with a long-barreled Smith & Wesson wedged in it from their pegs on the adobe wall. He removed his windbreaker, strapped on the shoulder holster and climbed back into the windbreaker. Walking toward the Jeep, he skirted the volleyball court. "Who's winning?" he asked.

A young lawyer who had been Swan Song's factotum in a previous incarnation said with a laugh, "Bolsheviks twelve, Mensheviks nine."

Minutes later Gonzales, with Swan Song next to him in the passenger seat, wheeled the Jeep through the double doors of the triangular fortress. Gonzales's cousin, a Brazilian contract employee armed with an Uzi submachine gun, guarded the narrow steel bridge spanning the arroyo over which cars had to pass to reach the fortress. He raised his hand in salute as the Jeep, kicking up a trail of dust on the unpaved road, sped past.

For half an hour the Jeep followed the trail snaking along the chalk cliffs until it came out on a bleak, arid no-man's-land swept by the wind and baked by the sun. Along an arroyo that filled with water in the rainy season but was passable now, the Jeep jolted down to the firebreak, which knifed through the thick forest of scrub oak. When the firebreak split, Swan Song waved the driver onto the right fork. Twice Gonzales had to pull up and haul away dead trees that had fallen across the break. The sun was sinking behind the hills by the time the Jeep reached the plateau above the oval lake.

Gonzales cut the motor and began to roll himself a cigarette. Swan Song took the night binoculars and, jumping down from boulder to boulder, made his way to a large overhang not far from where Rattlesnake Wash gushed out of the lake and ran down and around Watershed Station. Lying flat on the shelf of rock, he removed his Ray-Bans, trained his binoculars on the Apache village and activated the infrared night vision. Starting on the western end of Sore Loser Road, he surveyed the ramshackle wooden houses one by one. He watched the Apache women wheeling Indians in wicker chairs up a ramp and into the old-age home.

He observed several young Indians sitting around a small fire in a back lot, passing a pipe from one hand to the next. Half a dozen Indian women who had been weeding vegetable gardens on either side of Rattlesnake Wash could be seen trudging uphill carrying their hoes on their shoulders. Training his night glasses on the field behind the general store, he watched a heavyset Indian winch the motor out of a pickup.

A young woman with short-cropped hair appeared at the back door of the general store carrying a straw hamper covered with a dish towel. Leaving the motor hanging from the winch, the Indian met her halfway, took the basket and set out across Sore Loser Road and downhill. He crossed one of the wooden footbridges over the wash and waded through a field filled with shoulder-high corn. At the far edge of the field, he turned down a narrow path that ran parallel to a drainage ditch and wound up at the door of a two-room shack on an out-of-the-way rise above a curve in the river. A faint light glowed in one of the windows. The Indian with the basket stopped to talk to a thin Indian who materialized from behind some bushes. The thin Indian, who cradled a shotgun in his arms, melted back into the bushes. The Indian with the basket pushed through the door into the shack.

A few minutes later he and a younger one-armed Indian holding a pistol in his hand emerged from the shack. Sandwiched between them was a heavy man whose wrists appeared to be bound behind his back. The two Indians led him down to the river, where they untied his hands. The heavy man turned away and urinated into the bushes. Then he knelt down and splashed water onto his face and neck. The one-armed Indian pulled him to his feet. The other Indian bound his wrists behind his back again. Then the two Indians led him back up to the shack. Minutes later they came out with a second man, short, muscular, balding, with disheveled clothing and a bow tie hanging loose around his collar. He too was led to the river's edge and allowed to urinate and rinse before being led back to the shack.

Swan Song swung his night glasses back to the town. Lights—electric in the houses that had generators, gas elsewhere—were blinking on from one end of it to the other. A dozen teenagers were kicking around a white soccer ball on Sore Loser Road. From the shadows of a back porch came the faint notes of an accordion. In the shack near the river the one-armed Apache appeared at the door, smoking a cigarette.

So the Apaches *were* holding Early and Lahr prisoner, which meant they knew who had been milking the casino. Swan Song ticked off alternatives: he could send Gonzales and his Brazilian cousin and J. J. Knopf and even young Lefler, who was itching for a chance to play at cowboys and Indians, to free them, but that would end in a shoot-out, a shoot-out would result in deaths, and deaths would lead to a police investigation—which would end any hope the consortium had of making wetwork history, of shaking the Western world to its foundations. His twenty-nine-year career would fizzle out without a swan song.

On the other hand, he had to liberate Early and Lahr. Without them the Apaches could cry about being shaken down from now to doomsday, but they'd have no warm bodies and no proof.

If only he could find some leverage, something to offer the Indians in exchange for Early and Lahr . . .

Swan Song was mulling over the dilemma when he caught a glimpse of the beam from a powerful flashlight working along the path from Watershed Station. It blinked off and on as the figure carrying it disappeared behind boulders and bushes, then reappeared again. Lying flat on the overhang, Swan Song could hear someone whistling to himself as he came up the trail. About fifty yards below the overhang, whoever was carrying the flashlight set a plastic pail down on the ground, waded into the river and blocked the flashlight under his foot in the water. Focusing his night binoculars, Swan Song could make out an Indian boy standing absolutely still in the knee-deep water flowing around his bare feet, his hands poised just under the surface of the river.

The chief of the Adobe Palace station lowered the binoculars and pulled his worry beads from his pocket. Click, click. The Indian boy could be the solution to his problems.

50

Standing motionless in the icy water, Doubting Thomas felt the stiffness seeping into his limbs. He ached to move a leg or an arm, but he was determined not to return home empty-handed this time. He could almost see the satisfaction in his father's eyes when he showed up with a two-pound trout in his plastic pail. The waterproof flashlight wedged under his bare foot dispersed eerie fingers of white light upriver. According to Skelt, trout were hypnotized by light, which meant you had a better chance of snaring one with your bare hands. The boy saw something silvery slipping through the water and tensed, but it turned out to be a chip of bark. He wondered how long he could stand there without moving. Skelt had told him stories of an Apache who'd been found frozen like a statue in the swirling rapids of the wash, his fingers still hovering under the surface of the water. At the time Doubting Thomas had hooted in scorn at the unlikely tale, but now he wasn't so sure that Skelt had made it up to scare him.

His thoughts were interrupted by the crack of branches snapping on the bank of the river off to his right. Then a man's voice called, "Catch anything?"

Doubting Thomas could tell it wasn't an Indian. His first instinct was to wade across to the far side of the wash and head back to Watershed, but he felt an Apache's pride stir in his veins. He could hear Skelt's voice in his ear: an Apache sometimes felt fear, but he didn't show it—especially in front of a White Eye.

"Not yet," he called back. "Takes a while."

"Must be cold in the river at night."

"Bit cold," the boy conceded, trying to make his voice deeper. "Nothing an Apache can't cope with."

"You from Watershed?"

"You bet."

A second shadow loomed alongside the first on the bank of the river. The tip of a cigarette glowed. "We'ze got usselves lost hiking," he called. "If you was to look at our map, you could maybe show us where we is."

"He's only a kid," the first man said. "He can't read a map."

"Sure I can," Doubting Thomas said. Secretly he was happy to have an excuse to move. He fetched the flashlight from the bed of the river and, playing it on his feet in the water, started toward the bank. When he was close he raised the flashlight and shone it on the men, which was when he saw the pistol. The taller of the two men was gripping it in both hands and pointing it directly at his head.

Curiously, he wasn't afraid. "Is that thing real?" he asked, his voice so steady that even he was surprised.

"Bet on it," the man smoking the cigarette said. He reached down, took a grip on the boy's collar and hauled him up onto the bank.

"What's your name?" demanded the figure holding the pistol.

"What's yours?" Doubting Thomas retorted.

The man smoking the cigarette slapped him hard across the face. "Don't act smart-ass with the man," he said. "You got a name, spill it."

"I got a name. It's Doubting Thomas."

henandoah was vexed: at Finn, for disappearing from her life even though she had ordered him out of it; at Skelt, for being so goddamn casual about Finn's disappearance; at Doubting Thomas, for not showing up for supper. She was going to lay down the law when she got her hot hands on him. "Here's the deal," she muttered under her breath, rehearsing what she planned to tell him when His Highness graced them with his presence. "I cook the goddamn food, you get your warm body to the table in time to eat while it's still hot." She padded barefoot to the back door and called into the night, "Where the hell are you, Thomas? Kettle's on."

Shenandoah's annoyance gave way to fright when there was still no sign of the boy three-quarters of an hour later. It was in character for him to mosey in late; she guessed it was his way of making a show of independence. But he had never been *this* late. "I'll take a turn around Watershed," Eskeltsetle told her when he saw how worried she was. He grabbed a flashlight from the shelf. "He's probably off fishing and lost track of the time."

Eskeltsetle came across a circle of braves sitting around a fire in a back lot. "Anyone set eyes on my boy Thomas?" he asked.

"Isn't he kicking a ball around with the others on the road?" someone asked.

Eskeltsetle walked up Sore Loser Road to where the boys were playing soccer. Thomas's friend Eskinewah Napas was the goalie at one end of the makeshift field. "Where'd Thomas get to?" Eskeltsetle asked.

"Fishing," Eskinewah Napas said. "I seen him go off with his flashlight and bucket."

"Downriver?"

"Up."

Shining his flashlight just ahead of his feet, Eskeltsetle turned onto the path at the end of Sore Loser Road and made his way toward the Sacred Lake. The river flowed beneath the trail, murmuring with its almost human voice as it washed over and around boulders. Fifty yards or so below the lake, he came across the spot where two people had pushed through branches to the river's edge. He fingered the break in one of the branches. It was recent. Stepping off the trail, he discovered Thomas's red plastic pail.

"Thomas," Eskeltsetle called. Above his head the moon slipped behind gauzelike clouds. He took a deep breath, cupped a hand around his mouth and bellowed, "Tho-mas!"

Eskeltsetle bent close to the ground. In the beam of his flashlight, he could make out several sets of footprints. One came from a slight man wearing cowboy boots with worn heels and worn soles. The second came from hiking boots, fairly new, with thick rubber soles crisscrossed by deep gashes for traction. Judging from the depth of the imprints, the man must have weighed roughly a hundred and fifty pounds, which meant he was short and thickset or tall and thin. Where the prints started up the trail toward the Sacred Lake, the stride was long, which meant that the man was tall and thin.

Mingled with the marks of boots were another set of prints—those of a barefoot boy weighing around ninety pounds. The little toe on the right foot was folded in toward the other toes, a peculiarity that Eskeltsetle recognized instantly.

The footprints had been made by Doubting Thomas.

Eskeltsetle noticed traces that indicated a slight dragging of the feet, as if the boy was being pulled. His heart beating rapidly, he rose to his feet and gazed into the darkness. Then, following the trail of footprints and broken branches, he hurried up the path toward the Sacred Lake.

52

F inn had been trying to touch base with Pilgrim for days, but he was always away from his desk, engaged in a meeting that couldn't be interrupted, talking on another line or just plain not available. "I do see your problem," the secretary remarked when Finn informed her that Pilgrim couldn't return his call because he was using a pay phone and six people were lined up outside the booth. "I don't see what I can do about it." When he wanted to know the best time to ring back, she answered, "Your guess is as good as mine." "Could you narrow it down?" Finn asked. "Sure I can," the secretary said. "Try between eight tomorrow morning and midnight tomorrow night."

"Wait one," Pilgrim snapped when Finn, feeding quarters into the slot, finally lucked in just after 11:00 P.M. "I want to switch to a more secure phone." There was a series of high-pitched beeps. Then Pilgrim came back on the line. "Why didn't you call me sooner?" he asked. Before Finn could get a word in edgewise, Pilgrim was off and running. "Members of the select committee are scurrying around Room SH219 like chickens without heads," he growled, as if the whole thing was Finn's fault. "Here's why: I have a Special Forces buddy who hangs out with the National Security Middle East analysts. He's got a friend who hangs out with the Mossad, which is the Israeli intelligence service. The friend of my friend hears that a Russian intelligence defector recently passed through the hot hands of the BfV, which stands for Bundesamt für Verfassungsschutz, pardon my pronunciation, the only foreign language I ever studied was Spanish."

"What's the BfV?"

"It's the German intelligence agency. Turns out the Deutsche Gramophones thought they were doing a favor for their American cousins, but when you try to pin them down, which I did, they aren't sure which cousins they were doing the favor for."

"They passed the Russian defector to the Americans, but they can't remember which Americans?"

"Correct. They are mightily embarrassed about the whole situation. All they're willing to say for the record is that they were dealing with an agent who went by the code name of Swan Song. They assumed Swan Song was licensed because he turned up in Bonn waving letters of credit signed by people whose names, when pronounced, open doors. The Germans had the impression that Swan Song, who spoke perfect Russian, had been shopping around Moscow for a defector. And not just any defector, as you will soon see. When he came up with one he asked the Germans to act as shipping agents; they were to pick up the package in Kiev, provide her with documents identifying her as a German national and whisk her out of the country. Once she was on German soil Swan Song and his man Friday, who spoke Italian and looked like a central-casting mafioso, showed up to take possession. They flashed bundles of crisp twenty-dollar bills under the woman's nose and sweet-talked her into continuing on with them to the Promised Land, which in this case turned out to be Texas. The Germans I talked to were a bit pissed—in return for taking care of shipping and handling, they were supposed to get access to the cream during the milking process. But they never heard from Swan Song again. The Russian defector and her handlers disappeared from the radar screen. The Germans lodged several informal complaints with the CIA front office, which claimed they didn't have a Swan Song on their books or a female Russian defector on their hands. That's the last anybody heard of her until the police, alerted by a suspicious super who wondered how someone could live without occasionally going out for food, discovered her body in the Dallas apartment."

"What do you have on the woman?" Finn asked.

"The Mossad guy says his people think she wasn't as middle level as we first thought. According to the Jews, before the fall, before Yeltsin, she was a deputy to the chief of the First Department of the KGB's First Chief Directorate, who just happened to be the individual responsible for all Soviet espionage activity on the North American continent. . . . Just a sec."

Finn could hear Pilgrim talking to someone in the office. "Take his number," he called. "Tell him I'll get back to him before the Second Coming." He came back on the line. "This is radioactive," he said. "The feeling here is the whole thing is going to blow up in our hands." Again he called to someone, "Put him through. . . ." He told Finn, "I need to take another call." The line echoed with static, went dead, then was filled with chimes. After a moment Pilgrim returned. "Sorry. Where was I?"

"Something was about to blow up in your hands."

"Right. Okay. If the female defector had a foot in the door of the First Department of the First Chief Directorate, there's a good chance she could identify the KGB's agents in North America. So it sounds to us as if your consortium went shopping in Moscow, at a time when United States of America dollars could buy almost anything, for someone who could hand them a working Soviet network on a platter. You told me the Russian lady defector had been debriefed by de Wey, alias Dewey. We have got to assume she gave him a list of Soviet agents, along with the cryptograms that signaled to them they were being controlled by Moscow. We have got to assume that Dewey passed this information on, which means that Dewey's consortium is in a position to use these agents to further its own agenda. As long as the orders arrived with the appropriate identifying codes and cryptograms, the KGB agents would assume they were getting their instructions from the new KGB Center in Moscow."

Pilgrim must have covered the phone with his hand, because his voice suddenly sounded as if it came from another planet. "Tell the congressman to shove it up his arse. On second thought, tell him I'll be right there." He spoke to Finn again. "The select committee is sounding general quarters here. Decks are being cleared for action. We have a rogue group which calls itself the consortium and is staffed by former CIA agents who are supposed to have drowned. These former agents may or may not have ties to the DC flagship. That's something we're going to have to sort out when the dust settles. Or not sort out if the select committee wants to avoid destroying the CIA. We'll cross that bridge when we come to it. For now, thanks to the Apache casino, we know that the consortium has a cash flow, and they don't have to explain to us how they spend it. They have an agenda, and they have a group of highly trained Soviet agents who, thinking their orders are coming from Moscow, are ready to carry out that agenda."

Pilgrim called to someone in the office, "I'm on my way." To Finn he said, "What we have is a nightmare. I have to move my ass. I won't pin you down now, but next time we talk you need to confirm something I already know—that the joker who was going to kill you is a Russian agent who started to suspect his orders weren't coming from the new KGB Center in Moscow."

When Pilgrim had hung up, Finn dialed the number of Parsifal's mobile home in Truth or Consequences. "Do you remember Dewey's last words?" he asked when Parsifal picked up the phone.

Parsifal thought for a moment. "He said 'swan.' Then he said 'song.'"

"The agent who turned up in Germany to take possession of a Russian lady defector was code-named Swan Song. He spoke perfect Russian. He was accompanied by someone who spoke Italian and looked like a central-casting mafioso."

Parsifal laughed into his end of the line. "Dewey!" he said. "Parallel lines meet. Prince Igor and Swan Song are the same person."

H unched over, his eyes glued to the trail, Eskeltsetle followed the three sets of footprints until they disappeared onto the boulders at the rim of the Sacred Lake. Circling around to the other side, he scoured the ground for twenty minutes before he was able to pick them up again coming off the rocks. The prints, with traces of Doubting Thomas's bare feet dragging between the two adults, led to where a vehicle had been parked. Crouching, Eskeltsetle fingered the butt of a hand-rolled cigarette. The tobacco was still warm to the touch. The vehicle from which the butt had been thrown, a Jeep judging by the tread marks, had backed and turned and headed across the plateau and onto the firebreak that cut through the forest of scrub oak.

Quickening his pace, dreading that he would not be fast enough or skillful enough to rescue his son, Eskeltsetle followed the Jeep's fresh V-shaped tire tracks imprinted on the soft earth of the firebreak. Twice he came to places where the Jeep, outward bound toward the Sacred Lake, had stopped to clear dead trees from the trail. Where the firebreak forked, the Jeep's tracks veered off to the left.

Breathing hard, Eskeltsetle stared into the pitch darkness of the firebreak. He knew the terrain around Watershed Station; he had been roaming these hills and woods since his childhood. The firebreak led to only one destination: the arroyo that filled with water in the rainy season but could be negotiated now by a four-wheel-drive Jeep, above it the bleak no-man's-land swept by the wind and baked by the sun, the trail snaking along the chalk cliffs to the triangular Spanish fortress known as the Adobe Palace.

Turning off the firebreak, hurrying through the scrub oaks, Skelt cut across country until he detected the voice of Rattlesnake Wash coursing through the woods. Pushing himself, oblivious to the tangle of underbrush scoring his legs and arms with welts, he plunged through the scrub oaks parallel to the wash until he broke out onto the boulder-strewn flat eight miles beyond Watershed. Wiping the sweat from his eyes, he sank to one knee and drew a dozen deep breaths. As a child, he had been sent off every morning, barefoot even in winter, his mouth filled with river water so he would be sure to breathe through his nostrils, to run to the roof of the world and the Anasazi altar embedded in its heart, and back. Now, fifty years later, his breath came in shallow gasps and each gasp was accompanied by a stitch of pain in his chest, but the loping gait of the long-distance runner still seemed second nature to him. He ran on, splashing through shallow water as the smallest of the fingers of the river skimmed over water-smoothed shale into what was left of a two-hundred-year-old irrigation ditch. Wading through icy water, he continued along the ditch as it curled through a gorge with sheer sides. In places the opening narrowed to three yards and the cliffs towering overhead seemed to touch, blocking out the Milky Way.

Gasping for breath, his eyes stinging as the sweat dripped into them, his arms and legs smarting from razorlike cuts, Eskeltsetle burst out of the gorge into the box canyon. Sinking onto one knee again, he gazed across the canyon. Gradually it came into focus—the chalk white cliffs shimmering in the moonlight, the adobe walls of el Palacio Adobe on the rocky saddle atop the cliffs, the torreón at each of its three corners, the bell tower of the Church of San Antonio de Gracia floating over the walls.

The sight of the Adobe Palace provoked a flood of memories. His maternal grandfather, instructing him in the fundamentals of tracking, had taken him through the narrow gorge to the very spot on which he was kneeling and filled him with tales of the Adobe Palace: how Spanish *conquistadores* had flogged the naked backs of the Pueblo slaves constructing it; how the Apaches had heel-kicked their frightened ponies through the narrow gorge and angrily brandished their lances at the adobe walls; how the canyon, which had been an Anasazi burial ground from the dawn of time, had been turned into a killing field as the Spanish on the heights, their silver helmets sparkling in the sun, kept the Apaches at bay with muskets. Long after the Spanish had abandoned the fortress, Suma Apaches still considered the canyon bad medicine, a valley of death to be avoided at all costs. The bleached bones of animals scattered over the Anasazi burial ground—Eskeltsetle had spotted them the previous year when he came to check on rumors of trucks kicking up trails of dust on the unpaved road snaking along the chalk cliffs toward the fortress—reinforced the feeling that the Adobe Palace was cursed.

A light flickered in a window on the second floor of the church. Cursed or not, the canyon floor had to be crossed. Whoever kidnapped Doubting Thomas had taken him to the Adobe Palace. Pushing himself to his feet, Eskeltsetle murmured a prayer in Athapaskan. "I ask you, Wakantanka, to guide me over this killing ground so I can reach my boy Thomas before harm comes to him." He let another ten minutes go by to give the moon time to slip behind the cliffs. Then, stepping over or around the bones of dead animals, moving with great deliberation so as not to disturb the spirits of his ancestors haunting the ground, he started across the canyon floor toward the fortress.

Halfway across, with the cliffs and the fortress looming closer, Eskeltsetle sank again onto one knee and studied the situation. When the moon was still up he had noticed a steep ravine that led to a section of the fortress wall where the adobe had crumbled. The ravine was blocked by a coyote fence entangled with coils of razor wire. With at least four hours of darkness remaining, Eskeltsetle figured he had a good chance of squirming through the coils and reaching the fortress without being seen. He rose to his feet and headed in the direction of the bell tower, which was visible against the stars in the Big Dipper, and the ravine directly below it. Skirting the skeleton of a deer, he sensed something hard under his left moccasin. Horrified at the idea that he might have stepped on the bones of an ancestor, he flung himself to one side just as the small plastic antipersonnel mine exploded beneath his foot.

At first there was no pain, only a feeling of numbness spreading from his toes to his ankle. Reaching down in the terrible darkness, his fingers discovered something wet and sticky where his toes had been. Then the pain lashed at him in waves, starting at the sole of his foot and spiraling up his leg.

"I am killed," Eskeltsetle moaned.

High above him, in the one tower that was still standing, a spotlight snapped on and played slowly over the killing field. Biting down on the collar of his shirt, Eskeltsetle lay deathly still as the light swept past his body and moved on across the canyon. After a while someone on the tower cursed in Spanish. The spotlight stabbed into the sky and switched off.

Clinging to the ground in the still darkness, Eskeltsetle tried to cope with the pain that was branding the flesh of his foot and burning up through his leg. He shook his head violently to keep from fainting. The pain didn't recede, but he began to dominate it. He had, after all, an advantage . . . a working relationship with pain . . . the pain of his people, the pain of the young Apaches who scorned him, the pain of his lost youth and his lost pride and his lost dreams . . . the unbearable pain of his lost love. He would have liked to turn on his flashlight and inspect the wound, but he didn't dare. Fumbling with the buckle, he eased his belt through the loops of his corduroys and, twisting it around his left ankle, tugged it tight to stem the flow of blood. Curiously, the makeshift tourniquet seemed to dull the burning sensation in his leg. Willing himself to move, he staggered to his feet. The rim of the chalk cliffs and the sea of stars swam above his head. Squinting, he made out the mouth of the gorge at the entrance to the canyon.

Guided by an enormous reddish star poised over it, and over Watershed Station beyond, dragging his mangled foot behind him, Eskeltsetle set off on the long painful journey toward Betelgeuse.

ound and gagged, stretched out on the dirt floor of the tower, Doubting Thomas was startled out of a troubled sleep by a muffled explosion somewhere below the fortress. He could hear the man who spoke English with a Spanish accent leap off his cot onto the floorboards over his head; he could hear him racing up the flight of wooden steps to the roof.

"Re that noise, what was it?" a woman's voice called to the man on the roof of the tower. She was clearly jumpy, which Doubting Thomas took to mean that the kidnappers were worried someone was going to rescue the kidnappee.

From overhead came a sharp click, as if a great bolt had been thrown in a door, and then the dull hum of a motor.

"More to the left," a man's voice shouted. "Right about there. See anything?"

"Hold your water, J.J." Then: "Looks deader than Death Valley. Probably jus' another one of dem ani-mals stepping on a mine."

"Keep an eye peeled," the one named J.J. called back.

"That's what you pay me for," the lookout replied sourly.

Lying in the darkness, Doubting Thomas tried to think like a Suma Apache. When he failed to turn up for supper, Shenandoah would send Skelt to look for him. Eskinewah Napas, who had been guarding the goal at one end of the makeshift soccer field, had seen him heading upriver with his plastic pail and flashlight. "Where you off to?" Eskinewah had demanded. "Going to catch dinner," Thomas had replied. "River'll freeze your ass off," Eskinewah had said with a laugh. "Only thing you'll catch is cold." "Want to put money where your mouth is?" "Sure." "Quarter?"

"Sure." The boys had exchanged high fives. Eskinewah would tell all this to Skelt, who would start up the footpath parallel to the river.

Some of the younger Apaches could read a trail pretty good, but Skelt was by far the best tracker on the reservation, maybe the best Apache tracker in all of New Mexico. He was bound to come across Thomas's plastic pail. If he had his flashlight with him, he'd read the footprints on the ground; Thomas had dragged his feet as often as he could so Skelt would understand he was being taken against his will. Knowing Skelt, Thomas was sure he'd be able to figure out the height and weight of the two kidnappers from their prints. He would track the prints up to the Sacred Lake. He'd lose them where they disappeared onto the boulders, he'd pick them up again where they came off. But once they reached the Jeep, would Skelt lose the trail? Not in a million years! Oh, you just had to know he'd do it: he'd follow the tire tracks up the firebreak, he'd figure out where they were heading, he'd race back to Watershed and organize a rescue party. Any minute now Thomas was going to hear war whoops as the Apaches swept down on the fortress and freed the prisoner. He'd be a hero. Shenandoah would be real sorry she'd been angry at him for not showing up for supper. The young braves would punch him playfully on the shoulders. The other boys would crowd him with questions.

"Were you scared?" Eskinewah would ask.

"You got to be kidding. Me? Scared?"

Fighting back tears, Doubting Thomas trembled on the dirt floor. If an animal had touched off the explosion below the fortress, how could the Apaches ever reach him?

Fact of the matter was he was half-scared out of his wits.

55

Sunning himself on a park bench, his back to the river that flowed through downtown Santa Fe, Parsifal cracked open shells and tossed the peanuts inside them to the pigeons milling around his feet. Across the street, two stretch limousines pulled up in front of the Inn on the Alameda, and a dozen men, all wearing tan suits and metal aviator sunglasses, piled out. One produced a tiny cellular phone from his pocket, extended the antenna, punched in a number and strolled back and forth on the sidewalk, engrossed in conversation. The others pulled two duffel bags and half a dozen violin-size plastic cases (filled, Parsifal guessed, with Uzi submachine guns and spare clips) from the trunks of the cars and disappeared into the lobby.

Parsifal recognized the praetorian guard, come to town three days before the Jogger to organize local security arrangements. They would search and secure one floor of the hotel for the Jogger and his entourage, then confer with the Santa Fe police, pore over maps, make plans to divert traffic and close streets. They would draw up lists of known criminals and psychopaths with violent records and political crackpots and quietly invite them to leave town for a few days at government expense. They would arrange for an ambulance and a medical team to stand by at the hospital. On D day minus twelve hours, they would personally go over the route the Jogger would take, prying up manhole covers, removing garbage cans, towing away cars, posting sharpshooters on the roofs of buildings. On D day they would be joined by fifty or so more men in tan suits and aviator sunglasses. At the last moment each would be issued a distinctive lapel pin so that the local law-enforcement officers would let them through police lines. If everything went according to plan—and the praetorians were here to make certain it did—nobody who hadn't been cleared would get within shouting distance of the Jogger.

Smiling to himself, Parsifal kicked at a pigeon pecking at his shoe. To do what Prince Igor wanted him to do, he didn't need to get within shouting distance of the Jogger.

A white-haired woman wearing lace gloves and a pillbox hat with a dark veil draped over her eyes came limping up the street with the aid of a thin bamboo cane. She had on an ankle-length overcoat despite the heat, and sturdy lace-up shoes, one with a corrective heel. Drawing abreast of Parsifal, she paused to chase away the birds with the tip of her cane. "Pigeons are filthy creatures," she remarked. She spoke English with a middle European accent. "I read somewhere that they spread disease and death."

Parsifal had arranged to meet La Gioconda next to the river across the street from the Inn on the Alameda, but he had expected someone younger to turn up; on the telephone her voice had sounded as if it belonged to a woman in her forties. He delivered his half of the recognition cryptogram.

"Death is a debt one owes to nature."

The woman's painted lips stretched into a bitter smile. "Le Juif has paid."

She hobbled over and settled with an effort onto the bench next to Parsifal. Her right leg was stretched out stiffly in front of her; Parsifal noticed the tip of a metal brace around her bare ankle.

"So you are the legendary Parsifal."

He laughed under his breath.

Lowering her voice, she switched into Russian. "You were with Le Juif before he died?" she asked.

He nodded.

"Are you aware that he killed himself?"

"No, but it doesn't surprise me. Le Juif was a man of great integrity. There is a certain dignity in dictating terms to death when you reach the end of the quest."

With a flick of her head and a stab of her hand, La Gioconda raised the veil from her eyes. "Over the years Le Juif spoke highly of you. He said you had the most demanding job of all of us. He said you had to be mad to do what you did. Are you mad?"

"There are moments when I think I am searching for the Holy Grail. There are others when I think the quest is madness."

"Tell me what Le Juif said to you when you saw him in the hospital."

"He said we had made mistakes. He said the mistakes didn't matter. He said if something is worth doing—"

La Gioconda turned her face toward the sun and closed her eyes. "It is worth doing badly. That was a refrain he repeated many times over the years. It was more or less his credo. Le Juif was not a perfectionist; quite the contrary, he assumed that perfection was not something *Homo sapiens* could aspire to. As a child, you must understand, he saw a side to the human race that marked him—some might say warped him—for life. He was imprisoned in Auschwitz. His mother and father and two older sisters were selected for the gas chambers. It was only the timely arrival of our Red Army that saved his life." She looked at Parsifal. "Did he say anything to you . . . about me? Did he send any message . . . to me?"

Parsifal tossed another peanut to the pigeons milling around beyond the range of La Gioconda's cane. "When he told me how to find you, he instructed me to convey to you his . . . esteem."

"His *esteem* . . . yes. I can see him baring his tobacco-stained teeth in a twisted smile and saying that. I can tell you—where is the harm now?— that we were lovers once, Le Juif and I, a lifetime ago when people still made love, as opposed to the violent act of penetration that passes for love-making today. But love was not a word that could pass his lips. Yes, I can hear his voice in my ear. *Esteem.*" She shook her head. "I am. . . ." She smiled to mask her grief. "I am pleased to have had his esteem. He was a great idealist, and in his way a great man." La Gioconda smiled again. "We met in a center for displaced persons after the Great Patriotic War. We dedicated our lives to the cause of Communism. Together we volunteered to work for the KGB, we trained together, we labored together in this abominable country for twenty-eight years. We grew old, but not to-gether. Now and then I would receive in the mail picture postal cards from different places with innocuous sentences scrawled across them, and the words "Strive on" or "Victory is a foregone conclusion" written in mi-nuscule letters under the stamp. Are you able to visualize it, Parsifal? There I was, striving on because I could not conceive of an alternative; I no longer understood what victory was, and I certainly did not believe it was a foregone conclusion. Still, I sucked at Le Juif's postal cards the way a bee sucks at a sunflower."

Moved by her own story, she fell silent for a moment. Then she said, "In the beginning we would meet two or three times a year in cheap hotels in out-of-the-way cities. I would slip a ring on my finger and we would register as man and wife. We would eat dinner and leave a generous gratuity for the proletarians who waited on the tables and washed the dishes. We would sleep in the same bed. We continued to sleep in the same bed on these rare meetings long after Le Juif ceased to function as a man."

La Gioconda's tone turned professional. "How is it that you knew where to find Le Juif? How is it that you were able to talk him into giving you my coordinates? Le Juif was a stickler for craft. There was a method to our madness. Prince Igor contacted me, I contacted Le Juif, Le Juif contacted you."

Parsifal looked the old woman in the eye. "We have been betrayed," he announced. He saw her wince, as if she had been struck across the face. "The traitor had to be either you or Prince Igor. Le Juif vouched for you, which left Prince Igor." He went on to explain the sequence of events that had led him to this conclusion: how a rogue group of former CIA agents, working out of New Mexico and calling itself the consortium, had engineered the defection of a deputy to the chief of the First Department of the KGB's First Chief Directorate; how the man who ran the consortium, a former CIA Medici who went by the code name Swan Song, had turned up in Germany, along with an agent named de Wey, alias Dewey, to take possession of the female defector; how Dewey had debriefed her in a safe house in Dallas; how Prince Igor had surfaced to reactivate Le Juif's KGB network, which had gone into hibernation at the start of the Gorbachev era; how Swan Song's consortium had milked the Apache casino for operating funds; how he, Parsifal, had been called in every time one of the Indians threatened to take the matter to the police.

La Gioconda drummed the sidewalk with her cane. "You can prove what you say?" she demanded harshly.

Parsifal explained how two members of the consortium named Early and Lahr had planted marker messages with Le Juif every time they wanted to contact each other.

"Prince Igor told me they were subcontractors—"

"I interrogated both of them. They were at the bottom end of the consortium's ladder. Both had worked for something called Special Projects at the CIA, Early on a freelance basis, Lahr on staff, before signing on to the consortium."

"This could be explained in various ways . . ."

"That's only the beginning. When Swan Song and the consortium had gotten everything they needed from the Russian female defector, they decided to eliminate her. At which point Prince Igor relayed the order to you . . ."

La Gioconda was reliving events. "I passed it on to Le Juif, who passed it on to you."

"It was the perfect plot. The consortium got access to a KGB network, and then used us to do their dirty work for them."

"There was a young man . . ."

Parsifal nodded. "The Indians told him about the consortium milking the Apache casino. He went to Early with the story. Early passed word up the consortium's chain of command to Swan Song. Swan Song—who spoke perfect Russian, remember—had to eliminate the young man, so he put on his Prince Igor hat and passed word down our chain of command to you. You told Le Juif, who instructed me to kill him." Parsifal took hold of La Gioconda's elbow. "Something the young man said made me suspect that the order to eliminate him had not originated with the KGB. He and I both wanted to know who was behind the order, so we began to walk back the cat. We started with Early, who led us to Lahr. Lahr led us to the one named Dewey. When I was questioning him, he suddenly understood who I was. He said, 'You must be the Jew's Parsifal.' How could Dewey have known about the existence of Le Juif or Parsifal unless the consortium controlled our network? Unless Swan Song and Prince Igor were the same person?"

Across the street, two police cars pulled up to the hotel entrance. Squinting into the sun, La Gioconda watched as six high-ranking uniformed officers, each carrying an attaché case, filed into the Inn.

"Now Prince Igor wants you to eliminate the Jogger," she said. She regarded Parsifal. "*Pachimo?*" she whispered.

"I'm not sure why. The consortium may be doing the CIA's dirty work for them. Or the consortium may be a group of renegades who have decided they know what's best for their country and for the world. And what's best is to assassinate the Jogger."

"Le Juif used to say that there were seven levels to any intrigue," La Gioconda remembered. "You are only scratching the surface. Work through the problem from their point of view. If the only thing they wanted to do was assassinate the Jogger, they could do it themselves. Or they could hire professionals. God knows there are enough of them around if the price is right. They didn't have to go to all the trouble of gaining control of a KGB network. No. I tell you, the death of the Jogger is not an end, but a means to an end."

They talked in undertones for another twenty minutes, sorting probabilities, threading their way through plausible scenarios. Several times they started down avenues that looked promising; each time they came to a dead end and had to double back. As she listened intently, her lips parted, her eyes wide and brilliant, La Gioconda's face shed a decade, and Parsifal caught a glimpse of what she must have looked like, twenty-eight years earlier, when she and Le Juif arrived in America to do battle against capitalism.

Trying out one scenario, La Gioconda suddenly plucked at Parsifal's sleeve. "That may be it."

Parsifal nodded carefully. "All the pieces fit."

"What incredible arrogance! They think history is a river that can be diverted by explosives into a new channel!"

"They are aiming high," Parsifal agreed.

"They are aiming low," La Gioconda corrected him.

Parsifal didn't hear her; his mind had wandered into the rarefied world of wetwork tradecraft. "Pass word up the line to Prince Igor that, with the death of Le Juif, you have taken over operational control of Parsifal. Tell him I have figured out how to park an automobile filled with plastic explosives and a nitric-acid detonator along the Jogger's route."

La Gioconda saw where he was going. "You want to lure Prince Igor to the scene of the crime."

Parsifal spelled out the solution. "When you describe the parking of the car, specify which hill I will be on to activate the explosives."

By now La Gioconda was one jump ahead. "I will inform Prince Igor that you are ready to carry out his instructions, but given the gravity of the assignment, you must receive those instructions directly from his lips."

"If we are right, he will leap at the chance to meet me."

"I will provide him with the recognition cryptogram."

Parsifal recalled something else. "When Le Juif announced that we had a new Resident, he said you had actually encountered him."

"We met in the balcony of a darkened movie theater. He was just a silhouette—thin, tall, stooped shoulders. He wore sunglasses even in the dark and spoke Russian without an accent." She remembered something else. "When he was delivering to me the cryptogram that proved he came from Moscow, I became aware of something only a woman is likely to notice — the new Resident *smelled*. It was an unpleasant blend of something sweet and something tart — the kind of scent someone excretes when he tries to mask a strong body odor with a strong perfume."

Parsifal's nostrils twitched. "When Prince Igor turns up, I won't need a recognition cryptogram — I will *smell* him!"

La Gioconda lowered the veil over her eyes and, leaning on the cane, climbed to her feet. "We shall not meet again," she said, gazing down at him through the veil.

"What will you do now?"

"I have some money set aside. I shall return to Prague, where I lived as a child. I shall sit on a small balcony in the Malá Strana and close my eyes and imagine Le Juif when he was young and beautiful and thought he was more than a match for a windmill. And you, my knight of the Round Table, what will you do?"

Parsifal gazed across the street at the hotel, where another stretch limousine filled with young men in tan suits had pulled up to the entrance. "When I have reached the end of the quest, I shall attempt to follow in Le Juif's footsteps. I shall dictate terms to death."

hreading the silver worry beads through his fingers, Swan Song let twelve minutes slip by, then nodded at Miss Abescat, who dialed La Gioconda back at the number she had left on the answering machine. When a woman picked up the phone, Swan Song greeted her in Russian. At her console Miss Abescat hit a switch to record the conversation.

La Gioconda didn't waste words. "Le Juif died in the hospital," she said, speaking in Russian. "Acting on standing orders, I initiated contact with Parsifal and assumed operational control of him. He claims to have figured out how to park an automobile filled with plastic along the Jogger's route in the museum complex without having the automobile towed away."

"*Ya slishitya,*" Swan Song muttered into the phone. The worry beads clicked away between his fingers.

"He says it will not be possible for the police to tow away a hundred automobiles."

"How does Parsifal plan to get a hundred automobiles to park on the road along with his?"

"The morning the Jogger is due in town, an exhibition of Anasazi pottery is opening in the complex. When the parking lot in front of the museum fills up, cars overflow onto the access road. Parsifal proposes to print up a few hundred extra invitations to the pottery exhibition which will specify that the Jogger himself is to be the guest of honor. The day before the Jogger arrives in town, Parsifal will mail the invitations to the downtown art galleries. The next morning the parking lot will fill up, the automobiles will overflow onto the access road, where they will park bumper to bumper."

"I see that Parsifal is his usual creative self," Swan Song remarked. Click, click. "You are instructed to give him the green light."

"There is one thing more," La Gioconda noted. "Parsifal says that on an operation of this gravity, he will need to be pointed in the right direction by Prince Igor himself. Receiving his marching orders from an intermediary will not suffice."

Swan Song exchanged glances with Lefler and Knopf, who were monitoring the conversation through earphones. Lefler shook his head in disgust; what Parsifal was suggesting broke every rule in the book.

Swan Song let La Gioconda stew while he considered the request. Click, click, click. Then, barely able to contain a smirk of pleasure, he came back on the line. "Tell him I agree."

La Gioconda described the hill from which Parsifal planned to detonate the plastic stuffed into the trunk of a car parked on the access road. She mentioned a shopping mall, a supermarket. "You may leave your automobile in the employees' section behind the store. You will find a small hole in the link fence behind the garbage bins. A path winds up through a woods to the top of the hill." She passed on the recognition cryptogram and specified fifteen minutes before a particular hour.

Swan Song repeated the cryptogram and time and severed the connection.

J. J. Knopf, Adobe Palace's security chief, peeled off the earphones and swiveled in his chair. "I don't like it, Boss. This is a crazy idea. When it comes to wetwork, you build walls, you don't tear them down."

Swan Song turned to stare out over the killing field. From the very beginning, when he and Dewey had conceived the consortium and the operation that would make wetwork history, he had planned to be present at the denouement—he *needed* to be present at the denouement—but in his wildest dreams he never thought Parsifal himself would invite him.

Massaging a single worry bead between his thumb and forefinger, he permitted a rare smile to work its way onto his thin lips. He had devoted a lifetime to planning and executing wetwork operations, but his swan song was going to eclipse them all.

57

W hile one of the nurses from the Suma old-age home cleaned the wound as best she could, Shenandoah phoned down to New Jerusalem for a doctor and an ambulance. When the nurse had finished, Shenandoah let the Suma medicine man, who had brewed up some yellow clover and wild onion, spread the concoction on Eskeltsetle's mangled foot with a delicate spatula carved from the rib bone of a jackrabbit.

Her eyes red from sobbing and dark with foreboding, Shenandoah started to whisper in Skelt's ear. "The doctor'll be here before you can say . . ." But she saw that he had passed out again. She dipped the cloth she had torn from her petticoat in a basin of fresh water and gently wiped the sweat and dirt off his face. On the other side of the bed, the medicine man, wearing blue jeans and a headdress of eagle feathers, sprinkled to-bacco dust onto the yellow clover and wild onion, and continued to chant ancient Suma healing songs under his breath.

Finn touched Shenandoah on the shoulder. "It's incredible he made it back here," he whispered.

"Even with the tourniquet, he lost a lot of blood," she said. "He proba-bly didn't untie the belt often enough, or at all, because what's left of his foot looks real green."

Finn turned to leave and she accompanied him to the door. "There ought to be a better way," she said, but he shrugged her off and pushed through the door and walked out onto Sore Loser Road, where Alchise and Petwawwenin and Nahtanh were loading the balloon and the gon-dola and Eskeltsetle's giant fan onto the back of a pickup. The faces of the three Apaches were streaked with ash. Petwawwenin handed up Finn's pump shotgun, two M16s, Alchise's vicious-looking double-edged bone-handled knife and a Kellogg's Corn Flakes carton filled with ammunition.

A late-afternoon sun was flitting behind the trees. Shenandoah shaded her eyes with her hand for a moment. Her face contorted, she caught up with Finn in the street and grabbed his arm. "If Skelt's right, you'll never get near that Adobe Palace. For God's sake, wait for the goddamn police or the goddamn army or the goddamn government."

"The people up in the Adobe Palace *are* the police," Finn said. "They *are* the army. They *are* the government. The thing to do is get Doubting Thomas out safe and sound. Then we'll worry about the police and the army and the government."

From the thick of the scrub oaks came the distant whine of a siren as an ambulance made its way up the unpaved road toward Watershed. Shenandoah sucked in her breath. "Oh, sweet Jesus," she murmured, "who looks after the birds of the air, the fish of the sea, look after Skelt and Doubting Thomas and Saint Louis, and forget about your suffering servant, me."

Parsifal emerged from the shadow of a building. He was dragging on a cigarette as he watched the Apaches wrestle a single propane canister into the pickup and strap it to the back of the cab. "Whoever said the world would end in a whimper got it wrong," he remarked.

"Who's he?" Shenandoah demanded.

"A guy I met," Finn said. He looked at Parsifal. "A friend."

"How come he's not going with you if he's such a friend?"

Parsifal answered for himself. "I have a previous engagement," he said. He pulled Finn off a few paces. "We set out to discover who wanted you dead and expected me to kill you. Now we know. Launch the balloon so that it arrives just before first light. If I've figured right, our Medici will have left for Santa Fe by then and you'll have one less warm body to deal with." He flashed a cold smile. "If I've miscalculated and he's still on the premises, he's all yours."

Alchise and Nahtanh waved impatiently from the back of the pickup. Petwawwenin climbed in behind the wheel and gunned the engine. Finn went over to Shenandoah. His face was flushed, his eyes feverish. "I love the kid," he declared. "I love you."

Shenandoah stared deep into Finn's eyes. What she saw frightened her. "I don't know you!" she said fiercely. "You oughta go and smear your face with ashes like them. You're in love with war." She lowered her voice to a whisper. "What *did* you lose turnin' in squares back there in the desert, Saint Louis?"

"Whatever I lost," he said, "I found it here."

58

Finn stowed the meteorological gear and his pump-action shotgun in the back of the jeep, lowered the goggles over his eyes and slid in behind the wheel. Lieutenant Pilgrim set his M16 on automatic and climbed in alongside him. "Move it," he ordered, chopping his hand toward a point on the horizon.

For the first half hour or so Finn kept to the wadi, then swerved onto a desert track that cut across the Kuwait-Iraq frontier. They passed three dead camels, their stomachs shredded by heavy-caliber bullets, and, further along, a burned-out Iraqi water truck and an overturned Mercedes with the rotting bodies of two Iraqi officers in it.

Topping a rise at high noon, they saw an enormous khaki-colored earth-mover with the stars and stripes painted on its side. It crept across the desert on huge underinflated tires that dwarfed each of the eight troop-filled Abrams half-tracks escorting it. Two jeeps with unit pennants flying from long whip antennas brought up the rear of the column as the earthmover headed into the desert from what had been an Iraqi bunker complex. A Special Forces soldier manning the machine gun in the back of the last jeep spotted the scout jeep and waved happily. Lieutenant Pilgrim waved back.

Finn pulled the jeep up near an enormous drift of sand at the perimeter of the bunker complex. In the center of the complex a white sheet flapped from the top of a long pole protruding from a smaller mound of sand. It looked as if the Iraqi brigade manning the complex had raised the sheet in surrender.

Lieutenant Pilgrim treated himself to a swig of warm water from his canteen as he looked around. "Where'd all the Iraqis disappear to?" he remarked. Finn retrieved his shotgun, released the safety and, resting the tip of the barrel on his shoulder, strolled over to the great drift of sand to urinate. He was zipping up his fly when he became aware of a faint buzzing coming from the bowels of the desert; it sounded as if several dozen horse-flies were trapped in a shoe box. Then he heard the distant but distinct ring of metal striking metal.

"Lieutenant," Finn called. "Come on over and take a listen to this—something funny's going on here."

Pilgrim grabbed his M16 and joined Finn. He heard the faint buzzing too. Finn scrambled up the side of the mound and kicked at something half-buried in the sand. He knelt down next to it and, using his hands to scoop away the sand, uncovered an Iraqi helmet. Without thinking he leaned down and pressed his ear to it, the way he had done as a child with a seashell.

"What is it?" Pilgrim shouted.

Finn only shook his head. He looked as if he were going to vomit. Pilgrim climbed up to where Finn was kneeling in the sand. Sinking down next him, he bent his ear to the helmet. Then he looked up.

"They're all in hell," Finn whispered, "dozens of them, hundreds maybe. They're screaming in some strange language."

Pilgrim turned to stare at the giant earthmover. "Holy Jesus," he breathed. "They bulldozed a mountain of sand up against the exits. The poor sons of bitches are trapped in their bunkers." He gazed at the earthmover, which was crawling like a giant insect over a distant dune. "Like the man says, war doesn't decide who's right," he muttered with a bitter laugh. "It decides who's left."

Kneeling in the sand, the two men looked at each other. Finn started clawing at the sand. He kept at it until blood seeped from under his fingernails. Then he slumped back on his haunches and turned his head away and closed his eyes and tried to think his way into the lobe of the brain where emotions originated in order to root them out.

Eight days later, at a base camp in Saudi Arabia, Lance Corporal Finn got into a fistfight with a major who reprimanded him for failing to salute an officer. According to sworn testimony at the subsequent court-martial, Finn then caused "grievous bodily harm" to the three MPs who tried to arrest him. He wound up being sentenced to a high-security Seattle brig, where he served fifteen months: twelve for the original crime, and three more for breaking the arm of another prisoner. The night of his release, in a bar in south Seattle, he almost lost it again when a couple of drunken college football players made the mistake of joking about his shaved head.

A big red-faced Irishman with permanently bloodshot eyes stepped between them. "How the lad cuts his hair has to be his affair, doesn't it, now?"

The football players measured the Irishman, who stood six four in his stockings and blocked out the exit light over the door. Suddenly sober, one of them said, "You have got a point."

"I don't need help," Finn snapped.

"I wasn't helping you," the Irishman said pleasantly. "I was helping them." He climbed onto the stool next to Finn. "What's your name?"

"Finn."

The Irishman offered a thick paw. "Mine's Stu. Friends call me Irish Stu."

"Coming from the brig this morning, I bought breakfast at a diner up on the hill called Irish Stu's. They were launching hot-air balloons in the field behind it. When I was a kid, I had an uncle who flew hot-air balloons; he used to take me up with him and let me pilot them."

"Irish Stu's my place," the big Irishman said. "I'm the local hot-air-balloon guru." He sized up the young man. He liked the look of him, he liked that he made no bones about having been in the brig. "The johnny who washes my dishes just headed for greener pastures. Can't blame him none. In his shoes I'd have done the same." Irish Stu squinted down at Finn. "You wouldn't by any chance be looking for a job, would you, now?"

59

With Petwawwenin piloting the pickup as if it were a Formula One racing car, they careened down the S-curves into New Jerusalem, shot two red lights before doubling back toward the Colorado border on the long intestinal road over the mountains, then cut across the Jicarilla Apache Reservation on the single-lane tarmac that ended abruptly at the spot where the New Mexico Highway Commission had run out of funds. On either side of them the ground fell away in long sloping rocky fields dotted with stunted trees. Finn flattened Eskeltsetle's tattered logging map on the hood of the pickup. Alchise flicked on a flamethrower cigarette lighter, and Petwawwenin turned on his flashlight. "We're here," Finn told the three Apaches, stabbing at the map with a fingertip. "The Adobe Palace is eight and a half miles away as the crow flies. If it was light out and we had binoculars, we could probably see the steeple Eskeltsetle talked about. Okay, there's two ways of going in. The first is to follow the maze of firebreaks through the woods. Even assuming we could find a way through the maze, they'd see our headlights once we came out on the flat."

"Which leaves the balloon," Alchise said.

"I don't like it," Nahtanh said. "I'm for going in on foot."

"On foot we'd never get there before first light," said Petwawwenin. "They're sure to outnumber us. If we hope to save the kid, we need to have surprise on our side."

Alchise looked at Finn over the flame of the lighter. "What makes you think you can float us right up to the Adobe Palace with that balloon of yours?"

"It's a matter of plotting the winds," Finn explained. As the others watched, he pulled a wooden box from the back of the pickup, inflated a small balloon, fitted it with a battery-powered transmitter and released it into the darkness. He tracked the balloon on a miniature receiver for several minutes, transferred the bearing to the map, then shook his head. "We need to launch further south," he said.

They drove back to where they had seen a rutted trail angling off from the tarmac and bumped along it for half a dozen miles. Finn launched another of his small balloons. The Apaches passed a hand-rolled cigarette around as he plotted the flight path of the balloon on the logging map. "We went too far," he called.

"Make up your mind," Nahtanh groaned.

"Take your sweet time," Alchise told Finn.

Piling into the pickup, they backtracked several miles. Finn inflated another balloon, fitted it with a transmitter and released it. The Apaches stood around him, listening to the ticking of the receiver while he pored over the logging map. "Another five hundred yards ought to do it," he decided.

Finn released his fourth balloon and plotted its course on the map. "Ground zero," he said excitedly as the ticking grew faint. "Let's launch."

The Apaches unfolded Finn's great yellow-and-black air bag on the ground. Nahtanh pulled the pickup over, raised the hood, hooked up the giant fan to the car battery and started to blow air through the hooped crown into the hollow of the envelope. Petwawwenin loaded the two M16s, Finn's shotgun, Alchise's knife and the carton of ammunition into the gondola. Finn lashed the propane canister to the aluminum frame, hooked up the fuel lines and lit off the nozzles. As the nylon skin stirred on the ground, he sent a bubble of hot air into the envelope. *The Spirit of Saint Louis* swelled, then slowly began to right itself. The three Apaches scrambled into the gondola as it rose off the ground.

"Holy shit!" Petwawwenin cried.

"Take a look at us!" Alchise exclaimed.

Finn gave the balloon a long shot of hot air as it skimmed over the rocky fields on the edge of the Jicarilla Reservation, then soared up and over a sea of scrub oaks. He leveled off at a hundred feet as the dark folds of the hills spread out below. In the east the horizon was tinged with a hint of dawn. Far ahead, they could make out the faint glow of chalk cliffs shimmering in the light of the full moon, which was partly hidden by thin bands of clouds. As they sailed closer, they spotted the steeple towering over the dark walls of the fortress, and a dim light in a room halfway up the steeple. Petwawwenin slapped a clip into one of the M16s and worked the first bullet into the chamber. Gripping the double-edged knife with his only hand, Alchise polished the blade on the side of his jeans.

As *The Spirit of Saint Louis* approached the Adobe Palace, Finn tugged on the red strap attached to the rip panel in the crown, spilling hot air out of the envelope. The balloon gradually lost altitude. At fifty feet it drifted silently over a narrow steel bridge spanning an arroyo. A small shed with a light flickering in a window stood on the Adobe Palace side of the bridge.

"Looks like there's a guard posted at the bridge," Finn said.

"He's mine," Alchise said.

A ruined tower at the far corner of the three-sided fortress loomed out of the darkness. "Watch out," Petwawwenin warned.

Finn reached up, gripped the red strap and hung on it, spilling great gulps of hot air out of the balloon. With a bump the gondola touched down short of the tower and slammed into its adobe wall. Overhead, the nylon of the air bag collapsed into the roofless tower.

Clutching their weapons, Finn and the three Apaches leaped clear of the gondola. Huddled in the shadow of the adobe wall, they could see a woman stick her head out of a second-floor window in the church steeple. She listened for a long moment, shrugged and disappeared back into the room. Finn put his lips next to Alchise's ear. "Take out the guy guarding the bridge," he whispered, "then come back in through the main gate."

"I need to say it, man," Alchise whispered back. "We had you figured for a White Eye. You're one hell of an Apache."

Finn accepted this with a solemn nod. Moving soundlessly, Alchise vanished into the night.

Finn gestured to a breach in the fortress wall. Petwawwenin and Nahtanh grunted. Standing with his back to the wall, Finn waited until the moon ducked behind a cloud, then vaulted over the breach in the adobe and sprinted across the floor of the fortress to the side of the church. The two Apaches, their M16s swiveling nervously, caught up with him. Classical music drifted down from the second-floor room over their heads. With his back flat against the church wall and the barrel of his pump-action shotgun resting lightly on his shoulder, Finn peeked around the corner of the building and studied the fortress.

"Listen up," he whispered. "We got one lady on duty up in the church. She's all yours, Nahtanh. Then we got laundry drying on a roof, which means the long low building under the laundry is probably some kind of barracks. Judging from the laundry, I'd say we're dealing with six people in the barracks, eight at the outside. The building has two doors. Petwawwenin, you take the door on the left, I'll take the one on the right. When we go in, whoop it up so we sound like a war party as opposed to a church choir. Okay? Let's move it."

Bending low, Finn darted across the fortress to the shadow of the adobe wall, then made his way along it until he was standing next to one door of the barrack. He could make out Petwawwenin, his M16 at the ready, standing with his back to the wall next to the other door. He waited another thirty seconds to give Nahtanh time to reach the second floor of the church. Then, signaling to Petwawwenin with his shotgun, he stepped away from the wall and turned and kicked the door open and, whooping at the top of his lungs, burst into the barracks.

Out of the corner of his eye he caught a glimpse of Petwawwenin, his M16 in one hand, a flashlight in the other, as he came flying through the door at the far end of the long room. A heavyset man wearing boxer shorts and a white T-shirt rolled off an army cot and lunged for a pistol in a shoulder holster hanging from a chair. Petwawwenin pinned him in the beam. Finn cut him down with a blast from his shotgun, pumped a fresh cartridge into the chamber and looked around for another target. Across the room Petwawwenin twisted to his right and fired from the hip at a man diving for an Uzi. The impact of a quarter of a clip-full of bullets sent him reeling into a wall, where he collapsed.

Four more men came off their cots with their arms over their heads. "For God's sake, don't shoot," one of them whimpered.

"Cover them," Finn cried. He kicked in the door to the john and dove through it, his shotgun at the ready, but the room was empty. He kicked in another door that led to a small office with a cot in it. A pair of night binoculars and an empty shoulder holster hung from wooden pegs on the adobe wall. Returning to the barracks, he yelled, "Where's the kid? Where's Swan Song?"

The four men with their hands thrust over their heads stared at him, too frightened to speak.

Finn spotted another door at the far end of the barracks and kicked it open in time to catch a glimpse of a burly figure jumping out an open window. He plunged through the window after him, rolled once on the ground as a pistol coughed up two rounds from the darkness and came back up on his feet, his shotgun held in one hand in front of him.

"Where'd he go?" Finn yelled up to Nahtanh, who was leaning out of the church window, one hand gripping the shirt of a terrified woman, the other squeezing off single rounds from his M16 at the crumbling tower in the third corner of the triangular fortress.

The sky in the east was laced with streaks of gray, and Finn suddenly realized he was able to see. He inched his way along an adobe wall; in the Special Forces he had been trained in house-to-house combat, so the drill was second nature to him. He ducked under the sill of a paneless window and flattened himself against the wall on the other side of it. Taking two shotgun cartridges from his pocket, he tossed them through the window into the tower. A pistol shot rang out, and then a second. Whirling to his right, bending low, Finn dove through the door into the tower firing and pumping and firing and pumping and firing again. He heard a pistol clatter to the floor. A figure staggered out from the shadows under what was left of a staircase. Blood was trickling from the corner of his open mouth. He sank slowly to his knees.

Finn dropped to his knees in front of the wounded man. "Where's the kid?" he asked urgently.

The wounded man swallowed, then fell over backwards.

Finn strode out into the courtyard. Petwawwenin was covering the four prisoners lined up against the adobe wall, their hands over their heads. The Apache pressed the barrel of his M16 into the ear of the nearest man and was about to question him when the wooden door at the base of the single tower still standing in the fortress squeaked open. A thin man appeared in the shadows. He was clutching Doubting Thomas, bound and gagged, in front of him with one arm and jamming the muzzle of an Uzi into the side of the boy's jaw with his other hand.

"You want the kid alive, lay down your guns and back off," the man called in a high-pitched voice.

Petwawwenin looked at Finn, who brought the barrel of his shotgun back until the tip rested on his shoulder and started slowly toward the man holding Thomas. He sensed he was losing control over the demon in the pit of his stomach. He could feel himself slipping down the slope; he knew he wouldn't survive another atrocity. Rage mounted in him like bile.

"No," he said. Then he howled, "*Nooooooooo!*"

Alchise materialized from behind the great arched double doors. Finn could make out red stains between the three ash streaks on his face, and red glistening on the silver blade of his bone-handled knife. In one flowing gesture, Alchise reared back and sent the knife spinning through the air toward the man holding Thomas. The man must have spotted Alchise the same moment Finn did, because he lunged to his right as the knife flew past his head and embedded itself to the hilt in the adobe behind him. For the bat of an eye his grip on Thomas loosened. Twisting, the boy wrenched himself free. "Hit the deck," Finn screamed. Thomas flattened himself on the ground. The man started to lower the muzzle of his Uzi as Finn stepped forward and dropped the shotgun off his shoulder and holding it in one hand and pointing it the way someone points an accusing finger, fired into the man's startled face.

inn took Doubting Thomas up to the second floor of the church so he wouldn't see the Apaches wrapping the five dead bodies in sheets and laying them out side by side in the dirt. Parking Thomas in one of the swivel chairs, he examined the two computer-telephone consoles in the middle of the room and the coaxial cable that snaked up the wall to the dish antenna still tracking the communications satellite from the church's steeple. He started to pull out metal drawers, which were crammed with copies of deciphered cable traffic, when he noticed the red telephone on top of one of the filing cabinets. It reminded him of the red telephone Pilgrim had used in his holy of holies back in Washington. On the spur of the moment Finn lifted the receiver and held it to his ear. There was a crackle of static. Then a voice came on the line. "Federal Bureau of Statistics, demographic section," it said. There was another surge of static; the voice broke through it. "Duty Officer Phippen speaking. What can we do for you?"

"Send flowers to the Medici's funeral," Finn said, and he set the phone back on the hook.

or Parsifal, it was the bitter end of a bitter quest, the moment of truth; either he would discover his Holy Grail on a remote hilltop of a country he detested at the end of a century he detested, or he would dictate terms to death.

Could it be, was it possible—the idea came at him from his blind side—that dictating terms to death *was* his Grail?

Setting Le Juif's small black transmitter down on a rock, he took the binoculars out of their case and adjusted them, bringing into focus the two uniformed policemen two miles away coaxing their dogs as they sniffed at the cars parked along the road below the museum complex. At the entrance to the museum parking lot, two men in tan suits and aviator sunglasses were talking with three police officers with gold braid on the visors of their caps. Clearly annoyed, one of the men in a tan suit jabbed a finger into the chest of an officer as he drove home a point, then stalked off to call someone on a tiny cellular phone.

Parsifal looked at his wristwatch: it would be another twenty minutes before the Jogger, surrounded by an army of agents and journalists and cameramen and local runners, came swimming out of the heat of the asphalt, heading uphill past the cars now being searched by the dogs for explosives.

From behind Parsifal a voice called, "Shakespeare wrote somewhere that madness in great ones must not unwatched go."

Parsifal turned and delivered his half of the recognition signal. "Saint-Just wrote somewhere that nobody governs innocently."

A tall urbane figure of a man with stooped shoulders, slightly out of breath after the hike up through the woods from the supermarket parking lot, angled his head and narrowed his eyes and half-smiled, almost as if he recognized the agent he had never set eyes on before. "It goes without saying, they were both right," he remarked, speaking fluent Russian without a trace of an accent. "They were talking about the same sovereign." He studied Parsifal through his Ray-Bans. "So you are the famous—perhaps I should say infamous—Edouard Cheklachvilli, better known by the nom de guerre Parsifal, the namesake of the knight at King Arthur's Round Table who occupied the legendary Siege Perilous, the seat reserved for the one destined to find the Holy Grail and fatal for any other occupant."

Parsifal scrutinized the newcomer on the hilltop. "You will be Prince Igor, the warden of the heart of the heart of darkness."

"In which automobile did you plant the explosive charge?"

"The green Toyota, halfway down the line of parked cars."

"Are you absolutely certain the remote radio detonator will function at this distance?"

"Le Juif, who was a genius at electronics, made it and tested it."

Prince Igor took the binoculars from Parsifal, walked to the lip of the hill, inspected the line of cars and found the green Toyota. The two police dogs had already gone past it. "When it came to wetwork, Le Juif always said you were incredibly talented. You have lived up to your reputation." He turned briskly toward Parsifal. "I confirm the order. When the Jogger passes, you are to activate the explosive charge and kill him."

"Why? What is to be gained?"

A stillness, like the one that installs itself before a vicious storm, settled over the hilltop. Silver worry beads materialized in Prince Igor's left fist, and he began to work them through his long graceful fingers. Click, click. Click, click. "Isn't it sufficient that I confirm the order?"

"Under ordinary circumstances," Parsifal said, speaking softly, measuring his words, "it would be enough." His eyes narrowed and focused on the worry beads. He remembered Green Bow Tie's description of Egidio's Medici in the CIA screening room: "he was sitting in the row behind Egidio threading these silver beads through his fingers, you could see the light glinting off them, you could hear the beads clicking against each other." Parsifal looked up. "But given the importance of the target and the likely consequence of the wetwork operation . . ."

He let the sentence hang in the air between them.

Pulling at an earlobe, Prince Igor approached. "It suits our masters in Moscow that the Jogger should be eliminated."

Parsifal's nostrils twitched as they detected the sweet-tart scent of a strong perfume masking a strong body odor. There was no doubt about it: he was face to face with the Resident whom La Gioconda had encountered in the movie theater.

Sniffing delicately at the air, Parsifal said, "Out of curiosity, I'd be interested in hearing the logic behind this operation."

Prince Igor kneaded his worry beads thoughtfully. "Out of curiosity—I am curious to see how you will react—I will educate you. I suspect it will even give me a certain visceral pleasure."

From the waistband under his windbreaker Prince Igor produced a long-barreled Smith & Wesson with a silencer fitted onto its tip. Pointing it at Parsifal's knees, he drew closer. "The pistol is at the heart of the logic behind the operation." He glanced at the museum complex; a wedge of police motorcycles riding ahead of the Jogger had started up the hill. "You know me as Prince Igor, sent from Moscow by a rejuvenated KGB to reactivate the network of agents and pursue Russian interests in North America. In a previous incarnation I was a Medici who went by the name of Cleveland." As he talked, he worked the worry beads through the fingers of his left hand. Click, click. "You will not be familiar with the term *Medici*, at least in the sense I am using it; Medici was an in-house appellation at CIA headquarters in Langley. It described the handful of major players in the halcyon days when Congress could identify America's enemies and threw endless amounts of money at the problem. Then the Cold War ended, or so Congress, in its infinite wisdom, decided. Not all of us over at the CIA agreed, so we created a consortium of like-minded people. Cleveland disappeared in a boating accident and I surfaced as chief of the consortium. Our goal was to turn the clock back, to eliminate the traitors and fellow travelers in the military and civilian and intelligence branches of government who were sapping the free world of its moral and physical strength to resist Russia." Click, click, click.

"Americans," Prince Igor continued, "must learn that Greater Russia, whether ruled by so-called Communists or ersatz capitalists, always was and always will be expansionist. And what better way to convince them," he added, unable to restrain a note of triumph, "than to have a bona fide Russian agent assassinate the president and then catch him in the act. Better still, kill him *after* the act. The assassin was slain, so the newspapers will proclaim, by a local policeman who gunned his motorcycle up the hill after the explosion."

Parsifal appeared to breathe with difficulty. "It is not possible," he whispered. "How could you penetrate our network? How could you gain control of the identifying cryptograms?"

"Do you remember the woman you shot in Dallas? Later you told Le Juif that she was Russian. She was, in fact, a deputy to the chief of the First Department of the KGB's First Chief Directorate, which controlled the old KGB's espionage activities on the North American continent." Click, click. "Everything and everyone is for sale in Moscow these days, so our consortium went shopping there for someone who could sell us a genuine Soviet network operating in North America. The woman nibbled at the bait. We arranged her defection through the Germans. One of my associates debriefed her in Dallas. When she had given us the identities—Parsifal, Le Juif, La Gioconda—and the cryptograms that would permit us to control you, we had you kill her." Click. "Although you couldn't have known it, you were not working for the KGB but for the consortium."

It was almost as if Parsifal didn't believe the story Prince Igor was telling him. "You speak Russian without an accent."

Prince Igor leveled the revolver. "I am a third-generation anti-Bolshevik, my dear Edouard Cheklachvilli. My maternal grandmother came from an old White Russian family. You may have heard of the Kusmichofs; they exported tea before the Bolsheviks sent them scurrying for their lives." Click. "As a young girl, my mother looked out a window on the *bel étage* of a hotel when the Red Army captured the town she was hiding in. She saw Budenny's cavalry trotting past on the street below." Click. "She remembered that each of the heroic cavalrymen carried on the tip of his lance a severed human head." Click, click. "It is an interesting phenomenon, and characteristic of this century—how the trauma of the parents ends up driving the children."

Over Parsifal's shoulder Prince Igor could see the mass of joggers bobbing uphill through the heat rising off the asphalt. They seemed to move in a kind of unsynchronized slow motion. The target would be in the middle of the group, flanked by bodyguards who carried pistols strapped to their ankles under their sweatpants. Smiling slightly, Prince Igor said, "You chose your code name badly; Parsifal was never destined to find the Holy Grail. Once again the Siege Perilous has turned out to be fatal. Pity. The Grail was an interesting obsession." He expelled half the air from his lungs and blocked his breath and aimed the Smith & Wesson at Parsifal's chest and squeezed the trigger.

Parsifal never felt the bullet tearing into his body, or his body hitting the ground. He experienced a sharp pinprick under his left nipple and an instant loss of strength in his feet. Lying on the ground, his nostrils twitched as he smelled his own blood. He heard Le Juif's ironic laugh echoing in his head: "A life's work . . . *ne vozmozhna!*"

Stepping over Parsifal's body, Prince Igor retrieved the black box from the rock. He trained the binoculars on the stretch of road two miles away. He could make out the figure in the middle of the crowd of joggers; there was no mistaking him, husky, smiling, a baron bantering with the two young female subjects running alongside him.

Standing at the summit of his career, smiling to himself, Prince Igor, known to his consortium colleagues as Swan Song, extended the antenna on the transmitter and waited until the Jogger came abreast of the green Toyota. Then he pointed the antenna at the car and flicked the toggle switch to the position marked Signal On.

62

Petwawwenin, the Smoker, and Nahtanh, the Cornflower, had gone on ahead to prepare a funeral pit in the Suma burial ground and the ritual fire. As the sun knifed through horizontal blinds of clouds toward the mountains, Finn and Alchise and Doubting Thomas struggled up the trail with the makeshift litter bearing the corpse. Thomas was fine until he spotted Eskeltsetle's bandaged foot jutting from the white linen cloth covering the body, at which point tears spilled from his eyes. Shenandoah brought up the rear carrying three new Apache blankets and a burlap sack filled with Eskeltsetle's worldly possessions: his clothing, an eagle-feather headdress, beaded leggings and a beaded headband, several pairs of moccasins, his discharge certificate from the navy, a long ceremonial pipe, a shorter everyday pipe and the small beaded buckskin pouch filled with sacred pollen.

Making their way up the trail in the thickening twilight, the group broke through the forest of fir into the clearing the Suma Apaches thought of as the roof of the world and laid out Eskeltsetle's body on the great Anasazi ceremonial altar. Kneeling, Alchise struck a match with his thumbnail and touched it to a tuft of moist straw. Blowing on the embers, he ignited the tepee-shaped twigs that had been positioned upwind, then fanned the flames with his arm until the fire was roaring. Thomas fed the blaze with large pieces of dead wood stacked nearby. Chanting an Athapaskan death song, Petwawwenin carried the burlap sack filled with Eskeltsetle's belongings over to the deep burial pit, dropped it in and covered it with a layer of earth to prevent the dead warrior's spirit from returning to retrieve his possessions, which could bring ghost sickness and death to the Apaches of Watershed Station. On the altar, Nahtanh cast handfuls of dry sage into the flames. Thick white smoke from the sage drifted across the Anasazi altar, purifying Eskeltsetle's body.

When the death song was finished, Petwawwenin and Nahtanh and Alchise lifted Eskeltsetle's corpse off the litter, carried it to the Suma burial ground below the altar and lowered it on ropes into the pit. They abandoned the ropes in the grave and filled in the pit with earth and covered the earth with heavy flat stones to protect Eskeltsetle's corpse from wolves and coyotes. Returning to the altar, they stripped to the skin and wrapped their bodies in blankets and burned their own clothing in the ritual fire.

"Following our Apache custom," Alchise announced as the flames consumed their clothing, "I will no longer respond to Alchise, which is the name by which my father, Eskeltsetle, knew me. Alchise is reserved for when his spirit wants to summon me. From this time, I will be known as Paradeeahtran, the Contented."

"From this time," Nahtanh said, "I will be known as Natchinilkkisn, the Colored Beads."

"From this time," Petwawwenin said, "I will be known as Tatsahdasaygo, the Quick Killer."

Turning, the three Apaches, Paradeeahtran, Natchinilkkisn and Tatsahdasaygo, hurried down the mountain.

Shenandoah took out a pair of shears. Reaching back, she cut off a tuft of hair above the nape of her neck and dropped it onto the flames as a sign of mourning. "Here's the deal," she said. "From this time, I will use the name Sonseeahray, the Morning Star."

"From this time," Doubting Thomas said, struggling to control his voice, "I will use the name Sonsinjab, the Great Star."

Then Sonseeahray and Sonsinjab and Finn stripped naked and drew Apache blankets over their shoulders and fed their garments into the flames. Finn retrieved a worn paperback from the back pocket of his jeans before he tossed them into the fire. "This here was written by Mr. F. Fitzgerald," he said, turning to the last page. "I think Skelt would have smiled at it."

The valleys below the altar were already lost in shadows. Holding the book up to the last light of day, Finn read from the text. " 'So we beat on, boats against the current, borne back ceaselessly into the past.' " He closed the book and dropped it into the flames. "The past is where Skelt always wanted to get to," he said, "so I got to think it's where he's at now."

"*Metaka Oysin,*" murmured Sonseeahray, the Morning Star.

"*Metaka Oysin*," echoed Sonsinjab, the Great Star.

In the west the disk of the sun silently embedded itself in the horizon. A breath of wind stirred in the still mountains. Carried on the wind from a distant hunting ground, the proud hoot of an old owl reached the ears of the mourners.

63

A helicopter without markings delivered Pilgrim to the small airstrip which, according to New Jerusalem legend, had been laid out by Charlie Lindbergh. Alerted by a phone call to Watershed Station's only telephone, across from the Apache handcraft store, Finn was on hand to meet him.

"Want a ride?" he called across the tarmac.

Pilgrim waved off the sheriff's cruiser and strolled over to Finn's battered Toyota pickup with the rebored engine, Nissan suspension and a faded bumper sticker that read, "I spend my money on women and beer—the rest I just waste." "Good to see you're in one piece," he said, leaning in the window.

"Good to be in one piece."

Throwing his overnight bag into the back, Pilgrim came around and climbed into the cab next to Finn. "Move it," he ordered, chopping his hand toward a point on the horizon. Then he howled with laughter.

Neither man said anything as the Toyota climbed up the S-curves and started meandering along the wide dirt road through the hills. Then they both spoke at once.

"If I was in your shoes—"

"The record has got to be set straight—"

Pilgrim laughed under his breath. "My man Finn! You haven't changed all that much. Before we talk turkey, I need to fill you in on some facts of life. Back in Washington, back in the holy of holies of the Hart Office Building, all our calculations begin with the notion that the United States of America, for better or worse, has got itself one intelligence industry. Intelligence is an expensive habit; it costs the taxpayers in the neighborhood of thirty billion dollars a year. It's overpriced and inefficient and messy, and it makes big mistakes—it never alerted us to the possibility that the Soviet Union could collapse like a house of cards, to give you a for instance. But it happens to be the only intelligence industry we have. You need to think of the CIA as a moat. It maybe isn't as deep as we'd like it to be, or as wide, but we can't afford to face the world *without* a moat between us and it. We can't afford to dismantle our intelligence industry because a handful of its former employees went off halfcocked."

Finn downshifted going around a curve. "It wasn't a matter of a handful of employees," he said.

"I'm not sure I follow you."

"The Medici who was supposedly pensioned off from the CIA ran his consortium out of an old Spanish fortress called the Adobe Palace. The second floor of the Adobe Palace church had been turned into a fancy communications center. There was a dish antenna up in the steeple, there were two computer consoles in the room itself, and file cabinets stuffed with traffic. There was a red telephone on one of the filing cabinets. You had a phone just like that in your holy of holies, so I picked it up. It was the kind of phone where you didn't have to dial."

"Adobe Palace had a hot line?"

Finn glanced at Pilgrim and nodded. "A voice came on the phone. It said, 'Federal Bureau of Statistics, demographic section. Duty Officer Phippen speaking.'"

For a mile or so Pilgrim stared at the scrub oaks along the side of the road without seeing them. Drawing a deep breath, he turned back to Finn, his expression grim. "Remember what I told you back in the Saudi desert the day the horse you were riding stepped on a mine? Everyone needs to have a philosophy. Mine is: I don't want to know what happened. But I want to make damn sure it doesn't happen again. My white congressman, the other members of the committee I work for, they all come at this problem from the same direction. That's why they sent me to New Mexico—so they wouldn't know what happened, so they could be goddamn sure it doesn't happen again."

Finn said quietly, "It's kind of late to be sticking your head in the sand—there are too many loose ends."

"There are no loose ends, friend. Two dead bodies were found on a hill in Santa Fe. Big deal. The local law-and-order whizzes say there's no connection between the deaths and the passage of the president. Every single car parked along the Jogger's route was opened and searched. No explosives were found. The bodies on the hill were unidentified and are going to remain unidentified. The detectives investigating the case are leaning toward the theory that it was a homosexual murder and a suicide; one guy was shot dead, the other blew himself to pieces when a homemade bomb stuffed in a box he was holding exploded in his hands."

Rounding a bend, Finn could see the Rattlesnake Casino at the bitter end of Sore Loser Road up ahead. "You can't cover all the tracks."

"Wrong again. I can and I will. That's what I'm here for. Early and Lahr have disappeared back into cracks in the walls. I'll lay money nobody you know ever hears from either of them again. As for the Adobe Palace, it's true there were five bodies found. The state troopers up north think there must have been some kind of a showdown between the Mafia and the local Apaches—something to do with the Mafia shaking down a casino. That's the story that's going to appear in tomorrow's newspapers. In the back pages. The church up at Adobe Palace has been scrubbed clean; there's no dish antenna, no communications consoles, no file drawers filled with cable traffic, no telephones, no nothing. The joint is just an abandoned Spanish fortress with crumbling walls. There are Jicarilla Apaches who are Catholic who'll swear they've been going up there for Sunday services as far back as they can remember and never saw a white face." Pilgrim gestured toward Watershed Station as they bumped onto Sore Loser Road. "Your Suma Apaches will be quietly reimbursed for the money they lost paying Mafia protection. No questions will be asked. No answers will be offered."

Finn pulled around the side of the general store into the field filled with Eskeltsetle's used pickups and cut the motor. "What about me?" he asked.

A woman with short-cropped hair and a fringed skirt that stirred up dust around the painted toenails of her bare feet was directing an Indian boy and several Apaches who were spreading out a yellow-and-black air bag on the ground. Pilgrim looked at the wicker gondola with *The Spirit of Saint Louis* painted on a thin copper plaque bolted to its side. "There are people over at the Bureau of Statistics who want to have a word with you," he said. "I'd be lying if I said otherwise. They say you're a loose cannon, the only person who can put all the pieces of the puzzle together. Right now I'm going to get one of these Apache warriors to drive me up to Adobe Palace for a last look around. When I get back, if I was to see that balloon of yours gone"—Pilgrim started laughing; he laughed so hard he had trouble finishing the sentence—"I'd have to tell the folks at the Bureau of Statistics you flew the coop, wouldn't I?"

64

Using his one good hand, Paradeeahtran, the Contented, connected the giant fan to the pickup's battery, then hit the toggle
switch. Natchinilkkisn, the Colored Beads, raised the hooped
crown so that the fan blew into the hollow of the air bag. Its nylon skin rippling, the balloon stirred, then lifted lazily off the field. Scrambling into
the gondola, Finn angled the nozzles and fed a great bubble of hot air
into the envelope. It billowed and righted itself and tugged gently at the
wicker basket, which was anchored to the ground by two lines fastened to
stakes.

At the edge of the field, behind the two tepees, a burning tire sent a
thread of black smoke spiraling into the air. From far away it might have
looked like an Apache smoke signal.

In the gondola, Finn taped down the levers so that the propane sizzled
permanently in the nozzles. The *Spirit* pulled impatiently at the gondola.
Tatsahdasaygo, the Quick Killer, and the boy Sonsinjab, the Great Star,
drew knives from their belts and looked at Sonseeahray, the Morning Star.

"Here's the deal," she yelled, taunting Finn. She had wanted him to
sail away in his balloon. Now that he was doing it, she was furious. "If you
don't know where you're goin', why, any wind'll get you there."

Her eyes burning, she nodded at the two Apaches, who turned and cut
the mooring lines. At the last instant, as the balloon shot into the air, Finn
vaulted out of the wicker basket. On the back porch overlooking the field,
the old Apaches in wicker wheelchairs drummed their canes excitedly on
the railing in approval.

The Suma Apaches scattered around the field craned their necks and
gazed at the sky as the *Spirit* soared higher and higher. Paradeeahtran

tracked it with his good arm as the yellow speck drifted across the blue of the sky. "I sure hated to see Finn fly off like that," he announced to everyone within earshot. "Cut into strips, the nylon in his balloon would have made great banners for our feast day."

Squinting at the sky, Sonseeahray, the Morning Star, came over to stand next to Finn. The back of his hand brushed against the back of her hand, but she pulled it away. "Don't rush me," she said. "I need to mourn my Apache Gatsby."

Finn touched the spot where she had sheared a fistful of hair off the nape of her neck. "I got all the time in the world."

She looked at him as if she were seeing him for the first time. "Are you really finished turning in squares?" she asked.

"You bet."

Sonsinjab, the Great Star, joined them. "What you got to do," the boy told Finn, his eyes wide and serious, "is get yourself a new name like everyone else round here. That way Finn will have disappeared with the balloon and the bad guys'll never find you."

"If you're gonna go hog," Sonseeahray, the Morning Star, reminded him, a hint of a smile playing on her lips, "you might as well go whole hog."

Finn caught a last glimpse of *The Spirit of Saint Louis* disappearing into a cloud bank. He remembered what Eskeltsetle had told Sonseeahray when she was still called Ishkaynay. "You are who you think you are," Finn murmured. He could hear the old Apache's voice in his ear. "All you got to do is invent yourself over again."

The Amateur

Before Robert Littell vaulted onto the bestseller lists with *The Company*, *The Amateur* established him as a contemporary master of the espionage thriller. In this sleek and murderous novel, Charlie Heller is an ace cryptographer for the CIA, a quiet man in a quiet back-office job. But when his fiancée is murdered by terrorists and the Agency decides not to pursue her killers, Heller takes matters into his own hands. The fact that he is an amateur makes him all the more dangerous. Mind-blowing in its intelligence, pulse-pounding in its suspense, *The Amateur* is a stunner.

ISBN 978-0-14-303814-6

The Sisters

A classic among espionage aficionados, *The Sisters* features what the *New York Times* called "the plot of plots." Centering on Francis and Carroll, two enigmatic and extremely dangerous CIA legends dubbed "the Sisters Death and Night," *The Sisters* masterfully unveils an abyss of artful deception. By luring the Potter, a former head of the KGB sleeper school, into betraying his last and best assassin living secretly in the United States, Francis and Carroll set off a desperate race against time as the Potter tries to stop his protégé from committing the Sisters' exquisitely planned, world-shattering crime.

ISBN 978-0-14-303821-4

Legends

Martin Odum is a one-time CIA field agent turned private detective in Brooklyn, struggling his way through a labyrinth of memories and past identities—"legends" in Agency parlance. But who is Martin Odum? Is he a creation of the Legend Committee at the CIA's Langley headquarters? Is he suffering from multiple personality disorder, brainwashing, or simply exhaustion? *Legends* follows the life of a single CIA operative caught in a contradictory "wilderness of mirrors" in which remembering the past and forgetting it are both deadly options.

ISBN 978-0-14-303703-3

An Agent in Place

Deep in the vastness of the Pentagon and the bowels of the massive KGB center in Moscow are old Cold Warriors who refuse to fade away. Yet how can they wage their battles when there are no enemies anymore? Their answer is Ben Bassett. Sent to Moscow as a lowly embassy "housekeeper," Bassett meets a fiercely independent, passionate Russian poet, Aïda Zavaskaya, and falls under her spell. Together they become pawns in a dreadful game that leads to the clandestine heart of the Soviet system itself.

ISBN 978-0-14-303564-0

The Once and Future Spy

Inventive, imaginative, and relentlessly gripping, this tale of espionage reveals the dirty tricks and dangerous secrets of the subjects Littell knows best—the CIA and American history. When "the Weeder," an operative at work on a highly sensitive project for the Company, encounters an elite group of specialists and a clandestine plan within the innermost core of the CIA, disturbing moral choices must be weighed against a shining patriotic dream.

ISBN 978-0-14-200405-0

The Defection of A. J. Lewinter

For years an insignificant cog in America's complex defense machinery, A. J. Lewinter, a scientist, is now playing both sides against the middle. But neither the Russians nor the Americans are sure his defection is genuine, and as each side struggles to anticipate its opponent's next move, Lewinter is swept up in a terrifying web of deceit and treachery.   ISBN 978-0-14-200346-6